TORMENT, INCORPORATED

'So, tell me, do the Evil Twins have nice bodies?'

'Yes, they do. No doubt about that.' I was uncomfortably aware of a semi-hard-on stretching my jeans a bit, and a slight scent of the Twins' juice was still noticeable under my nose. I hoped Charlene didn't notice the bulge.

No chance of that. Her eyes dropped to my crotch for a long, significant moment, and then back up to my eyes. 'Looks like the Twins got a hook in you, hey? Thinking it might not cost you too much to head back there?' She shifted in her chair and I realised her nipples were erect, just noticeable through her Bettie Page vintage sweater. Pupils dilated, too. She was getting hot and bothered over my little adventure with the Twins. 'What part was the most exciting?' she asked eagerly. 'Licking their pussies or masturbating over Mimi's naked body? Seeing your fresh semen on her breasts?' She wasn't trying very hard to hide her arousal. A look of raw lust at me. The air over her seemed to shimmer slightly, like the air over a hot asphalt parking lot.

This book is dedicated to Jennifer Ellen Missler

TORMENT, INCORPORATED

Murilee Martin

This book is a work of fiction.
In real life, make sure you practise safe, sane and consensual sex.

First published in 2005 by
Nexus
Thames Wharf Studios
Rainville Road
London W6 9HA

www.nexus-books.co.uk

Typeset by TW Typesetting, Plymouth, Devon

Printed and bound by
Clays Ltd, St Ives PLC

ISBN 0 352 33943 8

All characters in this publication are fictitious and any resemblance to real persons, living or dead, is purely coincidental.

You'll notice that we have introduced a set of symbols onto our book jackets, so that you can tell at a glance what fetishes each of our brand new novels contains. Here's the key – enjoy!

Foreword

The book you now hold in your hands probably got there out of some sense of morbid curiosity; the year of relentless media coverage in Southern California and elsewhere, the grainy photos of me getting cuffed and stuffed into various official Ford Crown Victoria sedans in front of various trial venues, my cadre of high-powered attorneys issuing a steady torrent of gibberish about free enterprise while the cameras flash. All through the adventure I kept my mouth shut, figuring (correctly) that there was no point in trying to explain what really happened, at least until the frenzy died down a bit. And what a frenzy it was:

'$828 Million Unaccounted For in Sux-M-Owt.com Meltdown' *Southern California Business Week*, 27 July 2001

' "Devil Boss" Charlene Cabrillo Points Finger of Blame at Accomplice' *Orange County Sun*, 3 August 2001

'Sux-M-Owt.com Programmers Kept As Sex Slaves, Say Prosecutors' *Orange County Sun*, 1 September 2001

'Sux-M-Owt.com Sexual Harassment Suits Settled Out of Court; "No Comment" Says One Victim' *Los Angeles Courier*, 1 November 2001

'Justice Perverted? Sux-M-Owt.com Scamster Eddie Kelvin Gets Slap On Wrist' *Orange County Sun*, 12 April, 2002

On and on it went, as the cameras zoomed in for the kill. Investors had been bilked. Workers had been abused. High-flying, twenty-something execs had splurged on Ferraris and cocaine, against a backdrop of palm trees and brown sunsets. The image of my face was in the public mind in stark black-and-white, labelled 'Swindler', 'Con Man'. The good honest folks of Southern California, those who know there's no shortcut to the American Dream, they *knew* what had happened. I, Eddie Fritz, lazy blond beach bum turned overnight dot-com millionaire, had reverted to my white-trash Huntington Beach roots and fucked a lot of hardworking citizens out of a lot of hard-earned dollars. And now I was gonna pay.

All bullshit, of course. I never cared about the money. I'm not even getting any money for this book; it's being written for the state as a public service, to warn others not to take the path I've taken. All proceeds will go to Gleaming Road Foundation in Santa Ana, which teaches ghetto kids to avoid the soul-destroying allure of white-collar crime.

Now, as I sit in my cell in the minimum-security annex of the Wayside Honor Rancho, awaiting release on probation after six months served, typing on this fine state-owned Toshiba laptop and watching my fellow inmates play dominoes in the exercise yard outside the plexiglas slit that serves as my window to the outside world, I am gearing up to tell you what *really* happened at Sux-M-Owt.com. Take it as a cautionary tale, or a moralistic fable, or maybe just an entertaining story, coming right at you from the pen of this loathsome white-collar criminal.

One

Sure, I had it all. The penthouse office in that mirrored tower out by the airport. The chauffeured 1932 Cadillac V16 limo with full bar and Norma Desmond-inspired cheetah-skin upholstery. The beach house with paranoid ex-Green Beret guards trained, in fact *encouraged*, to use Unnecessary Force on any intruders caught inside the perimeter. The private chef. The private rock-climbing wall. The art collection. Getting high on the job, and not just a furtive high, the kind you get sucking frantically on a pinner in the warehouse workplace. No, I'd have my feet up on the desk at the office, dictating a memo while one of my crew of assistants packed my hookah and another applied the flame. And the women. Yes, the veritable cream of the lush Southern California crop of delectable femininity: from the still-green eighteen-year-old ready to move up from seven-second humps in the backseat of her Hesh boyfriend's 1983 Caprice to the world-travelling financial consultant with the conservative skirts and black-belt pussy musculature, drawn to the Southland from all continents, their ripe breasts and swaying hips straining for release from their clothes, and all seeking the touch of a man like me, a young, blond-haired dude with reasonably good looks, an artistic sensibility and, most important, a freakin' overnight millionaire with no hesitation to pop open that fat wallet. Cue the strip-club music. The pink spotlight.

But you know about all that stuff, from the TV news and the supermarket tabloids. No big surprise. Anyway, it really wasn't about the money. Or even the pussy. It was about the art.

The art? you ask, incredulous. For Christ sake! I spent $6.99 for this paperback and this cheating, embezzling, arrogant 23-year-old punk whose well-deserved demise I prayed for as my own bills stacked up like a death sentence says he defrauded all those investors and abused all those employees for fucking art?

Yes, indeed. Read on.

The whole scam got rolling when I met Charlene on the job, driving for Colonel Sausage's Pizza Shack over on Bristol Street on the Newport Beach/Costa Mesa County line. I was delivering eighth-ounce sacks of Mendocino-grown marijuana of the *Cannabis Indica* variety, in the guise of a simple pizza delivery man. The arrangement there involved a very rational division of labour and a foolproof system: weed-starved loadies would call up and order some edge-case pizza, like a small thin-crust with double ground beef and pineapple, which resulted in an eighth of green bud being delivered pronto by me. But there was no edge-case pizza on the menu. Legit, hungry pizza-eaters would order a normal pie and get delivery by Juan or Thor, the other drivers. Juan made the most money, thanks to his ride (a stock-looking 1979 Ford Fairmont stuffed with a super-charged 347 grunting out about five hundred horse-power – all the good stuff. No cop would admit being outrun by such a grandmotherly-looking car, so Juan had de facto exemption from the California Vehicle

Code. Meanwhile, Thor's sleepy-eyed stoner demeanor made him a much-loved fixture in the lives of his regulars, resulting in healthy tip money, but I had the highest overall job satisfaction. All of us had our regulars, our chosen routes, etc., though the non-perishable nature of a bag-o-weed meant that I could drive at a more leisurely pace. It was an easy job and a dignified one. My customers were almost always glad to see me and, thanks to the reasonable prices of my wholesale connection, I didn't have to work many hours to pay the rent. In between deliveries I could spark up a fattie with Juan and Thor by the dumpsters and we would sing our special dope-smoking song:

Why don't you get me lit,
You useless piece of shit?
Why don't you get me high?
We'll smoke pot 'til we die!

If feeling particularly mellow, with a cool Pacific breeze taking the edge off the blazing white sky and a nice dope-brother vibe in the air, we'd all add a little air-guitar part between the lines, making crunchy guitar noises in our throats:

Chunk-a chunk-a chunk-a chunk-a,
Chunk-ch-ch-chunk-ch-ch-CHUNK!

Sometimes, standing in that lot and watching the cars suck down gas at the Exxon station across Bristol Street, the sunbeams cutting between the palm fronds would create patterns in the smog in just the right way, the sound of the freeway would mingle pleasingly with the seagull screams, and I would find myself in the eye of a perfect Southern California Moment.

As the joint passed to me, time would slow, the baked coworker with the Primo Beer T-shirt would be my brother, and I'd feel the sheer unironic optimism with which Southern California was sold back in the day, when swarms of Midwesterners poured out of trains and straight to the land of oranges and sunny skies. Sure, the whole place was built on a blood-drenched foundation of union-busting and institutionalised racism, but we could pretend that wasn't so if we squinted into the sun just right.

When my delivery rounds took me out to the Anaheim/Yorba Linda area, I would stop by the Richard Nixon Birthplace, park the car, and contemplate the little house built by Frank Nixon for his young family. I felt a strange connection to Richard Nixon in spite of our ideological differences and the fact that he died before my twentieth birthday; I'd read all the biographies I could find and I could see that we both felt the same love and alienation for and against our native Orange County landscape. But his was a cautionary tale for me; the descent into paranoia, the sense that the seemingly benevolent Southern California environment served as a camouflage for more menacing human threats, all these were paths to avoid. The nice old ladies who ran the Nixon Birthplace and Museum were used to seeing me there all the time and sensed my respect for the man and his place, if not his presidency. Sure, I'd thought of showing up one day with a five-gallon bucket of fresh pig blood and sloshing it all over Frank Nixon's handbuilt house, screaming about two million dead Southeast Asians, the betrayal of the American people's faith in the Presidency, et cetera – I mean, who *wouldn't* think of doing such a thing after learning the dives and swoops of Nixon's life? But I never acted on my impulse.

With my Nixonian fascination, totally incomprehensible to my friends, I set about trying to build my own monument to Nixon the Man and His California Dream. Hours spent in the garage welding, cutting, rigging wires, all that good stuff, and I pieced it together: the Vacuum-Powered Richard Nixon robot, which, though you never read about it in any of the stories or exposés on the rise and fall of the Sux-M-Owt.com Empire, featured prominently in the whole twisted drama.

Two

Like everybody else I knew, I was in a band for a while. Randy Kraft and the Dead Marines, we called ourselves (you may remember serial killer Randy Kraft, who was busted at the side of the 405 with a couple of dead, diced-up Marines from Camp Pendleton in his car). We'd gone through a series of names (The Sniffdogs, Tinhorn Dilemma, The Weasel Piss Demonstration) but Randy Kraft seemed to be just the right theme for our target audience. I played a piano harp rigged up with a bunch of guitar pickups, fed through about eight crappy analog distortion pedals into an amplifier/speaker combo once used to broadcast flight arrivals at Burbank Airport. My fingers would get sore from plucking the strings, so I switched to a sander, which made my solos sound like fifty bad teenage metalhead guitarists locked in a shipping container with fifty Marshall stacks, and jamming on 'Highway Star' until the onset of full testicular liquefaction.

'Dude, the freakin' Datsun solenoid isn't working the hammer on the oil drum!' Larry the drummer came at me as I unloaded my crap from the van for our Friday night gig at The Doll Nipa Hut, a feet-stick-to-the-floor sort of headbanger bar in Huntington Beach that served beer by the tallcan, whiskey by the paper cup. Larry had a bunch of oil drums and car horns operated by automotive starter solenoids – we got a shitload of noise from the stuff but the gear was unreliable, often reducing Larry to beating on the 55-gallon drums with tire irons. This exhausting labour would then prompt him to start hitting the Slimeball Specials (one part ouzo, two parts anti-freeze-colored Island Lime Soda, with a sprinkling of salmon eggs on top) extra hard, and we'd have to bring him from the gig to the van on the dolly. I dug through the crap and found a replacement solenoid.

While cranking it down on the oil drum on stage, I checked out the early arrivals for the night's audience. The Doll Nipa Hut tended to attract a mix of lower-income white freaks: full-on ragin' dudes fresh from spinning doughnuts with their Camaros in the Circle K parking lot, the scent of scorched rubber on their Motorhead T-shirts; wallet-chain-equipped wannabe hipsters trying to look badass with their tatts, and a trashy assortment of rocker chicks with beer breath and well-stuffed Spandex outfits. I felt comfortable there. Nobody looked twice when I hung my feet over the edge of the stage, packed the bowl of my travelling pipe and fired up, and the bartender didn't object to the cooler full of cold King Cobra tallcans we hauled in from the van.

It was a good night. I had a police scanner set to the CHP's frequency fed into a crude spark-gap transmitter and out through fifteen Kraco AM radios packed into a toilet tank, and the audience was grooving on my sander-on-the-piano-strings solos. The cop voices shrieked out of the toilet tank: 'Roger ... roger ... roger ... roger ... four-oh-five ... four-oh-five ... four-oh-five ...' Our singer, a club-footed speed-dealing warehouseman from Downey who went by the name Yum El Monster Shoe, opened up with our latest song, 'If You Don't Shut Up I'll Kill You':

If you don't shut up,
If you don't shut up,
If you don't shut up,
I'll kill you!
If you don't shut up,
If you don't shut up,
If you don't shut up,
I'll kill you!

And so on. I had been pushing for the band to adopt some of my more complex lyrics, but I could see that the Doll Nipa Hut crowd was happier with Yum Shoe's concepts. Wall-to-wall Orange County lowlife moshed around the club's fetid confines, taking swigs from random glasses and smoking uneven-burning jerntz of low-end Mexican Brown coughweed, no doubt sold by the bale from a horse-drawn wagon in the parking lot. An indoor smog of Marlboro, weed, and rubber smoke burned the eyes, the parking lot having become the setting for a high-stakes burnout contest featuring a 1972 Plymouth Satellite packing a tunnel-rammed 440 taking on all comers while a screaming crowd bet on the best smoke clouds. I swigged cherry brandy with Olde English 800 chasers and staggered around the stage, howling stuff like 'Orange County uber Alles!' and 'Fuck you, ya fucking fucks!' at the audience while jamming out fiendish solos with my overdistorted sander-enhanced instrument (I called it 'The Punisher').

The gig was a wildly successful deal during which I introduced my new stage persona, Phillip McScrewdriver. Shaving the top of my head in such a way as to resemble the business end of a Phillips screwdriver (kind of a Mohawk but with a stripe of hair running left-to-right across the head to intersect the traditional front-to-back hair to create an 'X'), I spent the gig aiming the top of my head at the crowd, twisting it in a counterclockwise direction, and promising to 'unscrew your brains' while a slide show of 1970s Chrysler promotional slides touted the benefits of The Hang Ten Dart Swinger and Plush Cut Pile Carpeting on the puke-stained wall behind the stage. Once the last car horn finished blaring and the last hum ceased from the amps, I took a seat at the bar and ordered up a Master Cylinder of Schlitz Blue Bull, taking a break before lugging all the gear back to the van.

'You gonna drink that beer to your head, McScrewdriver?' A trashy Surf City metalhead chick, maybe nineteen years old, had sidled up to my tall can of the Blue Bull. Stuck in the 1980s, complete with crypto-punk spiked leather and a trowelled-on layer of waxy eye makeup around her baby blues. Hard, narrow face, nose running from a recent application of speed. Cheap Beach-Boulevard cooze, but I lusted after a thousand girls like her when I was growing up within spitting distance from Beach, and I felt . . . interested. Her hand-stamp was a crudely inked phony, no doubt applied with a marker pen outside to avoid the five-dollar cover charge.

'No, feel free to take a swig,' I offered pleasantly, handing her the can. She chug-a-lugged the remaining quart of malt liquor, then crushed the can on her thigh. Belched fetchingly. Pleather pants, of course, and cheapo slut-style stiletto heels, right out of a Ratt video, circa 1984. I wanted to do her, preferably in knee-trembler fashion against the alley wall behind the club, or perhaps in the trunk of her car (I imagined a full-size mid-1970s land yacht, something in the Chrysler New Yorker family). Something sleazy, a fitting capper to a good Randy Kraft and the Dead Marines show.

I figured the direct approach was best. 'Seeing as how I'm with the band, how about we go someplace else and you give me some ass?'

She giggled. 'You know the old bumper sticker? *Gas, Grass, or Ass, nobody rides for free.*' She slapped her left ass cheek, with a moist pleathery sound. 'What's in it for *me*, other than your rockstar peenie?'

I ordered another can, the stronger Country Club Malt Liqour this time. I figured I'd want to have the spins by the time I stuck it in, just on the edge of puking. It seemed the best way. I decided a quick, demeaning experience was just the ticket. 'How about an eighth of green bud for a blowjob in the men's room?' I patted my crotch. 'And I get to come in your hair,' I added for good measure.

She laughed, enjoying this. 'You like it scuzzy, huh? *Dirty.*' I nodded, tilting back my head and guzzling half the can of vile-tasting warm beer. 'Me too. But *I* want more out of it then a bag of weed and splooge in my *hair*.' She indicated her greasy, shoulder length hair; the home bleach job and black roots were dead-on perfect. The room spun a bit; alcohol and gritty apocalyptic lust, the kind you get when the Chinese missiles are coming down on the final reentry and you have eighty seconds to get off in the last ass you'll ever see.

She leaned into me, sliding her hands into my back pockets and grinding her tits against my chest in a mocking manner. 'How about this? You can fuck my mom in a dumpster for fifty bucks, and if you have any juice left after she's done with you I'll suck it out for that eighth.'

The room was definitely spinning now. Beer and noise gurgled around in my head. Her *mom*? Juice? A *dumpster*? What's the story here?

'What's the story here?' I asked. 'A dumpster full of trash, or with say an old mattress in it?' But I did have the fifty bucks, which I snapped between my hands like a riverboat gambler setting up a big bet with a sucker. Her hand snaking out, grabbing my belt buckle, dragging me off the barstool. *Go with it*, I thought, as she guided me through the crowd, out the door, past the burnout contest, and down the alley behind the Doll Nipa Hut. The rest of the band would just have to load the gear without me; I tried to signal as much to them on the way out, pointing to my date's ass and then my bulging groin, but it was clear they understood none of it. I was loaded, really staggering, but we managed a few blocks into an area of loading docks wedged between the hot-sheet El Conquistador Motel and the South County Water District Sewage Treatment Facility. The smell of low-grade crack smoke from the motel and percolating shit in the open treatment tanks made my stomach flip-flop queasily. We came upon a grimy, primered-out station wagon parked between the truck ramps and a row of dumpsters, a true Homeless Special – a 1977 Olds Vista Cruiser wagon sitting on four bald, half-flat tyres, with crap piled high on every available horizontal surface, a pink temporary registration sticker (the type referred to by the more racist local cops as 'Mexican Licence Plates') slapped on the back window, and the finishing touch: a coat hanger for a radio antenna.

As it turned out, the *real* finishing touch was inside the wagon. Darlene (that was the name she'd given me during her cottonmouthed speed-addled rambling during our walk from the bar, although I would have been hard-pressed to recall many other details of our one-sided conversation, which seemed to be some kind of downward-spiral family history) rapped on the windshield with a big dime-store ring of the Lemmy Kilminster Screaming Skull variety. 'Hey Mom!' she shouted, 'Wake your ass up! We got company!'

A heap of rags in the back of the Vista Cruiser stirred. I heard the clink of empty Crazy Horse forty-dog bottles rolling off the heap as Mom's head emerged, blinking in the pink mercury-vapor light. Mom didn't look so bad, I thought as she extricated herself from the pungent U-Haul blankets and shredded beach towels that made up the 'bedroom' of Darlene's family home. She was about forty; her face showed some hard miles, but she packed a tough-looking plump body into her beer-stained thrift-store print dress, and I caught a glimpse of a prison-esque flower tatt (the blue ball-point pen color was the giveaway) on her inner thigh as she struggled to a sitting position. Darlene opened the tailgate and proceeded to consult a whispered negotiation of some sort with Mom, who groped around in the junk for a bottle with some life left in it. Hitting pay dirt, she swigged the dregs of an Olde English 800 forty-ouncer while appraising me and my fifty bucks. Eyes locked with mine. I couldn't look away. She had a couple of gold teeth and some foam-rubber car-seat stuffing stuck in her hair. The mercury-vapor light on the warehouse wall hummed louder and I fought down a wave of nausea and lust. The sound of a scream followed by broken glass and someone shouting *¡Chingados!* wafted over from the motel. Shit bubbles blooped. The atmosphere was perfect.

'All right, big spender,' she snapped, swinging her legs over the tailgate and onto the ground. 'Fifty bucks and we'll have enough gas money to get to Reno.' She lifted one leg onto the tailgate and started working her panties down. They didn't look clean.

'So let's get down to *business*!' She tossed the panties at me; not knowing what else to do, I balled them up and stuck them in my back pocket. Darlene lit up a joint and sucked half of it down before passing it to Mom. I felt like little men in motorcycles were buzzing around the interior of my skull, but I called upon years of experience to dredge up some cool and gather my shit together.

Mom strode over to a nearby dumpster. Her ass cheeks were big and powerful-looking and her bare feet seemed unscathed by the broken glass beneath them. She yanked the latch on the end door of a six-by-twelve rollaway and dragged it open. The dumpster was full of what looked and smelled like Chinese restaurant trash – cardboard boxes with Chinese labels and rotting vegetables. Darlene plucked the two twenties and a ten from my hand and leaned against me, whispering 'Save some for me and I'll earn that bag-o-weed from you,' shooting a little tongue in my ear.

Mom cleared a space in the garbage and polished off the joint, flicking it away. 'All right, you've always dreamed of fucking a down-on-her-luck woman in a heap of garbage at the low, low price of fifty bucks, here's your chance. I ain't no whore, but that fifty bucks is our ticket outta this shithole, so I think this business arrangement oughta work out fine for both of us.'

I felt vaguely evil. Had it been *my* idea to fuck this poor homeless woman in a dumpster? What I'd really wanted was to get sucked off in the Doll Nipa Hut men's room by the daughter, but now my cock was apparently swelling for a shot at the mother's grimy vulva in a reeking bed of week-old bok choy. This whole scene didn't jibe with my enlightened vision of the act of love, but events seemed to have gained the momentum of an unstoppable train.

Mom leaned over and settled into the cleared area of the dumpster, face down and ass in the air. She pulled the dress back over her hips and wiggled her legs far apart. A rat scurried past her knee but she seemed indifferent. Her parts glistened in the humming pink air. A PA voice in the sewage plant recited a series of numbers. 'Four . . . four . . . four . . . nine . . . nine . . . nine . . .'

'Now, because I don't normally do this shit, we're gonna go about this a little differently from your usual trick/john transaction.' Mom's head was twisted around as she explained, but her round white ass had most of my attention. 'We're not just gonna have you dick me for fifteen seconds and then pop your load while my face gets jammed in the trash. Maybe that's the kind of thing you Huntingdon Beach surfer boys like to do with your women, but that's not how *we're* doing it. That right, Darlene?'

Darlene was sitting on the Vista Cruiser's lowered tailgate, fiddling with a small handgun. 'That's right, Mom.' Armed rocker chicks and their moms. The Vista Cruiser. All in a night's work. I wanted to explain that I wasn't a surfer boy, but it seemed an inappropriate time.

'So, as you can see, Darlene is going to be the Good Behaviour Enforcement Agency. And good behaviour means that *I* get off, *then* you get off.' She licked her fingers and applied some spit to her cunt lips, carefully separating them and generally preparing for action. 'Darlene, you know what to do.'

Darlene slid down off the tailgate, stuck the gun in her back pocket, and approached me. I was transfixed, a deer in the headlights. What this situation needs, I thought, is more chemical enhancement, so I fished my pipe from my pocket and lit up as Darlene unzipped my jeans and started working them down my legs. The soothing smoke put a nice fuzz over the scene. Obediently, I lifted one leg, then the other, as she removed my pants. My eyes remained fixed on Mom's cooch, with the spit globules gleaming on the edges of its pink folds. Then Darlene's slim fingers were working into my shorts, unreeling my tackle. While my forebrain wasn't firing on all cylinders, my reptilian brainstem was still sending out all the appropriate signals and my goods were in perfect working order. Darlene knelt and ran a lizardy tongue-tip over my stuff; I had a decent hard-on and it was ready for action. 'You'll like this one, Mom,' she called. 'Not real long, but good and hard and a nice texture to it.'

'Well, let's get *busy*!' snapped Mom, digging a few fingers into her parts to spread some juice around and settling more firmly into the trash. Mom was getting a little excited, I sensed, more than fifty bucks' worth. Darlene pinched my cock tip between thumb and forefinger, the way you use one of those bull nose-rings, and led me in the direction of the dumpster. Mom wiggled her ass invitingly as Darlene steered me into position: me standing at the dumpster entrance, Mom with ass in air and face in a crate of slimy cabbage. *Here we go*, I thought. I grabbed a couple of handfuls of ass (just as hard and muscular as I'd imagined) and leaned in. Her labia parted a bit and I felt an almost unpleasant heat as I pressed a bit more. Mom's application of spit had clearly been unnecessary; as the inner lips opened a bit more I sensed a hot trickle of cunt juice building up at the base of my cockhead, then rolling down the underside of the shaft and dripping down over my balls. I pushed in another half-inch or so, but felt like I'd hit some kind of bottleneck or tight corner in her candy. Mom moaned. The night was looking better.

Darlene produced the toylike handgun again. Looked like a real small-caliber job, like the kind Nancy Reagan carried for shooting Salvation Army Santas in the eyes. 'Remember, Mom gets off before you do.' I looked questioningly at her. 'Is that a threat?' I slurred.

Darlene smiled. She had found an eighth of bud in my jeans pocket and dangled it. 'Save it *all* for me,' she whispered, 'I want this sack.' I got a better grip on Mom's ass and pushed a bit harder. I felt her stuff give a bit and I worked in another inch or so. Mom seemed to have a body temperature of about 130 degrees. She jammed her face into the trash and panted while I put a little more force in my thrusts. Something in her cooze still seemed to be keeping me from getting more than about halfway in, but it didn't feel like your ordinary, everyday vaginal tightness, more like a slippery fist was clamped down on my fuckstick and refusing to yield. Judging by the way Mom was pushing back and gabbling gibberish into her garbage pillow, it wasn't interfering with her enjoyment any. Unable to get a real purchase on her ass – too much muscle for me to really grab a handful – and going crazy with the need to bottom out in that maddening roadblock of a pussy, I grabbed hold of her dress and wrapped the thin cotton around my fist a couple times, then yanked back on it like a set of reins and gave Mom a couple of brutal thrusts. No dice; her grip wouldn't ease at all. I pulled harder on the dress and the cheap fabric shredded like wet newspaper, leaving her naked. I'd have to chip in for another two-dollar dress, I figured. Mom's bulging tits mashed into the trash with every thrust. I was starting to think maybe Mom was just born with only three inches of poozle length and I was just futilely beating my head against some other of her innards, maybe her liver or spleen or something. The few inches of meat I couldn't get inside was acquiring a coat of girl-lube dripping down like molten fat from a barbecue grill, and the cool ocean air was making my exposed parts feel frozen compared to the few inches of Mom's slimy furnace I was permitted to enjoy. God . . . *damn* . . . it! No danger of me popping my rocks prematurely and possibly getting shot full of small-diameter holes by her loving daughter, but I figured my head might explode from sheer frustration.

Darlene eased in behind me as I struggled with Mom's unyielding cooch. Her small, hard breasts flattened on my back as she crossed an arm across my body and got a grip on the exposed part of my stalk. She gnawed on my neck a bit, then made a helpful suggestion: 'You need to give her a reach-around.' Those words bounced around in my head with no apparent results, so Darlene found my hand and worked my fingers down Mom's mound, just south of my hopelessly stuck shaft, and gave them a bit of a wiggle up and down in the general area of Mom's clit. It was a big one, about the size of a peanut kernel and very firm. Ah, a reach-around! I did a bit of separating and probing among the squelching folds and corners and got a couple of fingers set up on top of her fat little button. Working in little circles, I got a rhythm going that seemed to have quite an effect on Mom, judging by all the noise coming from the heap of vegetables she'd buried her head under. Quite an effect on Darlene, too, who now had my nuts cupped in her hand and was grinding against my back. Finally, Mom was there, howling like a wounded mammal and squeezing great curls of garbage paste between her spasming fingers, her spleen or whatever it was slid out of the way and I was finally able to hit bottom dead centre and start fucking a proper cervix instead of whatever gristly gynaecological oddity I'd been running into before.

'Fuck my mom! Fuck my mom!' howled Darlene, bracing herself and shoving on my ass with both hands, so as to fuck her mom with my equipment. Even by my unusually broad-minded standards, this scene was getting a bit disturbing. All that malt liquor in my gut sloshed forward and back with every frenzied push by Darlene as she used me to fuck her mom, and the action of Mom's upper body getting jammed into a heap of fermenting Chinese food was releasing great gassy clouds of Moo Shoo Dioxide . . . I was more or less a rag doll at this point, concentrating on not chirping a stomach full of cheap beer all over my date for the evening. Darlene worked into a steady rhythm, body-slamming me into Mom's trim with a breathless 'Fuck . . . my . . . mom . . . Fuck . . . my . . . mom . . .' Mom meanwhile was gurgling sounds of pleasure into the ever-gooier layers of dumpster slime as the action forced her deeper into the trash. I realised that my only escape from this prize mother/daughter team would be my own climax, but the building nausea from the beer, trash, motion, and general weirdness was giving me porn-star-like stamina.

Darlene seemed to grasp this fact, because she yanked me out of Mom, wrestled me over to the Vista Cruiser, propped me up against its rusty flank, and jammed her slobbery mouth over my aching rod and commenced with the old oil-well action, up, down, up down, drooling and gasping in most undisciplined fashion, teeth scraping and tongue rasping. Mom, meanwhile, had extricated herself from the dumpster and limped over, naked, coated in sweat and stanky food waste. Wrapping herself in a piss-stained sheet from the Olds, she watched her daughter approvingly as I finally came, screaming for mercy and seeing stars as I short-circuited every breaker in my brain. Darlene, remembering our deal, yanked my dick out of her mouth at the moment of truth and milked the spooge into her hair.

All vestiges of cool spent, I staggered away and puked, with a terrible case of the spins. Mom and Darlene dragged me, half-conscious, into the Vista Cruiser's back seat, then jumped in and fired up the engine. *Bad exhaust leak*, I remember thinking as the 307 caught, then I blacked out when Mom jumped on the gas. Next thing I knew, we were sliding sideways in front of the Doll Nipa Hut, the door open and Darlene shoving me out onto the pavement. 'We're done with this one!' she shrieked as I tumbled into the gutter in my fuck-juice-soaked boxers and vomit-soaked shirt, roaring off toward Reno in a cloud of oil smoke. Naturally, the rest of the band was just wrapping up loading the equipment at that moment, so the Randy Kraft bass player, Swede, took the opportunity to take some really humiliating Polaroids of me crawling, bruised and beaten, out of the gutter and pleading drunkenly for help. 'We'll use these shots on our flyers!' Swede chortled as I limped into the van. And I knew they would, just as I knew a grainy, fourth-generation Xerox copy of a high-contrast Polaroid of my begging, spent face printed on Day-Glo paper and stapled to every telephone pole in the 714 area code would only *enhance* my standing among my peers.

Three

I preferred being on the road to working in the restaurant. Aside from the surly customers and their squealing children, I had to deal with the whip-crackin' management style of the Evil Twins, Corinne and Mimi. Colonel Sausage's owners rarely showed up at the store, leaving day-to-day operations in the hands of the Twins; some sort of profit-sharing and/or till-tapping deal made the arrangement work well for them. I'd prefer to say that they *looked* the part of the hateful bosses I knew them to be, with warts and faces twisted by hate into hideous masks of evil, but in fact the Twins were stunningly attractive women, still fairly young and equipped with French accents and attention-grabbing hourglass shapes. Working a relentless 20-hour day (no doubt fuelled by large quantities of potent Orange County speed, if I interpreted their nervous chain-smoking and lack of appetite correctly), they abused, ridiculed, and generally hammered on the hapless employees, the nadir being reached when they snitched Ramon, the long-suffering dishwasher with a little girl dying of kidney failure back in Sinaloa, to the Immigration and Naturalisation Service because he showed up seven minutes late for work. I'll never forget his tearful face as the thugs from *La Migra* dragged him into their van, Mimi elbowing Corinne as she mocked Ramon's weeping, Corinne laughing out a lungful of Marlboro smoke before whirling to the horrified crew and ordering them back to work. Their little faces wilted before her Hate Rays, and she showed no remorse in the face of the certain death of little Senaida once Ramon's payments for the dialysis stopped showing up (in fact, she and her twin would often imitate Ramon's pleading – *por favor, por favor* – and break down in fits of giggles at the recollection of his anguished face as *La Migra* zip-tied his wrists).

The Twins knew something was off about the delivery-driver setup, but as the money from deliveries rolled in and I was rarely in the store they chose not to probe too deeply on the subject. The driver crew was treated with contempt, but we were hard enough to replace that the Twins pulled their punches with us.

The crew that actually made the pizzas suffered under the Twins' lash. Signs in gimpy French-distorted English warned ominously: NO EATINGS OF THE TOPPINGS – POLICE WILL CALLED or WASTE TIME IS TO STEAL TIME and so on. They patrolled like bailiffs, their cruel eyes scanning constantly for infractions and inefficiencies, seeing everything. A pure example of managerial evil, purer than most of us are ever privileged to witness. I feel bad about it now, but my stories of the exploits of the Evil Twins provided inspiration for Charlene later on, as she cranked up her own version of the Colonel Sausage slave ship in the basement of Sux-M-Owt.com.

But I maintained a comfortable distance between the day job and what I *really* cared about. I went from being a rock star to being an artist, at first because it seemed to promise more in the way of pussy and giggles, but then because I enjoyed it more and, God help me, I was *good* at it. Here's how my life took such a strange turn down a weird offramp:

Thanks to my dope-dealing day job, I had a fair amount of interaction with various artists and artist-hangers-on. I made plenty of deliveries to galleries and studios in a territory ranging from Long Beach down to Laguna Beach. I always enjoyed the company of the artistic types, even the total dingbats, and figured myself to be a kindred spirit, a product and student of the same ironic American Dream milieu, et cetera.

One of my regular, half-ounce-a-week customers was a performance artist called Gennifyr Xebrius (I'm assuming this was not the name her parents inked on the birth certificate, but she took on a wishfully-mysterious dazed look when questioned about the origins of her name and nobody felt like pushing it after about three minutes of her maddeningly unfocused conversational style). Gennifyr was a very big, soft, dark-haired, crazy babe with a very high-calorie set of compound curves and creamy small-pored white skin. Monica Lewinsky was big in the news at the time, and I had a hard time keeping my mind off the similarities in appearance between Gennifyr and Monica, although Gennifyr was a good head taller and much meaner, and would have kicked my ass up between my shoulder blades if I'd mentioned such a resemblance (like all substantially-built hipster chicks from the southern half of California, Gennifyr felt herself to be the living embodiment of Tura Satana, even to the point of driving a battered kit-car Porsche 356 clone with an unconvincingly spluttering VW engine). But she and Monica both had pretty mouths . . . mighty pretty mouths . . . I knew it was the sight of that fellatio-enhanced mouth that had driven Bill Clinton to his marital indiscretions. I would doze off watching Monica's inviting-looking, heavily-lipsticked mouth on the TV news and I'd think I was seeing Gennifyr licking her equally enticing lips in preparation for the best head I'd ever receive.

Gennifyr had a day job running a gently failing art gallery in the Fashion Island shopping mall in Newport Beach. Her bosses were world-travelling homosexuals who didn't give a damn if anything sold, provided Gennifyr put in her time at the joint each day. The expectations were low, and any customer who came into the gallery would usually do a quick U-turn upon seeing a 6-foot-tall Monica clone wearing sprayed-on nylon mechanics' coveralls with no underwear (her pecan-sized nipples just about tearing through the sheer fabric), her eyes crazy and red from non-stop bong hits on the loading dock behind the shop, talking confusing crap in an unsalesmanlike manner. At night she would head out to various 'experimental' artist venues (usually Pabst-Blue-Ribbon-serving dives in hipster districts), strip down to a G-string, smear mud all over her acres of voluptuous flesh, and jabber really terrible poetry that read like ransom notes or punk album covers with a background consisting of a mountain of black-and-white TV sets showing all 31 flavours of static. Heavy stuff. The audience would sit there, stunned as much by her monstrous mud-caked rack as by her bewildering act, and applaud crazily when it was apparent that Gennifyr had reached some kind of artistic climax and stalked off the stage. This seemed to satisfy both her and her audience.

I went to a couple of her shows – her act even opened up for Randy Kraft & the Dead Marines once – and I saw her frequently in my role as her dope connection. I don't think she'd drawn an unstoned breath since early childhood – she'd already told me how her particular wake-and-bake method worked:

'So you see I pack the bowl of my morning bong – that's the one that looks like Satan's claw holding a screaming skull – with a measured gram of your skunk-bud as ordained by my chrome-plated Taiwanese balance scale. I pack that morning bong at night, before going to sleep, with that measured gram I was telling you about, and then the bong – that's the Satanic screamin' skull from the headshop in Garden Grove – ends up next to the alarm clock with lighter and gram-o-weed ready for instant action, so's the first conscious act I take in the morning is to get high right away. Get it?'

Oh, I *got* it, all right. She was crazy as a bedbug and mean as a snake, as my grandpappy would say before he keeled over from a burst bile duct, and a steady parade of bong hits every fifteen minutes hadn't done much to stabilise matters. But all that *flesh* – 180 pounds of it, bulging every seam – and that Monica mouth! Oh, I could put some stains on her blue Gap dress. I couldn't even tell if she had any interest in sexual contact in any form, with men, women, Shetland ponies, or whatever, but Gennifyr's incomprehensible monologues and 48–34–46 measurements were doing a boogie-woogie on my sensibilities every time I saw her, and I admit she inspired more than one session of onanism. Even more shameful, I imagined I was grabbing a big armful of Gennifyr when I was fooling around with my righteous girlfriend (but more about her later) and blasting off as she gobbled me like a White House intern slamming to her knees for the Commander In Chief.

Since such lust seemed pointless, I kept a tight lid on it during my interactions with Gennifyr. But things changed one day when she asked me to participate in one of her performances. She wanted me to get 'in the diving submarine' with her. I was confused.

'The *sub*marine. The sub-ma-*rine*! You know, we fill the tank with water, the underwater microphone, the strobe light on the sheet.' She made a strange undulating gesture with her hips, which resulted in me involuntarily licking my lips. I felt the need to adjust my parts, as they were starting to feel cramped by a seam in my pants. 'The *sub*marine!'

I never like to feel confused, it being more my style to be the one *doing* the confusing, laying my bewildering rap on the cringing minds of the squares and so on, but there was a fascinating overtone to her talk of the submarine and I couldn't resist. 'The underwater microphone?'

'Yeah – oh, hold on a sec,' she saw a customer enter the gallery and whirled away from me. I nonchalantly slid the quarter-ounce sack of Mendocino Mayhem I'd been delivering into my sleeve while an elderly couple scoped the harmless paintings. Gennifyr did her customer-service thing: 'Sorry, grandma, we don't sell our shit to decrepit old pieces of fascist *shit*! So get out of my fucking store!' Just like Tura, only crazier and more 1990s. The customers backed out, stunned. She went to the door and locked it, flipping the sign with the CLOSED/CERRADO sign face out.

She produced pen and paper and started drawing a complicated diagram. There were little humanoid stick-figures and what could have been electrical schematics. It looked like one of those conspiracy-theory flowcharts, the type with the Trilateral Commission at the top and every arrow leading to a need for brainwave shielding.

'Do I have to wear an aluminum-foil-lined baseball cap?' I asked, just to mess with her. 'With one of those Afrika Corps flaps hanging off the back, made of corrugated steel? To keep the *rays* out?'

But she was caught up in her diagram. Finally, she flipped it around, so I could see it better. She droned on about her usual mystical-ass shit for a few minutes, then tapped a crudely drawn symbol that looked kind of like an 'X' with a circle around it. 'This is the part where you spurt.'

Well, *that* got my attention. 'Spurt?' I asked. 'Is that some kind of submarine thing?' I felt odd. Inside my head, a little Bill Clinton was pounding his tiny fists against the inner curve of my skull, trying to get my attention: 'The *mouth*, dude, her *mouth*!' But Bill never had an intern who could crush him like a roach, the way Gennifyr could doubtless do to me if she got mad enough. And I was pretty sure the real Bill Clinton wouldn't use the word 'dude'.

'Yeah, that's why I need a man for the piece. A man spurts. Like this . . .' She moved in close, covering me in a huge shadow. That big, red Lewinsky mouth I'd fantasised about so many times was at my eye level. *Ai-ya!* as my Chinese friends would say. She reached for my belt and hauled me the last couple of feet to her. I'm not a small man, but in her grip I felt like balsa wood. Powerless. Her free arm wrapped around me and settled on the small of my back. This was a *lot* of woman. She smelled good, even the faintly bongwaterish scent from her breath. She had to duck a bit to look me in the eye. 'You didn't see, but I had thoughts about you. Thoughts, Mr Dope Man, Mr Pusher Man. Dirty thoughts.'

I wasn't sure you even had those kind of thoughts, you fucking freak, went through my head, but I figured she might wig if I voiced such a sentiment. I felt hot, but a little scared. What now? One-handed, she expertly unbuttoned my pants and worked the zipper down. Started reaching into my skivvies to free up my goods. 'Well, Gennifyr, now that you mention it, I, on occasion, had some similar thoughts about *you*. What a coincidence!' It seemed best to speak clearly and enunciate carefully – I didn't want her interpreting something indistinct as *God wants you to break me in half*.

In fact, what she was gearing up for with her dirty thoughts about Mr Dope Man was a good old-fashioned American red-white-and-blue blowjob. Once she had my cock freed up, she got down on it with true vacuuming action and slapped that purty mouth into place with true skill and grace. It was turning out to be a pretty good day, I thought as she did all the little things that separate a quality hummer from a run-of-the-mill suck job: the anatomy map of nerve endings consulted mentally, the right combination of cold and hot, the teasing-and-satisfying cycle. Gennifyr knew her way around male genitalia, and she went about her task with precision, the only sign that maybe she was getting a little jolt out of it being a tight grip on my thighs as I spurted.

Apparently this was her introduction to my role in her show later in the week. She became very calm and reserved as I shakily rearranged my clothing. I was to arrive at the Café Bataille on Goldenwest Avenue and we would perform her piece 'The Submarine' on the stage. And I would 'spurt' again during the course. Maybe she would, too, but it was hard to tell what she had in mind. It would all become clear to me.

At the gig, I met her on the stage where she was rigging up a big sheet of white cloth that completely covered the front of the stage. Behind the sheet was a big oil drum, the same proportions as a 55-gallon model but twice the size, full of water and sprouting a bunch of wires and hoses, and behind that was a bank of strobe lights and slide projectors. Big amplifiers and what looked suspiciously like an air compressor stood off to the side. It looked like the sheet would form some sort of back-projection shadow-puppet theatre for whatever was going to happen in the water drum.

The Café Bataille was a real shithole, sort of like the Doll Nipa Hut but without the cheap beer. Big posters advertising 1920s French porn novels decorated the walls. The place smelled like ass. I smoked a blunt with the manager, an ageing hippie who looked similar to the portrait of George Washington on the one-dollar bill, and waited for Gennifyr's next move. She was screwing around with the equipment but angrily cut off my offer of technical help with a hiss and a chop of her hand. Finally, she had finished twiddling wires and adjusting the cloth to her satisfaction. I was to go through the 'airlock' and enter the submarine.

'What fuckin' submarine? You mean the water tank on the stage?' Yes, the water tank. I needed a beer. Gennifyr was insistent, and what's more I had to be *naked* in the submarine. Well, at least the audience of art geeks wouldn't see much of my exposed hide from behind the sheet, especially considering I would be deep inside the U-boat. Her eyes were redder than usual and I noted that she hadn't brought her usual g-string-and-mud outfit for the show. OK, I peeled off my clothes, climbed up the stepladder next to the water tank and climbed in. She handed me an air hose and fired up the compressor. 'Go underwater and breathe this air.'

I went along with the thing, partly because I owed her something for the top-shelf blow job she'd given me before, and partly because she'd probably unscrew my head if I didn't do what she said. I found myself breathing rubbery compressed air out of a hose, completely submerged in a metal tank my fellow artist referred to as 'The Submarine', all this taking place on a stage in a foul-smelling hipster café in central Orange County in the Year Of Our Lord 1999. I couldn't hear much, but I could tell from the muffled vibrations and thumps that the audience was filing in and the show was beginning. The strobe lights and slide projectors started working and amplified unpleasantness buzzed through the water. Peeking above the surface of the water, I saw Gennifyr naked and doing a strange mutant dance on the illuminated side of the cloth between the stage and the audience. The audience saw just the shadow of her glorious shape, distorted by flashing strobes and what looked like slides of close-up photos of pigeons. *I* saw her in full undiminished, illuminated view and the sight of supersized portion of femaleness just *got* to me. All right, I figured, I'll put up with her silly show, but I'll be riding that ass into the sunset later tonight. *Tappin'* that ass! My cock was getting ready for action as I contemplated the ways I'd be wrestling with that healthy specimen of womanhood, and I couldn't help but give it a few strokes.

Meanwhile, the audience was starting to gasp, giving out some nervous muttering. I took a closer look at Gennifyr and realised with a shock that she had three or four fingers dug into her pussy and was thrumming her clit as if possessed by the spirit of some ancient Pagan sex god. Even with the shadow effect the audience had dug the score. She flipped around a bit, kept going, really *grinding* with her fingers. On her back, she arched her cunt to the audience. If not for the soundtrack (seemed to be whale songs played at half speed, maybe mixed with some Top Fuel dragster sound effects) I'm sure we'd have heard her enthusiasm too. I began to beat off in earnest. She'd never notice a little spunk floating in the water and I'd have plenty more for her when I finally got her alone.

But wait – she's climbing up the stairs and joining me in the old U–92! I noticed the howling soundtrack fading in volume and a new sound coming from the amps as I ducked my head back underwater and went back to sucking my air from the compressor hose. Holy shit! The drum was miked up with insulated, underwater sound pick-ups! Every slosh and gurgle was being broadcast in full garbled underwater glory to the audience of befuddled art patrons in the folding chairs. I pulled the hose from my mouth and tried to ask Gennifyr what was gonna happen next, but it came out 'Grglglurgmurgl?' no doubt echoing hideously around the muddy acoustics of the Café Bataille.

'Glrrgmnglrb bloogrrmlgrgle,' she replied softly, putting a finger over my lips and inserting her own air hose into her mouth. Underwater, she was graceful, with her long hair billowing around. The scene was almost downright romantic as she tenderly embraced me and pinned my back against the curved metal wall of the tank. The oily rubber-scented bubbles from our air hoses mingled as our bodies met; we were like a couple of divers scrubbing oil-fouled rocks in Prince William Sound after the Exxon Valdez oil spill, finding true love among the dead seabirds. Well, maybe not, but I figured out the reason for her masturbatory interlude prior to jumping in the water – there'd be no way to wedge a dick into a cunt if you used plain water as lube; it would probably strip the epidermis off a man like skin off a roasted marshmallow. But with her pump primed, as she'd done, she effortlessly slipped her cunt down onto my cock, which had already reached full tumescence before she entered the water. The water welled pleasantly around our bodies. She braced her hands on the lip of the tank and leveraged down onto me. In fact, the very noise itself was picked up and broadcast to our audience, as was all the sloshing and underwater moaning and gurgling coming from us as we tried to synchronise our bodies with each other and continue breathing compressed air.

Everything about the underwater public amplified fuck was great, except for the shortage of breathable air; while the compressor gave us enough for a resting heart rate, it couldn't meet the oxygen needs of two people exercising hard underwater. I kept gagging on mouthfuls of water and was starting to see a red haze around the edges of my vision. Gennifyr wasn't going to quit until she got off, however (or 'spurted' as she so charmingly referred to an orgasm for either gender). Come or die trying. I gazed longingly up at the surface of the water, about eighteen inches above my head and propped my feet against the opposite tank wall in an attempt to get more oomph into my thrusts. Her eyes were huge and round as she sucked that air hose and slid up and down on my cock. In spite of my oxygen deprivation and exhaustion, her cunt felt incredible. It was a nice grippy cylinder to begin with, no doubt even under normal non-watery circumstances, but the hydraulic effect of the water inside it really added a sensation like nothing I'd experienced. Just when I was about ready to give up and come inside her, committing an act of great sexual impoliteness just so I could get some air, she commenced with the 'fixin' to blow' routine. I'm sure the speakers made some crazy noises as we went off together – I was pleading for some O_2 and saw brain-damaging anoxic stars when I popped. Then I was pleading for release from her crushing orgasmic grip around my back with her powerful arms. My ribs were creaking and my innards were getting rearranged when she finally finished and whooshed to the surface to gulp down some air. The audience, shocked, gave us a jittery round of applause as we clambered out. Another success.

After that I began collaborating regularly on projects with Gennifyr. Then I started doing some solo work. The World War I Santa Installation was the first one I did that got much attention outside the insular world of Orange County weirdness connoisseurs. It was around Christmastime and lots of folks in the wealthier white-trash suburbs were putting up huge, costly Christmas displays: Santa and reindeer flying across roofs, Gingerbread Men marching in goose-step formation between topiary sculpture, Baby Jesus and the Wise Men on the lawn in front of the 1950s ranch-style, seemingly flinching as Mexican gardeners blasted them with leaf blowers in a swirl of dust and two-stroke oil fumes. Driving Gennifyr home one night and seeing several such Christmas tableaus in her neighbourhood, a switch clicked in my head and I got her permission to do my own version: Santa Kills the Hun.

I needed to turn the lawn in front of an Art Deco Santa Ana cottage into a World War I battlefield. First, I dug trenches in the yard and banked them with sandbags. Bullet-pocked French signs leaned at odd angles and coils of barbed wire trailing bits of cloth and rotting flesh (cheap pork from the 'Day Old' butcher shop) gave the scene a proper atmosphere. The streamers of pork also attracted real live rats, for that feel of trench warfare (unfortunately, they also attracted very un-European desert visitors such as vultures and possums, but I figured the viewers would be willing to overlook such a minor historical inaccuracy. I made a couple of 'corpses' which I half-buried in the yard. Then I set the sprinklers to soak everything on an hourly basis, for that impossible-to-fake muddy look. Hitting the local strip mall, I picked up a huge Korean-made motorised Santa statue, which was rigged up to endlessly extend its arms, retract its arms, extend its arms; apparently the purchaser was supposed to put a big present in Kim Il Santa's hands. When I completed my modifications, however, Santa was jabbing a bayonet into the gut of a German soldier (complete with spiked Kaiser Wilhelm helmet). A pump-and-reservoir setup caused 'Chunky Vegetable' tomato soup to spew from the ruptured abdomen of the Hun, and his face was a mask of agony. Speakers played sounds of machine-gun fire, bugles, shouts in French and German, and so on. I wanted to rig up some device for shooting flares overhead on an hourly basis, but flare prices turned out to be quite high and I figured Johnny Law would probably then find cause to demolish the whole shebang.

The overall effect was even better than I'd imagined. Santa, his face chubbily beaming with Korean good cheer, would s-l-o-o-o-wly lean forward, thrusting his rifle at the prostrate Hun's midsection. The mechanical apparatus would sometimes seize briefly, giving the motion a disturbing, palsied appearance. *Creak . . . creak . . . creak . . .* 'AIIIIIEEEEEE!' The Hun would scream my recorded voice from the loudspeakers (and startled crows would take a few flaps away from the scene). Drivers passing by would stand on the brakes and stop, staring in horror at the sight of World War One Santa Spearing The Hun.

Well, this had Gennifyr and friends busting up with laughter in the house, pounding each other on the back, beer spraying from noses and so on, all in a massive thundercloud of dope smoke. After a few days of this they'd set up a couple of couches in front of the street-facing window, so as to permit the viewing of reactions to the Santa/Hun spectacle by larger audiences, and a crowd of hipsters from throughout the Greater Los Angeles Metropolitan Region would show up each night. And my rep as an edgy artist grew.

Naturally, during my visits, I would usually guide Gennifyr into the nearest empty room and sink my cock into her eager flesh the second the door slammed, usually tearing as few clothes aside as were needed to gain access – it seemed best to dispense with the preliminaries. Her friends on the couch would roll their eyes disaffectedly, but secretly envied her weird hatefulness and lack of sexual shame. After the first few times we didn't even bother to head for another room. I'd just bend her over the coffee table and pound away while the visitors reached over her for their beers and chatted calmly about current events in the art scene. We might as well have been playing Scrabble, although it did get some attention when Gennifyr's bulk collapsed the legs of the table and spilled everyone's beer and sloshed bongwater onto the white carpeting. 'Can't you two go do that *else*where?' came an outraged cry from the couch. There was a fine sense of detachment from reality about the setup; outside, Santa gutting the Hun for eternity while rubber-necking drivers scraped parked cars, unable to deal with the Christmas tableau before them.

The group at her place was a willing audience for my tirades, rants, and bewildering quizzes. Just to keep my ranting chops sharp, I'd get them going on some incomprehensible proposition, something to get the brain looping in a tizzy of self-biting confusion.

'OK, since you folks seem to enjoy the abuse of illegal and probably highly dangerous drugs, I have a theoretical proposition to put forward,' I'd start as they chopped up lines of crystal, poured warm water mixed with heroin into their artistic-type nasal passages, and so on. They'd nod, half-interested.

I'd go on, packing a bowl of my own Schedule One drug of choice and gesturing wisely with the bong, trying to look like a wise old nineteenth-century German philosopher. 'So let's say you have the ultimate drug high available. Its effects are like a combination of orgasm, total awareness, love for your fellow humans, and the ability to fly, with no unpleasant side effects of any sort.'

They liked that idea: 'Sure, sign me up!'

'Not so fast. You see, there's a price to be paid – as you'll always find with anything so worthwhile. The thing is, the act of ingesting this drug might strike users as somewhat repulsive, and the preparation is long and involved. Basically, the ultimate high involves smoking a specially prepared type of catshit –'

This turned the group of sophisticated artist-hipster chicks into a bunch of sixteen-year-old San Fernando Valley Girls: 'Eeeew!'

'No, hold on. You can't just grab a log of dried-up catshit out of the litterbox and bong it up on the spot. Oh, no. The only way to get the genuine, ultimate-high-producing Holy Catshit, for that's what I call it, is to feed the cat a diet of nothing but oysters and asparagus for a week prior to harvesting the good stuff. And you can't force-feed the stuff to the cat, because only a happy, completely content cat can produce the ultimate-high grade of Holy Catshit. Unhappy cat, no high. So you have to scour the world for cats *willing* to eat an oysters-and-asparagus diet, cats who *love* this diet, and at the same time you must minister to the cat's every whim or its unhappiness will render the shit totally worthless.'

They thought about this: *hmmmm . . . ultimate high . . . kowtowing to a cat weird enough to like a crazy diet like that . . . but the ultimate high!*

'Then, when the full week of the special diet is done and the cat has experienced nothing but pure happiness the whole time, the cat will shit out the Holy Catshit. Now, considering the bizarre diet the cat has been eating, the shit will be less than solid. Well, let's face it, you need to smoke cat *diarrhoea*! And it's only good for about fifteen minutes, so there will be no dealers, no pushers, just "do it yourself!"'

Their brains would be churning like hamsters on exercise wheels at this point.

'So my question is: would you do this for the Ultimate High? Would you fill your pipe with a blob of freshly excreted steaming catshit and apply a flame to it, sucking its essence into your waiting lungs?' I had a million such questions I could pose for them; it came from all those hours sitting in Southern California traffic with nothing to do but think.

One time I stopped by while in a particularly lustful mood, horny in a drunken Texas redneck sort of way, just looking for some sleazy trim. I'd guzzled a sixpack of Meister Brau and watched a couple of Russ Meyer films and needed some hot girly action. Gennifyr was busy doing a fingerpainting on a huge canvas, using her own menstrual blood for paint; the painting seemed to depict a burning city with a heroic woman kicking Superman in the balls in the foreground, much to the oohs and aahs of her artist buddies who stood around watching her create. I wasn't going to be getting any 'leg' from her, so I motioned to Yma, a slender blonde morsel with complicated acupuncture-diagram tatts over most of her body and plenty of stainless-steel hardware stuck through various flaps and folds of her anatomy. Yma had locked herself in a car trunk parked in the Knott's Berry Farm parking lot for nine days, living on Pop-Tarts and club soda and filling many notebooks with her cryptic, tiny scrawl – she was way too far into Chris Burden to make any kind of sense and would probably go right for the .22-bullet-in-the-arm routine in homage of her idol – but I wasn't interested in making sense. Nothing like a head full of bottom-shelf beer and a brainpan stuffed with images of jiggling 60s jugs to bring out the crude redneck in a normally urbane California gentleman:

'Hey baby, what say you and me head out to my van and, like, *get busy*?' I slurred, winking lewdly. I patted my bulging groin. 'I got something for you, eh?'

She was charmed, interpreting the whole routine as some kind of incredibly sophisticated irony from a fellow artist. Next thing I knew, I was helping her into the van and shoving aside enough crap to make room for us to lie down. I scrabbled through some cardboard boxes and hauled out a greasy canvas sheet, the one I would put under the van during particularly greasy repairs. Spreading the canvas on the van floor, I sat down on it and pulled her to me, pawing her portions in a most drunken-sailor-esque manner and jamming my tongue as far as I could get it into her mouth. The studs in her tongue really sent me as they clacked on my teeth. 'Get them clothes off, woman!' I commanded, getting into the character but also feeling genuine white-trash randiness. She giggled – in her mind, we were probably acting out some kind of archetypal reification narrative. Stripped, she was a petite young thing, about a third the volume of Gennifyr, but every inch of her save the face and hands was a vividly tattooed acupuncture diagram, complete with Chinese characters and symbols and that got my motor revving a bit. 'I'm gonna split your jelly roll wide open with my rooster-head, baby!' I crowed, beating my chest. 'Git down on it!' I commanded, unzipping my fly and barely suppressing a Dukes of Hazzard 'Yee Haw!' as I unreeled my tool. If I'd had a wooden kitchen match at that moment I'd have lit it on my zipper and ignited a 5-cent cigar. I rummaged through one of the many boxes in the van while she fumbled for my unit and found a warm can of Milwaukee's Best Lite, the kind of beer best consumed while dynamite-fishing for radioactive catfish downstream from the Savannah River plutonium-processing plant. She wrapped her lips around my stuff as I gurgled the warm, vile beer into my mouth and down my shirt. 'Take it, sweet-heart! Take it *all*!'

What had started out as a simple beer fuck had turned into another irony-corrupted bit of playacting, but by Jesus I was gonna get righteously laid in the process. Her pink-and-yellow-dyed hair was cut too short for me to grab a big handful of it, so I put my hands on either side of her head and extracted her from my schlong with an audible cartoony 'pop'. Reclining on the oil canvas, I pulled her on top of me and, grabbing the points of her hipbones, guided her cooch into place against my mushroom-head. We hadn't really been at it for long enough for her to get seriously wet and permit a smooth to-the-hilt penet-ration, but she had enough juice flowing for me to work it in a couple inches with a bit of jiggling and twisting. Redneck sex, baby! She was panting through clenched teeth, pushing harder against me, impatiently trying to get all of my wood in her.

'Damn it, gimme some *more*,' she groaned, grinding away. But I *was* trying. Then we must have hit the wet spot inside her, because she suddenly slipped all the way down, her ass meeting my thighs with a loud slap. Once that obstacle was passed, we got a mighty rhythm going, my hands gripping white-knuckled into her hard-muscled ass cheeks, our timing synched up to permit full bottom-dead-centre to top-dead-centre movement, with no fear of the old 'broken dick' nightmare when the parties pull away from each other at an inopportune moment. It was glorious. No holding back – we were going to kill each other. The van's tired springs creaked and boxes of crap started to overturn from the savage jouncing. I tried to talk dirty as befitted the scene, but I couldn't catch my breath enough for anything other than gasped monosyllables: 'Shit . . . yeah . . . awk . . . oh . . . damn . . .'

She seemed to be in better physical condition, burying her face into my neck and gasping much more complex statements than I was capable of even *thinking*: 'There it is, right there . . . keep doing that . . .' She seemed to have unlimited energy, bashing the small of my back into the mean steel floor of the van. Her ass grew slick from sweat, and beads of the stuff dripped from her hair into my face. My heart seemed on the edge of ventricular fibrillation. I was literally about to get fucked to death. It was great. I figured I wasn't going to wait for her to come more than once – first time she peaked I was gonna be there with her – but she surprised me with a no-warning climax, going all stiff and silent, holding her breath for a long time and emitting a few little squeaks from her throat. I let go and tried to join her in the climax, but came a few seconds later.

After we sneaked back into the house, filthy from sweat and van-dirt and smelling like cheap beer and spunk, we tried to put on an innocent routine, but Gennifyr wasn't buying it. Not that she'd ever show any emotion as bourgeois as jealousy, but there was disapproval in the way she slapped the blood on the canvas. Flies buzzed around the painting. I figured I should wrestle her to the floor and give her a long ride, but I had nothing left. Yma had gotten it all.

Four

My rig was a '63 Ford Econoline van, the type with the engine mounted between the driver's and passenger's seats and the driver's face inches from the windshield as he cranked on the horizontal bus-driver-style wheel. Shaped like a brick, painted white with a faded LUCKY GOLDEN MEAT CO logo in Wild West-style gold leaf, drawings of chickens and pig, displayed in various stiff unnatural Chinese angles, and a bunch of Chinese characters on the sides. It accelerated wearily and made scary clanking noises while cornering, but police didn't notice the thing and I could haul large amounts of gear and assistants to my shows. Best of all, I got it from a Phishhead for a quarter-ounce of midgrade barrio Nibley, and all it needed was a new distributor cap.

The van wasn't just about delivering pizzas and penetrating various female specimens in every proffered orifice. Sometimes I hauled along the Vacuum-Operated Richard Nixon Robot, a sort of parody of a Disney Animatronic robot I had rigged up using hundreds of vacuum solenoids yanked from various junked cars at the Ecology Auto Wrecking lot in Santa Fe Springs (I'd learned something from the construction of the World War One Santa project). The whole setup was powered by vacuum (or 'Suck

Power' as my crude-tongued bandmate Swede would have it) from the Econoline's engine via a network of hissing rubber hoses snaking out of the Vacuum Nixon's left foot and into the engine compartment. The setup could be controlled by a system of switches on the dashboard, or from a random-impulse generator triggered up from an electromechanical pinball-machine cam device, augmented by a 4K mechanical-relay memory device out of an F-102, purchased cheap from the Air Force salvage yard out in Chino. On the random setting, the Nixon (which featured a very realistic rubber mask for a face and a period-authentic late-60s dark blue suit) would often seem almost human in its (or *his*) movements; when set in the van's passenger seat, he would sometimes whip his head around and wave spastically at occupants of other cars, who would then cringe in horror as he punched himself in the side of the head and then bit his own hand like an epileptic schnauzer. As with all my work during my Artist Period, I had one eye on somehow making a buck and/or promoting some pussy with the thing (any other goals seemed somehow phony for an artist of my calibre), so I always looked for an open door-o-opportunity into which to jam the Vacuum Nixon's foot.

One morning I hit the road with Swede to hit the Pick-N-Pull junkyard in Wilmington and score some more starter solenoids for the Randy Kraft & the Dead Marines 'drum kit' and I didn't feel like disconnecting the tangle of vacuum hoses from the Nixon, which we left in the passenger seat while Swede perched on a barstool in the back, among the car parts and assorted crap. Swede was the bass player/roadie of the band. About halfway there, the van's fuel pump gave out and I had to pull over and jimmy up a field-expedient fuel system to get us to the yard. Swede wasn't all too happy about having to manually pour gas into the carburettor, but I figured we could just grab another fuel pump out of any 6-cylinder Ford on the Pick-N-Pull yard and a mere fifteen minutes sniffing gas from an open jug was a small price to pay for the overall *efficiency* of the scheme.

'Holy Jesus! Watch where you're spilling that *gas*!' Swede squawked as a pothole sloshed a healthy pint of Regular Unleaded out of the smile-faced red plastic Kool-Ade jug onto the Econoline's exposed engine (the between-the-seats location made this type of van popular with surfers, who could sit on 'the Warm Seat' on the drive home from the beach), sending up a blinding cloud of gasoline vapour from the hot exhaust manifold. The Vacuum Nixon flashed a palsied peace sign, its jaws clattering rapidly. The speaker in the Nixon's head was blaring out a lo-fi speech, complete with dramatic pauses and applause, about elections in Saigon. Swede tried to steady himself on the wobbly barstool that served as the van's remaining passenger seat, trying to pour a steady trickle of gas from the Kool-Ade jug into the tiny cooking funnel duct – taped to the carburettor's fuel intake. The van jolted and swerved its way down the 57, barely under control, with particularly violent bumps accented by showers of sparks from the under-dash wiring or from the muffler dragging on the highway. The van had already stalled several times due to fuel starvation, gasping and jerking, angry drivers fist-shaking, screaming obscenities as they roared by on both sides, my van having forced them to piss away several precious seconds in their race to The Goal. A dozen gas-filled wine bottles and peanut-butter jars jittered around in the back of the van among the bald tyres, fishing tackle, odd-shaped chunks of rotting plywood, stacks of wet newspapers, soup bones, and other scavenged loot that I had accumulated in my travels. I enjoyed the experience, crowing with delight as the cars screamed past us and into the hydrocarbon-scented future. 'Why don't you get a damn *gas tank* for this thing?' Swede demanded as the sludge-coated 170 motor backfired into his face, making him spill a dollop of gas through one of the holes in the floorboards. 'And move Nixon somewhere else . . . can't he stay at *home*? Does he get *lonely*? Swede was kind of a whiner, and a silky-boy as well, with his fashionably-ripped Iskendarian Cams T-shirt and oh-so-vintage Converse high-tops.

'I keep telling you, dude, the gas tank is *fine*,' I admonished Swede as the gas dripped from his long, 1971-junky-style hair and into his eyes. 'It's the *fuel pump* that's busted. And we'll have a new one as soon as we get to Wilmington. They're five bucks at Pick-N-Pull, bro!' I found myself slipping into Californian dude/bro-speak when I spent any amount of time with Swede. He grumbled incomprehensibly, but I figured the experience would be valuable for him. Swede groaned, flicking ashes from his joint into a puddle of gas by his feet. The Nixon trembled all over, then suddenly lashed out, knocking the jugful of gas into Ned's crotch. '. . . take this action not for the purpose of expanding the war into Cambodia, but for the purpose of ending the war in Vietnam and winning the just peace we all desire.' The Nixon lurched forward, slamming its rubber face into the windshield, then back, again and again, as the van began sneezing into a stall. I scrambled to open a jar of gas to refill the jug.

After our gasoline-soaked jaunt unmarred by any explosions or serious burns, we arrived intact at the junkyard. Swede headed over to the Import section to grab a dozen or so Japanese solenoids (bitter experience having taught us that solenoids pulled from Detroit or European products tended to crap out halfway through a typical Randy Kraft & the Dead Marines gig) while I plucked a ratchet, screwdriver and a 7/16″ socket out of the toolbox and proceeded to extract the fuel pump from a '77 Mercury Monarch.

Heading out to the parking lot with our greasy load of automotive swag, I dropped the parts off at the van while Swede stopped by the Taco Zapateca roach-coach near the yard's entrance (junkyard roach-coaches always have the best food) and picked up some *tacos de lengua* with sides of pickled radishes and a couple bottles of Jarritos tamarindo soda. I alternated bites of beef-tongue tacos with turns of the wrench on the fuel pump, hot sauce mingling with gasoline and oil sludge. Once finished, we smoked a job-well-done joint of Canadian Government-issue Chemotherapy-Grade marijuana and headed back down to Orange County.

'Hey, can we stop at my girlfriend's house?' asked Swede. 'She just distilled a fresh batch of banana gin and I want to try some.'

Banana gin? What the hell? Had the world gone *insane*? 'Did you just say she made some banana gin? Like, am I hearing you correctly, dude?' I lapse into a thick Valley Girl/Jeff Spicoli California-dude accent when with another native son for any length of time.

'You're hearin' me right, brah! She got a recipe from somewhere and made *gallons* of the stuff. Only you have to let it ferment for a few weeks before you distill it. I've been, you know, waiting for it to be ready.' I had to experience bathtub banana gin for myself, so I set a course for Cerritos.

Once we got to Jessica's place, an apartment in a decaying complex full of screaming aficionados of domestic violence, I found that technically she had made banana *brandy*, not banana gin. She was a perky one: 'You guys have to have a drink of my gin right *away*!' She'd read someplace that the cheapest possible fruit-based alcoholic beverage you could possibly make could be made from bananas. She bought about fifty pounds of low-grade bananas, mashed them up and mixed them with hot sugar water. Adding wine yeast, she fermented the mix to get the max non-distilled alcohol level. Then she rigged up a stovetop distiller, which was a teakettle hooked up to a bunch of copper coils and started running the mash through it. Sure enough, after a few passes through the distiller, she had a credibly alcoholic beverage, tasting like sour, rotting bananas with a shudder-inducing bitter aftertaste. Blobs of congealed yeast clung to the sides of a glass filled with the vile drink. No wonder banana-based booze had never caught on. I downed a couple of swigs and burped up a few bubbles of stuff that smelled like a tyre fire in a banana plantation. She was very, very proud of her project, even prouder than she'd been after getting promoted to assistant manager at the flower shop around the corner.

Swede felt it politically wise to show great enthusiasm for the drink. 'Hey, this is some smooth stuff, sweetheart! Gimme a refill!' I politely refused her offer to top off my glass, claiming that such fine liqueur should be savoured, not guzzled in a crude, oafish manner.

After a few minutes sitting at the kitchen table while Swede knocked back several glasses of Jessica's Banana Gin and we discussed matters of great import, I started to feel very relaxed. Not just mellow, but downright *melted*, like my hands and feet weighed about five times normal and I just wanted to hold really, really still. 'Say, Jess, what *else* did you put in this stuff? I mean, besides the bananas?'

She giggled. 'I put my, like, secret in*gred*ient in it. From the flower shop. It makes it hella good!' She opened the fridge and pulled out a bag full of what appeared to be little balls on sticks. On closer inspection, I realised they were dried poppy pods. *Opium* poppy pods. Jessica's Banana Gin had a kick all right – enough opium to sedate an entire Chinese province. 'At work, we sell them for flower arrangements and I found out they can get you *high*!'

No shit. I turned to Swede. 'Uh, dude? You might want to, like, *mod*erate your consumption of this stuff . . .' Too late. He blew a couple of spit bubbles and then toppled forward, very slowly, ending with his face against the table and his eyes rolled up in his head. He drooled and mumbled. I checked for a heartbeat, just to make sure we didn't have an OD on our hands, and he seemed fine, just unconscious.

'What a lightweight, eh?' I said, toasting his snoozing form with my glass. I brought out my stash. 'Care for a dube?' She did. I patted my pockets for rolling papers but I had none. 'Got any papes, Jessica?' She did not. I figured we could just pack a nice pipe bowl, but her mind was locked on a genuine, honest-to-God joint, preferably a mid-70s monstrosity out of a Cheech and Chong movie. It made sense to me. 'Let's take the van down to the head shop – we can get a sixer of Sierra Nevada on the way back.' I had a powerful craving for some hippie beer. 'Not that your banana gin isn't the bee's nuts,' I hastened to add, 'but beer goes with a dube like guns go with Texas.'

But that plan was blasted to hell the moment she saw the Vacuum Nixon in the passenger seat. 'Holy shit!' she squealed, her flip-flop sandals skidding to a bewildered halt on the sidewalk. 'What the hell is *that*?' Jessica wasn't the brightest bulb in the old marquee, but she caught the humour behind a mechanical, vacuum-driven replica of the former president. I started up the engine to provide a good vacuum and ran the Nixon through its paces. I showed her the manual mode, which permitted me to control the Nixon's movements from a switch panel on the dash, and the automatic mode, which caused random flailings. She was delighted. Then she had an idea – I could almost see the comic-strip light-bulb over her head. 'Wait here – I need to go get something!' She turned and ran back to the apartment. Her bare legs flashed in the sun and her long bleached-brown hair shimmered behind her in an extremely 60s flower-child manner, reminding me of those stick-on non-slip daisies folks used to stick in shower stalls back in The Day. Sparkly and simple and without cynicism, but steeped in a true California stoner sensibility.

She returned in a few minutes with a brown paper bag. Climbing into the van, she whipped out a glossy red dildo from the bag. It looked translucent, like a Gummi Bear, and seemed an awfully large, porn-star-sized implement for such a small girl – Jessica couldn't have stood more than five feet even. It smelled of plastic and flower-scented lube. I tried and failed to visualise her stuffing that monster into her body. 'Nixon needs a DICK!' she shouted gleefully, waving it. The dildo flopped around. It had veins and balls. The deluxe model. 'It's *mean* to not give him one!'

Well, sure. I hadn't thought of it, but what right did I have to deprive Tricky Dick of that crucial implement? I could probably rig up a vacuum device to make it go from flaccid to erect, maybe even shoot some sort of spooge-like fluid.

Jessica was at the Nixon, fiddling with his pants. She got the zipper down and worked the dildo into the mechanism where his legs hinged off the backbone. I'd welded a metal brace in just the right spot, and the balls wedged into place perfectly. There was Nixon, sitting in my van's passenger seat with a raging translucent red hard-on protruding from his dark-blue wool pants. A disturbing sight, to be sure, but a thought-provoking one as well. Maybe I could do a show in which the Nixon humped some symbol of innocence, like Frosty the Snowman or the Pillsbury Doughboy. Hmmmm . . . that idea had potential . . .

She looked at me funny. 'Hey, do you think we could take the van someplace more, um, *private*?' She had one tiny hand wrapped around the Nixon's new appendage and was giving it a little strokage. Oh, *man*. 'I was thinking, you know . . .'

I knew. My visions of the newly-minted manhood of the Vaccum Nixon getting some action could be realised right before my eyes. An extremely complicated morality logic puzzle whirled around in my head, concepts of honour and betrayal spinning like souped-up slot-machine reels. Eventually they came up cherries, straight across. Sure, she was my bandmate's girlfriend, but if I didn't actually *touch* her and we happened to try a little Nixon-Jessica experiment, what harm could that do? Sure, it was hardly even a grey area! I jabbed the key into the ignition and lit the fire in the Econoline's engine.

We needed privacy, but the van's engine had to be running in order to produce the vacuum source necessary to run the Nixon. I thought of pulling it into my garage and running a hose from the tailpipe outside, but it would get too hot and loud with the engine roaring indoors – not much vacuum was produced at idle; I'd have to keep the engine racing at about 2,500 RPM to keep the ideal 20 plus inches of steady vacuum necessary to operate the tangle of vacuum motors, solenoids and switches working. Below about five inches mercury the Nixon slowed to a creaky government-employee pace.

I remembered a huge, empty parking lot at a shopping-mall construction site in Orange. Plenty of pallets and parked tanker trucks to shield us from curious eyes, and big enough that nobody would hear the racing van engine. I merged the van onto the 57 East and gunned the thing up to its maximum cruising speed of 71 MPH. Jessica was still fascinated by the Nixon and his freshly installed gear, adjusting it a bit and secretly playing with herself a bit when she thought I wasn't looking. I looked at the vacuum gauge. 23 inches. Flipping the master switch on the Nixon's control panel, I turned some knobs to set him on the RANDOM mode.

It always took a few seconds for the vacuum to build up in the lines and the switches to start distributing the vacuum signal. The Nixon hissed and twitched a bit; one eye snapped open and the eyeball jittered left-to-right. Jessica jerked back in shock and stared. I hit the Soundtrack switch and started the recording of the 1972 Inaugural Address, playing from the speaker in the Nixon's head: '. . . rrrrrRRR . . . and because our strengths are so great, we can approach our weaknesses with vigour . . .' I hadn't really worked out the jaw motions so well – his face *was* just a $19.95 rubber mask – so his mouth just clacked open and closed randomly as he spoke. After a moment, his jaw stuck in the open position while the speech continued. I felt around under the driver's seat and found the tyre iron. Reaching over with the tyre iron, I whacked the Nixon on the back of the head to free up his jaw. Jessica went 'Eep!' at that, but it fixed the problem. Now the vacuum lines had charged up completely and he was fully operational. While the '72 Inaugural (or was it the '68? I could never keep them straight in my mind) droned on, the Nixon went through his usual quivers and strange hand motions that he'd do when I had him on the RANDOM setting. Of course, with the gleaming Gummi-red dildo protruding pruriently from his pants, the strange motions took on a far more disturbing aspect than ever before. I wondered why I'd never thought to equip him with boy-parts . . . it seemed to add so much to the Nixon's effectiveness as a statement on the American Way Of Life.

Jessica was hypnotised by the Nixon's actions. She wasn't even trying to hide the fact that she was giving herself a good diddling any more; both hands under her skirt and a facial expression like a chimp doing something shameful at the zoo. Nixon's presidency ended before Jessica was even born, and he had been dead for almost five years, yet his vacuum-powered, well-hung representative seemed to have struck some primal chord in the reptilian portions of Jessica's overheated brain.

We rolled into the mall-to-be's parking lot and I eased the van between a shipping container and a gigantic mound of gravel. I turned off the Nixon's master switch and his motions gradually slowed and halted. I exited the van and walked around to the passenger-side door. I looked at the Nixon sitting in the seat, then at Jessica and her expectant face. She sucked absently at her sticky fingers while staring straight at the Nixonian hardware glowing red in the afternoon sun. How was I going to get the two of them together? Nixon was tethered to the engine compartment by a relatively short leash of vacuum lines, but I could manoeuvre him into the area behind the passenger seat and then position Jessica in the proper orientation to accept his vacuum-powered ardour.

I climbed in the van and guided her to the back of the vehicle. Her skin felt hot and dry and she seemed in a strange sort of trance. No doubt the stupefying rays of the Man From Yorba Linda's essential Orange County manhood, having wandered lonely about the county for years, had worked their magic on Jessica. I had her take off her panties, which took quite a while in her state; I was tempted to help but figured I'd be breaking some kind of rule involving the undergarments of one's bandmate's girlfriend. I arranged her with her palms on the underside of the van's roof, her feet spread out wide, and her ass sticking out and toward the rear of the passenger seat. Scrupulously avoiding touching her flesh, I lifted the hem of her skirt between my fingers and pulled it up and out of the way. Her ass was stunning – healthy, peach-coloured cheeks and not a zit or ingrown hair to be seen. Her cooch, with its downy blonde tufts, glistened pleasantly. I believe her position was the one referred to by primatologists as 'presenting'.

Next, I went over to the Nixon and wrestled him out of the seat. He wasn't very heavy, but all the hinges and joints made him quiet unwieldy. Horsing him around the seat, I grabbed a roll of duct tape from the glovebox and proceeded to wrap it around his chest and the seat, taping him to the seat back facing rearward. His schlong quivered in the air about a half-foot from Jessica's eager cooch. She remained obediently in presenting position, trusting me to get the party set up properly. I then applied duct tape to his Size 11 Shiny Black Shoes, sticking them firmly to the van's floor. The final step was a bit trickier; now that the Nixon was firmly anchored to the van, he needed to remain attached to Jessica or he'd just flail aimlessly, squandering his presidential grit and determination on thin air.

Digging through a milk crate full of random car-related crap, I found a couple of bungee cords. Eureka! I placed the Nixon's hands (actually rubber gloves filled with silicon sealant over a crude hinged skeleton) on her hips, then bungeed them to each other. The cords provided enough tension to keep the hands firmly clamped on her hips. I jiggled him around and he stayed attached to the van and to Jessica. Now I had the Nixon in a slightly hunched standing position, clutching his latest conquest's bare hips with his glowing red phallus locked and loaded.

'OK, Jess, get him started.' She turned her head around to look at me, confused. 'Oh, all right,' I sighed. Clearly she was expecting Tricky Dick to take some vacuum-assisted initiative. Some amount of touching would have to be acceptable; I took the Nixon's rubbery rod in one hand and pulled her toward it until its tip just touched her cunt lips. She gasped at the touch, but held still. Making an inverted peace sign with my fingers, I laid them on either side of her labia and spread them open enough to manoeuvre Dick's dick into the correct angle and location at the vaginal opening. Then I pushed her back against him, just enough to get him worked inside her a bit. This definitely got her attention – I could see her pulse in her neck and her heart rate was way up. Thanks to all her masturbation on the drive over, she was good and wet; no need for me to scavenge around the van for some transmission fluid or other Field Expedient Lube. 'OK, now hold it right where you are,' I told her.

Heading back to the driver's seat, I sat down and put my foot on the gas pedal. At about 2,400 RPM I got maximum manifold vacuum, so I slid a cinder block against the pedal to hold it in place and flipped the Vacuum Nixon control panel's master switch to ON. This time I set the main dial to MANUAL control. As his vacuum lifeblood coursed through his system, he came back to life. Jessica started to hyperventilate a bit as she felt him shudder and hiss. Since this was a special occasion, I popped the 1952 'Checkers Speech' cassette into the tape deck that fed the speaker in his head, and a tape of John Philip Sousa marches into the van's own cassette deck. *The Stars and Stripes Forever* blared jauntily from the 6x9s in the back, while Nixon began to speak to Jessica in a harsh and metallic, yet strangely soothing voice:

'... not one cent of the eighteen thousand dollars or any other money of that type ever went to me for my personal use ...' His jaw worked smoothly; no need for any tyre-iron persuasion. The Sousa tubas oompahed majestically and he quivered with anticipation. '... no contributor to any of my campaigns has ever received any consideration that he would not have received as an ordinary constituent ...' he continued, fighting for his spot as running mate to Eisenhower and, by extension, his political life. Jessica started to moan softly, like a distant cow mooing, just barely audible over the march music and the van's engine roar. I could see the Checkers Speech had *her* sold on his essential goodness.

I detached the Nixon control panel from the dash and set it in my lap, for a better sense of the controls. With the twin joysticks controlling his upper arms beneath my fingers, I tried to make his arms pull her toward him. At first I couldn't get it right, but I found that he would push forward with a combination of arm action and a leg push. My fingers danced over the switches like a 9-year-old with a video-game controller; a little more left arm, now some hip action, and finally a push from both legs. A little jerkily at first, then smoothly, I worked the Nixon's tool into her cooch. She kept up a steady droning moan, which increased in volume as inch after inch of Nixon's plastic manhood slid into her.

'. . . our family was one of modest circumstances and most of my early life was spent in a store out in East Whittier . . .' he told her, thrusting more energetically as I got the hang of the controls. Jessica started to push back. She was starting to sweat. Her lips were parted now, her teeth clenched, and she breathed through them with an urgent hissing sound. '. . . Pat Nixon has never been on the government payroll . . .'

I started getting fancy, making the Nixon do little fishtailing pelvic flourishes and synchronising his thrusts with hers. I made him bend over her so his talking jaw could bite her on the neck. Note to self: I'd have to install some more realistic teeth in the Nixon during his next overhaul.

As he worked his way through the speech, Jessica seemed to have a searing climax each time he made another convincing point about his overall integrity and honour. As he reached the part of the speech in which he listed the Nixon household finances in excruciating detail ('. . . a 1950 Oldsmobile car . . .') her breathing and moaning took on a desperate, sobbing sound. All the opening and closing vacuum switches and venting vacuum motors gave the Nixon's body a hissing, clicking runaway-locomotive sound.

When Nixon reached the point in the speech at which he mentions the cocker spaniel, Checkers, after whom the speech got its name, I figured I'd finish off the Nixon's genital inauguration with something special. Cranking the volume on the Sousa marches up another few notches and then adjusting the Speed slider to MAX on the Nixon control board, I flipped the main dial to RANDOM and leaned back to watch the finale.

With the speed turned all the way up and his impulses now totally random, the Nixon began having a fit, almost a seizure. As he was still taped in place and bungeed to Jessica, he didn't pull out of her, but he shook, flailed, and jittered crazily. His head whipped up and down, side to side, while his eyeballs rolled crazily, often pointing in strangely different directions and sometimes rolling up in his head completely, showing only the whites.

This frenzy had quite an effect on Jessica. Probably sensing that Nixon was about to wrap it up, she built up to a siren-like wail and continued thrusting her hindquarters into him. It was impressive how she managed to absorb that plus-sized dildo into her petite slit, but she'd had plenty of practice with it prior to its installation on the Trickster. I noticed some pretty gooey snail-tracks on his pants and vest and wondered how hard it was to clean cunt juice out of a vintage wool suit. While I debated dry-cleaning versus another suit from the Salvation Army, I heard Nixon enter the homestretch of the speech: '. . . I would suggest that under the circumstances both Mr Sparkman and Mr Stevenson should come before the American people as I have and make a complete statement as to their financial history . . .' Switching the Nixon back to MANUAL mode, I had him thrusting as hard and fast as I could work the controls. When he reached the final line of the speech (. . . and a vote for Eisenhower is a vote for what's good for America), I snapped off all the noise, dropped the engine back down to idle, and shut down the Nixon. He was finished. Trembling, Jessica retracted herself from his unit. Although he hadn't ejaculated or lost his hard, she understood that the 'vote for Eisenhower' line was his climax.

Well, I definitely wanted to keep the Nixon sexually active after this pleasant experience. I thought of how I would go about rigging the Nixon up with a pump that would squirt some kind of homemade jizz-like substance; it would have to be heated somehow, and he would need to have firehose-like quantity and velocity. I wanted gushers of Nixon jizz to fill the vaginal vault and then come spraying out around the shaft of his schlong, and to have the process continue for several minutes. *That* would make an impression.

But that would have to wait for later. I had to take Jessica home and back to her banana-opiated, none-the-wiser boyfriend. But I had big plans for future Nixonian adventures.

Five

I had a fair number of prized regulars, including a bunch of gnarled redneck construction workers staying at the Ali Baba Pleasure Dome, a pseudo-Moorish domed motel compound on Newport Boulevard, while they worked as imported scabs on some union-busting project, the evening-shift cashier at the Minute Pit convenience store at Bristol and Warner, a poet-in-residence in the beach cabañas of the U. of Mission Viejo, and so on. One of my steadiest regulars lived in a cottage behind one of those 1920s Hollywood monster homes on the beach edge of Costa Mesa: Charlene Cabrillo, aka Mistress Carlotta. The cottage, a stucco job with a phony Spanish mission bell in a tiny tower atop the red-tile roof that suggested orange groves, endless sunshine, and other postcard Southern California pre-apocalyptic subjects, served as Mistress Carlotta's home and office. I later found that she came up with the Mistress Carlotta persona as a means of turning the cheery-looking cottage into an ominous Spanish Inquisition-style dungeon for her clients; a certain suspension of disbelief apparently being a prerequisite for your typical Orange County businessman seeking humiliation from a 27-year-old punkette-turned-unemployable-waitress with a respectably hourglass shape and

Irish/Mexican ancestry that could be mistaken for Spanish with a hopeful squint through tear-filled eyes. I could sympathise – after all, the audiences for my so-called performance-installation pieces were just as desperate for some sort of relief and just as willing to make-believe they were getting the Real Deal without having to go up to LA. After bringing her several eighths of Kind Bud over the course of a month, I suggested that we simply schedule a weekly delivery, with an extra Bud Of The Month thrown in. The Bud Of The Month was my contribution to Southern Orange County dopelore; I'd just toss in a nice-looking gram bud to each regular.

I was vaguely curious about Charlene and her line of work, though her whole setup reeked of flakery and wishful thinking, like a pet store full of half-dead lizards waiting for the landlord to show up with big evictin' boot forward, and I didn't usually have the time to burn one with customers while making my appointed rounds. It seemed clear that her clients numbered in the single digits – I never saw one – and that some shameful source of income, like a trust fund or insurance settlement, really paid the bills. Really, I thought she was basically full of shit with her self-consciously edgy lifestyle and inability to find a better-paying scam to avoid the 9-to-5 horrors of Slaving For The Man. Still, the way her goodies swelled those black Nick Cave T-shirts (and, once, her cheapo vinyl dom getup; those curves projected on my mental TV screen a shameful number of times while simu-schtupping my girlfriend and during self-pollution sessions) and her never-ending supply of quality Mexican beer had me looking forward to her part of my Appointed Rounds. Found myself scheduling her place as the last stop of the night and then shooting a few hours through the head while bullshitting and passing the bong around. She had an impressive library of true-crime and serial-killer books, which she was willing to loan out, and framed portraits of the Manson Family on the walls (ominous signs that didn't mean much to me until it was too late). As it turned out, of course, I'd badly underestimated Charlene, both in the smarts department and in her seriousness. Charlene was and is *extremely* serious about certain things.

Now, anyone who knows anything about the Sux-M-Owt.com story knows there's some bad blood between us now, what with Charlene's slimy ratting-off of yours truly in order to save her own worthless hide, etc., but I'm doing my best here to be honest. Why would I lie? I've done my time (well, almost) and there's nothing to gain from flogging her already foul image with a bunch of made-up gibberish. I knew at the time that her whole 'dom' routine was mostly crap, that she was getting trust fund checks and insurance settlement money from a phony back injury and probably income from other nebulous non-Horatio-Alger-type sources, but I believed that there was *some* truth to it, that she basically knew what she was doing when she strapped on the vinyl suit and picked up the Goebbels riding crop. Later on, when she had the whole code crew hooked up with catheters and banana-pellet dispensers and had her bodyguards administering disciplinary beatings for 'loyalty lapses' and 'time theft', I began to suspect that she was on territory completely uncharted by the International Sisterhood of Dominatrices.

One day I cruised into the parking lot to start my shift and idly noticed that most of the crew's cars were absent. Inside, chaos. The smartest and evilest money-saving move yet by the Twins. Taking advantage of their evil relatives back in France, they had recruited a dozen or so French high-school kids into working at Colonel Sausage's for the winter. Apparently promises of Beach Boys-style high living on the beach, beautiful apartments, etc. had been made. The reality was that all the French Pizza Slaves, or FPSs as we came to call them, were made to live in one squalid room in Mimi's apartment, where they lived on pizza leftovers and muddy Southern California tap water. Sleeping on chunks of packing material beneath U-Haul blankets, they spent most of their free time, of which there was very little, smoking generic cigarettes and watching Salvadoran religious UHF TV while the flies bonked against the mini-blinds. They had been chosen for their docility and lack of English skills, with unnamed threats against their families back home keeping them from running to the French consul in LA and the use of a single rusty bike to take on trips to the beach enabling them to receive beatings at the hands of skinheads. Sharing a beer ripped off from the walk-in fridge at work with Ferdinand, the least incompetent English speaker among the FPS squad, I asked why he didn't just fucking grab his plane ticket and blow town. 'Passport, airplane ticket, Mimi keeps them. Shit. Summer finish soon, then home.' Resigned to his fate.

The poor fucking FPSs had a hell of a time at work; the Evil Twins tried to keep them in the sweltering heat of the pizza assembly area in the back, but occasionally an FSP would be required to man the cash register. Naturally, this led to some pretty severe language-based conflicts with customers. Your typical Southern California pizza consumer, upon being faced with a service employee who doesn't understand English, will automatically assume the employee is a Spanish speaker and start barking orders in primitive Spanish:

'Gimme uno pizza grande con pepperoni y . . . y . . . *mushroomos*!'

Spanish-speaking customers went through a similar routine. The end result was an angry customer screaming at the confused FSP, who knew terrible things would happen at the hands of the Evil Twins if he or she started screaming French obscenities at the asshole. The rest of us tried to be nice to the FSPs, sneaking them beers from the walk-in fridge and so on, but we knew any attempt to turn the Evil Twins into The Man would be fruitless; it was clear that the proper hands had been greased, and there were dark rumours about the Twins providing sexual services for officials at the French Consulate in Los Angeles and even the Newport Beach cops. It all seemed quite plausible.

Of course, the efficiency of the bitter, non-English-speaking FPSs wasn't really up to even Colonel Sausage's sorry-ass standards, so there were normal employees, mostly gringos from the white-trash flats of Costa Mesa and Anaheim, trying to scrape up the cash to put themselves through one of the local junior colleges. Parents mostly boozed up, in jail, missing teeth and tinfoil on the TV antenna in the Huntington Beach Aztec Tacoburger dingbat apartment building. We had a fair number of babes working behind the counter – making pizzas, taking orders – and one, a dirty little redhead number named Becca 'Possum Girl' McTeague, was selling ass for $50 a pop. Her days flew by in a whirl of pizza toppings, bong hits in the parking lot, and half-C-note humps with coworkers on the green corduroy couch at her place at Park West. California Potato Chips (the crackly circles of dried fuck juice that result from postcoital drips on the rough fabric of a thrift-store couch) would flake off and be replenished as the old springs took another 30 seconds of abuse from the thrustings of a 19-year-old pizza cashier. I had never purchased Possum Girl's services, and in truth wasn't much interested at first – she resembled a possum in both small, sharp-toothed face and low-watt brain, though I must admit the view of her mean little ass as she bent over the counter to feed logs of Nearly Dairy Simu-Cheese into the grater got my goods a-twitchin, just a bit. Not only was her ass mean; by all accounts her *cooch* was downright satanic: 'It's, like, got *calluses* on it, dude,' Thor hissed at me, holding in a lungful of some quality Thai-Indica hybrid as we got red in the vinyl luxury of his 'civilian' car, an '87 Mercury Grand Marquis. 'Ten-dons. Or *some*thin' weird . . . it's *hard* to stick it in, and then it, like, *resists* the whole time, while she's screwin' that little possum face up all hateful and shit.' Thor was one of the other delivery guys, well-known for his somewhat-frightening ability to make the Grand Marquis's vast, old-lady-land-yacht bulk thread the needle through the grimmest traffic jams as he cruised to the swift completion of his appointed rounds. Word was, no man could stay on more than one minute in the Possum Girl's Mean Coochie without blowing his oats right off and then spending the rest of the evening sitting with her on the Couch Of Spooge, watching bad UHF TV and smoking Santa Ana Coughweed to the accompanying drone of her insights into the nature of reality.

I tried to stay out on the road as much as possible during my delivery shifts, as the scene at Colonel Sausage could be depressing if not soul-damaging. Beaten-down sorry bastards toiling under the wicked verbal lash of the Evil Twins, or facing hordes of assholistic customers at the counter or on the phone. I gave my coworkers an Employee Discount on my wares, figuring a good high might help make the drudgery tolerable.

Six

At this time, I had a regular girlfriend. Violet Tran, born on a shrimp trawler full of refugees in the South China Sea. Schoolteacher parents fleeing the Cong death camps or some such grim shit. One of those boring stories involving terrible wrongs committed by guys with AK-47s and floppy camo hats. Raised in Garden Grove, attending Chapman College on a *volleyball scholarship*, of all things. It was Violet's very wholesome Orange County straightness that attracted me; I figured I needed an anchor like her to keep from spinning off too far into my weird shit. Without her hitting me square in the nuts with the occasional sneering 'You're so full of shit!' I'd start believing my own various fuck-with-heads schemes and would likely end up a workplace rampager, single-interest collector, or worse. Her conservative, immigrant-Republican-patriotic parents didn't quite know what to make of this crazy blond-headed roundeye romancing their daughter, but I could usually charm Mr Tran if I showed up with a 12-pack of Brew 102 and started him on The Evils of Communism after we'd knocked back a few while listening to some wailing Saigon crooner on the static-blasting AM radio. Once he got going there was no stopping him: 'Fuck fucking Ho Chi Minh!

He kill my BROTHER! He kill my UNCLE!' I'd be screaming along with him, swearing that I'd love nothing better than to wade hip-deep in a lake of freshly-spilled commie blood. I'd yank back the bolt on an imaginary M-16, squeeze off a couple rounds at Ho Chi, and chug down another watery beer.

Once lightweight Papa-san passed out, Violet would usually ask me to take her 'to the library' to 'help her with her physics homework.' When the parents weren't around, I'd always refer to our destination as 'the *Li*brary' with appropriate quote-mark finger motions. Mama-san would beam approvingly. What a nice American boy, to humour crazy lonely old Papa-san and take daughter-san out for some homework assistance.

What we'd *actually* do is park the van someplace and indulge in some good wholesome blue-ball-inducing, window-steaming, high-school-style make-out sessions. She was plenty willing to get on with some real mucus-membrane action, but whenever she started trying to yank off the burning clothing over her more tempting zones, I'd put the brakes on with a firm hand over the buttons or snaps or whatever her shaky fingers were tearing at: 'No . . . no . . . our relationship isn't *ready* for us to do that yet.' At this point, of course, she'd spent about 45 minutes probing the outlines of my pulsing blue-veiner through my jeans in a futile attempt to drive me to such a paroxysm of lust that I'd shred her clothes with my testosterone-pulsing meathooks and *throw it in*. Truth be told, I really get off on sexual frustration – a harmless yet endlessly entertaining minor kink – and Violet was so good-natured as to put up with it. A virgin at the time, of course. She'd missed out on serious Boy Contact in high school, being a shy immigrant Asian girl in a school full of sleek boob-job-equipped white girls and aggro big-haired Chicanas, and figured my reluctance to stuff her various aching orifices with a healthy segment of Man was just a temporary phase that all guys went through with a new girlfriend. I'd take her home looking a lot more agitated than one might expect from a physics study session, and she'd run right up to her room for some well-deserved self-pollution. Yeah, I admit it – I had a sick misogynist virgin/whore thing going on with Violet, in addition to my little frustration games, and if she ever reads this she's probably going to track me down and de-ball me with a broken beer bottle. She probably suspected I was messing around a bit with other females, but the frequency and twistedness of such contacts would likely have pissed her off in a big way.

Possum Girl, like a radio station of negative vibes, beamed a fair amount of resentment toward my own person; this situation stemmed partly from her (accurate) belief that I was the origin of her hated nickname and partly because she read my reefer-scented blond good looks and thick 'like, dude' Southern California accent as sure indicators that I was a Surfer. She hated surfers, fancying herself more of a crypto-goth Angry Chick. Though I had never set foot to surfboard in my life, it never seemed worth the energy to correct her when she made sarcastic references to my surfin' lifestyle. Although I am technically a tall, blond-haired, suntanned Southern California white boy, perhaps vaguely resembling a surfer if the observer squints or has a head injury, I got my tan lounging on vinyl lawn furniture in the backyard while sipping very non-surfer Whiskey Sours and reading *extremely* non-surfer Russian novels. After a few months, I realised that her conception of what made up a Surfer was, in her own dim marsupial way, a fairly interesting mental construct and perhaps worth more study. Surfer Time stood still in the eyes of Possum Girl, and the ur-Surfer standing sunburned and tall on the flickering screen in her less-than-spacious cranium seemed a weird mix of 90s aggro-pierced-and-tatted skinhead, brandishing a jailhouse shank to a rap-metal beat, and wholesome early-60s Jan & Dean hodad, complete with '50 Woody wagon, zinc oxide on the nose, and big striped swim trunks, with discordant hints of poi-scented Hawaiian-ass themes throughout. The more I thought about the massive disconnect between the surfer reality surrounding her and her conception of it, the more fascinated I became. With fascination came a certain amount of schlong-twitching interest, alloyed with a fair measure of contempt – enough to make me unwilling to pony up the $50 Possum Girl price tag. As she was a loadie supreme and I was the Dope Man, I knew we could work something out. While stuck between deliveries I imagined a plan – a cruel one-act surfer drama with her as unknowing participant – that would be one of my finest pieces yet. One warm evening, with the brown sunset sinking into the petrochemical horizon and the Econoline idling in the Colonel Sausage lot, I called her over to the car as she left her shift. Producing a pinecone-sized bud of Hayward Haywire and drawing it under my nose like a plutocrat applying a sneef to a fine cigar, I suggested that perhaps we might find a satisfactory arrangement.

'But I'm, like, extra perverted, you know,' I oozed her way, with a used-car-salesman wink, 'so you'll have to do this *my* way.' I wanted her disgusted and feeling superior at first, but at the same time experiencing a sense of foreboding at the way she would be *used* by me. Her face showed disgust, for sure, but her baby-blue beads were locked on that $200 bud – her head would jerk around when something interfered with the line of vision to the bud, much like a cat will do if you block its view of a prey animal. I started talking the Surfer talk, based on all the millions of conversations I'd had to listen to from my wave-riding customers and twisted into what I figured fit her image: 'See, queeb, me and the mokes was talkin' about taking the ol' van up to HB to spend some time in the green room with the Man In The Grey Suit, and we got to nostalgifyin' about the old days, back when a, like, surfer boy would take his best surfer girl for a love-ride into the desert in his Woody, a good Beach Boys tune on the AM, and so on, and it came to me – nobody can *do* that anymore. The early 60s are *gone*.'

She could see where this was going. My Little Surfer Girl fantasy. Ah, my little possum, just you wait. This won't be the same garbage can you always rummage around in with your sharp little snout.

'I fucking hate surfers, and I hate you too, asshole!' She was giving me the squinchy-face, lips pulled back from her tiny sharp teeth.

'Ah, peace out to you, my pretty gremmie,' I soothed. 'Just think of how stratospherically *high* you'll get when you smoke this . . . big . . . fat . . . nug!' I joggled the bud in a little dancy-dance, in time to the last four words, to make it more attractive. 'In fact, before we have our little surf party I'll load you up an extra-special bowl of pure THC crystals, screened off the tops of a pound of Northern Lights hydro-weed.' This was the key moment; I whipped out a tiny ziploc full of the stuff and let her handle it – no mistaking the red hairs mixed in with the crystallised tetrahydracannabinol deltas 7 and 9 – the stony essence of a pound of good weed. Even I, with my legendary Iron Head, was a little scared of the stuff. She couldn't speak, eyes glazed. I had her. 'Pick you up at home tomorrow at seven.' I drove off packing some serious wood in my jeans.

Figuring I'd sharpen my sexual-tormenting skills on the uncomplaining surfaces of long-suffering Violet, I dropped by her place. The parents were gone, visiting one of her many medical-student brothers up at UCLA, so we retired to her room. She was on me as soon as the door closed. A simple Garden Grove tract-home bedroom; I mused on the optimism of Orange Country back in the 50s as she wrapped her lithe body around me, her mouth on my neck and her breath coming ragged already. Out the window, I could see the neighbours Bar-B-Q-ing up what looked like human lungs; a GGPD chopper nosed through the brown early-evening sky in search of crime. My attention veered back to Violet, who seemed more worked up than normal, as her teeth gouged into my ear. Embracing her, I allowed my hands to move slowly along the little knobs of her spine, enjoying the sensation of her fuzzy sweater under my fingers. When I reached the bottom of the garment, however, I felt . . . *skin.* Damn! She'd managed to wiggle out of her jeans and panties while I contemplated the weird scene outside, and now I was having great difficulty finding the will to remove my hands from her bare ass. Flawless smooth skin over hard striated volleyball-induced glutes. She giggled and ground against me, hard – all those years on the volleyball court made her strong as hell to begin with, and now my own resistance was melting like a Cong village under a napalm attack. I still felt somewhat confident that I could still stop before I found myself squirting a full ration of spunk into her eager cervix, but it would be quite a challenge.

I nudged her leg outward a bit with one foot, getting a very accessible bit of spreadsky up higher; she understood and obligingly parted her legs as much as possible while still remaining standing. I was half-holding her up as her mouth sought mine. My fingers rested at the top of her ass crack, the palm curved around the muscled cheek. As I probed behind her front teeth with my tongue tip, I began to slide my hand down and around her ass, leaving the fingertips in the crevice – but not too deeply – until they brushed pubic hair. At that point, I curved my fingers so as to cup the entire length of her labia. *That* sure as shit got her attention; for a nanosecond I felt like a real jerk for my cruel teasing, but that didn't stop me from pushing my index finger between the outer lips and into the magical land inside. 'That's it,' she whispered, putting her hand over mine and rubbing it around, hard. Joy-juice squeezed between my fingers and onto hers. She figured she'd finally get properly fucked after paying all those dry-humping dues.

I considered it. I really liked Violet and didn't want to think about all the bad-karma chips I'd be stacking up on The Big Table if I continued to leave her with a head full of confusion and a distinctly vacant vagina due to some strange ideas about sexual control. I'd probably turn into a full-fledged crazyman without her stabilising presence, and any sane woman would have no choice but to dump a man (like a monkey dropping a hot penny – I flashed on a vivid image of a tiny primate hand yanking back from the scalding copper, a high-pitched 'EEEEEK!' from simian lips) if he continued jerking her around like this.

I figured I'd better make her come at least once, or she'd probably show me the door for good. I steered her onto the bed, a sensible twin-size, devoid of stuffed animals and other accessories of the stereotypical Southern California Vietnamese chick. Trying not to seem too knowledgeable about the geography of Girl Parts, I arranged the wisps of pubic hair to one side or the other of the outer lips with my tongue tip, all the while holding my forearm across her belly, to prevent excess wiggling. She was digging this in a big way, and dug it even more when I commenced with the full *lengua*-gynaecological exam. *Don't make her think you've done this too many times before*, I thought as I made sure to keep missing her clit by a maddening eighth of an inch on each pass. I worked a little finger in – no doubts about her virginity – and gave her a little gentle in-out stimulation while I munched rug. Eventually, like I'd stumbled on the magic spot through sheer patience, I allowed myself a few fancy flourishes and kept her in a state of climax for quite a while – she was a 'skimmer' rather than a 'big bang' type and made a lot of tiny strangled noises.

Dizzy and flushed, I staggered to my feet. She sat up and went right for my zipper. I was frozen. Off with the pants. She wrapped her hands around my crank and got right down to business. What she lacked in experience, she made up for in enthusiasm, even getting a little fancy once she got the hands and mouth coordinated and figured out the most sensitive areas. *Finally* she was getting some real action. I didn't hold back on the groaning and heavy breathing – to be honest, it would have been hard to do so – and felt that *here we go* feeling of approaching orgasm rolling up on me. She slowed down, stopped, and looked hard into my eyes. Taking a page from my book, apparently.

'You need to give me *more*,' she said, stroking the underside of my shaft with her nails. There didn't seem to be much room for debate here. I'd burn in hell for eternity if I left her room without giving her at least a little taste. 'I just want to *feel* it. Just let me feel it, kiss me a little, and then we can finish like *this*.' She wrapped her tongue lightly under the head and applied a few inches of vacuum. Fast learner. 'I know we can't go all the way'. More than fifty years after the invention of the atomic bomb, and it was still possible to hear the phrase 'all the way'. Strange world.

Fair enough. She reclined on the bed, legs wide, gazing fascinated at my schwantz as it approached her nether regions. She was certainly wet enough for a trouble-free entry, but I wasn't sure how to go about slipping it to a virgin without undue pain. Not that I'm hung like a Shetland pony, but my wang was a good bit thicker than my little finger, which had encountered fairly stiff resistance. Just plunge in, like jumping into cold water – get the shock over with quickly? I decided on the slow approach. Guiding her hand to my shaft, I had her slip the head up, down, up, down, the length of her slippery trough, while I applied a bit of thrust. After a bit of this I'd penetrated the inner labia; I took her hands and pinned them beneath mine, next to her head. Her fingers laced with mine. With a slow, steady push, I slid inch by inch into her heat. Extremely tight fit – almost painful for me – but she clearly enjoyed it as much as she'd hoped. Once I bottomed out, I maintained the pressure and held it there, still, while lowering my face to hers. We kissed. Concentrating on our kissing, I tried to pretend I didn't feel her feathery little contractions as she had a couple of peaks while wrapped around me, and refrained from the thrusting that seemed so instinctive. After what seemed like hours but was probably a couple of minutes, I pulled out as gradually as I'd entered.

Quickly, she drew herself up and applied mouth to cock. Nothing fancy now, just an excited straight-out oil-well motion. I popped my rocks fast, yelping out as I shot – no doubt causing some knowing glances between the Lung-B-Q-ing neighbours. Violet was startled by her sudden mouthful of jizz, but recovered fast and swallowed like a veteran. A *trooper*.

She'd done a fine job of enticing me into crossing the Line In the Sand, and it looked like I'd be seeing a lot more of Violet in the future. Sure, there'd be a reckoning when she found out about my extracurricular activities, but I trusted my finessing ability to spin my way out of the frying pan. I was probably better off just settling down with Violet; who knows, if I'd done so at that point I would have had a lot less hassle with Johnny Law later on.

Seven

During my frequent visits to Charlene's place, our discussions gradually took a turn toward the business side of our chosen professions. Though we were dwellers in the so-called 'shadow economy', we felt that the titles of Dope Dealer and Dominatrix were in fact badges of honour. Hallowed traditions, passed down from generation to generation. Rituals and secret languages. I was a proud member of an elite group and could look back at my predecessors selling 'tea' in 20s jazz clubs with the sort of respect a modern astrophysicist might give to Galileo (this sort of line of thought, when coupled with a head stuffed full of my wares, tended to lead to lengthy reveries involving me as The Reefer Man in speakeasy Chicago, driving a cord and selling 'sticks' to various hepcats). While I still didn't take her all that seriously as a *successful* dominatrix, I at least gave her credit for being an affable bumbler, feeling her way to what might end up being a marginally competent career.

I began noticing Charlene a bit more during this time, too – I mean noticing her in a male-female sort of way – especially her nice, fully-packed round ass and small waist. I had always been *aware* of her in a pussy-hound-type way, of course, but I tried to avoid slipping the meat to customers. Business with pleasure and all that. I knew she was thinking along those lines as well, but there were some weird pride issues on both sides and, as it turned out, some dark better-left-unexplored rooms in her basement.

My deliveries to her place had become a twice-a-week affair, and I dispensed with the pizza-delivery schtick for the stop at Charlene's, hitting her house after the completion of my appointed rounds with Colonel Sausage. I was beginning to view my visits to her place as more of a social event, a chance to kick up my feet on her coffee table, suck down a few Pacifico Claros, pack the four-footer with my finest dealer-quality weed, and shoot the shit with her for a few hours before rolling home. And my respect for her began to grow, grudgingly, over time, as I discovered her evil, cutting sense of humour and her quick wit with the ol' language. Sure, she was full of shit and coasting on a fat layer of grease provided by her trust fund and god-knows-what-other-sources-of-income, but she did it with such *style*, a sense of entitlement, that I shed most of the contempt I had once harboured for her. We talked a lot about my projects and installations, coming up with plenty of those buzzed ideas you like to kick around in such discussions: getting the video equipment together to start our own public-access cable TV show, on which we would show a conceptual series of driver-training films entitled *Brains On The Pavement* . . . or modifying the signs marking the entrances to the City of Buena Park (*Work Where You Must, But Live In Buena Park*) to include a huge plywood cutout of a stereotypical Redneck Southern Sheriff brandishing a shotgun, with a big speech balloon stating 'Don't Let The Sun Set On You Here, Commie!' and so on. Naturally, all this took place to a young-urban-nihilist soundtrack of vintage Throbbing Gristle and Negativland on her high-end audio system.

I even told her about my exploits with Possum Girl. Charlene was impressed and more than a little excited by it. She looked at me with new respect for having put Possum Girl through the sexual wringer like I had; that kind of stuff was right up her alley. After a few more drinks, I even told her about my latest evening with Violet, since we were on the subject. I was bragging a bit, showing that I had more control over my sinful drives, etc., than your typical male, and that I could always retain the upper hand in a tense sexual situation.

So, one night, with the screams of the flock of wild parrots that had chosen to roost in Orange County for the summer (apparently they were the survivors of a 1967 fire at a massive parrot-breeding facility out in Lancaster, augmented by singleton escapees over the years) mingling with the dull thuds of fireworks celebrating the nightly Electrical Parade and Triumph Over America's Enemies in nearby Disneyland, I had a decent buzz going and mentioned that the dope business had been pretty good to me recently; I had a big stack of dope-money $100 bills sitting in an ammo can in the garage and figured I might want to invest in a hydroponics growing operation my wholesale connection was setting up in a Quonset Hut on the outskirts of Tonopah, Nevada.

'I could double my stack in six months,' I mused as I cleaned the four-footer's screen. 'But it wouldn't be a whole lot of fun.' I was beginning to feel more like Daddy Warbucks than the Reefer Man. 'Maybe I should put it all into a huge installation, like the World War One Santa but fifty times bigger, you know?'

Well, gears started turning. Light bulb over Charlene's head, et freakin' cetera. 'I've got a few bucks, too – well, more than a few – stashed away and I'm getting a bit bored myself.' And she started describing her dream – yes, it was *her* dream, at first – of the Ultimate Dungeon:

'All of my customers are quasi-powerful mid-to-upper-level managers,' she began. *Yeah, all five of them*, I thought, smirking, but I said nothing. 'They come here and have me piss on them, figuratively and, if they're paying for it, literally. What they want seems to be a sort of role reversal from their everyday lives, which involve pissing all over the poor fuckers under them in the office. You know, they inhabit this weird world of fluorescent lights overhead, some shock-jock DJs lame-ass 'morning show' on the radio as they go to work, dreading, cubicle walls covered with that strange dried-burlap fabric in various vomitous colours –' she paused to take a lung-scorching hit from the four-footer (HHHHSSSSSK!) '– and then they see the temp receptionist – she's about 23, trying to pay off her student loans from pharmacy school or vet school or something, doesn't give a fuck about the job but knows it's a real pain in the ass to get a new one so she just smiles when the boss tries to make her feel stupid for not kissing ass with quite enough vacuum when the customers call – they see the receptionist and they have this lazy sort of powerful feeling, like *I could crush you* out of a bad sci-fi movie, kind of overlaid with this low-fidelity lust as they stare at her tits on the way into the office, and, uh . . .'

She'd lost her train of thought, in fact the train had left the station and promptly got sidetracked into an obscure switching yard full of rusty abandoned locomotives. An occupational hazard of the stoner lifestyle. 'You were saying something about the Ultimate Dungeon, I believe,' I prompted helpfully, reaching for the bong. Don't mind if I do (PSSSUUUUUCK!).

'. . . oh yeah. So, here's your typical rich Orange County businessman who spends his day piling petty humiliation upon petty humiliation on the couple of dozen poor schmucks who have the misfortune to toil in his salt mine for forty hours each week. Now, these same boss-types often feel the need to be humiliated in a sexual-type way by someone, as the abstract idea of being on the receiving end of such humiliation seems exciting to them. But, since they're used to being in charge, the humiliation is purchased like any other commodity. A Lexus. A new cleaning system for the pool. Or a few hours at the receiving end of the whip of Mistress Carlotta.' She gestured to the display of Tijuana's finest cats-o-nine-tails, bullwhips, etc. Then she paused, zoning out stonedly, watching residual weedsmoke curl from the bong's mahogany bowl.

'And?'

'*And*, they show up here and I take them into the basement, which I have decorated in the cheesiest straight-from-central-casting, cliché-assed manner everyone who plays this game has come to expect as the standard for such a setting. Plenty of suspension of disbelief is required for my client to enjoy himself; *both* of us have to kind of half-squint and do a lot of pretending.' She got up, gathering empty beer bottles from the coffee table. 'Come check out what I mean.'

So, she dumped the empties in the recycle bin, grabbed a couple of fresh ones from the fridge, and headed down the basement steps to the Dungeon of Mistress Carlotta. Once there, I could see what she meant about suspension of disbelief. Her client, wishing to spend a few hours feeling genuinely *at the mercy* of the cruel Mistress, would be required to overlook such fantasy-shattering elements as the Sears water heater with its big yellow Energy Star sticker, or the stack of old paint cans, or the fibreglass-wrapped heating ductwork, *before* he could even get around to pretending the flimsy 'torture rack' with its easy-to-break 22-gauge chains was actually going to be the place where he confessed his crimes to the Mistress. The other 'tools of torment' were equally crappy – more Tijuana leather, some dime-store shackles, and so on.

'I see what you mean,' I told her, keeping a poker face. But I was starting to get some ideas. 'Even if his big thing is traditional, bread-and-butter, mom-and-apple-pie torture – which, from the way you describe your clients, it isn't – he's gonna have to do a lot of work to believe any of this.'

'Exactly. And that cuts into my bottom line. I'm not making my clients truly satisfied, and that means I'm not doing my job right.' She smacked her palm on her ass, which I couldn't help but notice was clad in some very tight denim and in perfect grabbing range as she stood with one foot on the stairs. 'And my wallet could stand to gain some weight, if you follow my drift.'

'That's a big ten-four, good buddy,' I pretended to say into a CB mike, playing the clown a bit to distract myself from her increasingly *interesting* presence. In my super-stoned state I was sure I could *smell* that pussy. It smelled good, like what you smell when you stick your face into a jar of fresh pennies and take a big whiff of copper. To paraphrase Hank Williams, I was getting ready to start howling at the moon. She laughed politely, no doubt sensing an extra charge to the air. I could see her eyes darting around nervously; she was thinking about offering me a sample of what she gave her clients, just for laughs of course. No way – I'd be the one giving *her* something to cry about. Back to business. 'So, it seems to me that what you ought to do is, you know, set up your office to require a little less make-belief and a lot more actual humiliation.'

'Roger. And the way to do that is by creating a setting that's *familiar* to the client, then work within that environment to provide him the sort of twisted pleasure he feels compelled to seek after a hard day of writing negative quarterly reviews.'

The possibilities opened up before me like a brand-new 18-lane freeway through a once-pristine desert landscape. 'A familiar environment, eh? Like you recreate his cubicle world, complete with ringing phones, photos of triple-chinned offspring gnawing dispiritedly on corndogs at a urine-soaked waterslide park, and the stench of microwave popcorn?' I shuddered, thinking about all the 9-to-5 jobs I didn't want. 'The *break room*, God help us?'

She nodded, like a used-car salesman sensing a deal. But I didn't need any more selling. I was imagining how much fun it would be to set up such a place. Carlotta's Office of Torment . . . too bad the questionable legality of such a venture would prevent us from getting a big animated neon sign out front; I could already imagine it: an animated Vegas-style job, with a suit-wearing dude at his desk, cringing from the neon whip of Carlotta as it bore down on him. And, I admit, I may have had an inkling that this scheme might result in us making a buck or two.

We headed back upstairs, to settle down on the couch for some serious discussion. 'All right, I'm interested,' I told her, holding up a skeptical finger, 'but I don't see how we could get your basement to resemble a typical office. We can't do that, it won't work.'

'No, that's the part that costs the money. We need to rent some actual office space somewhere cheap, and furnish it with real office furniture. Clocks on the wall. Beige carpeting. You know, get the phones to ring. Maybe pay some folks to sit at the desks wearing depressing office clothes and . . . look busy. Whatever it is they actually *do* in offices.'

I had about 30 grand available. 'I have about ten grand available,' I told her, 'which should be enough for a couple months' rent and the furniture. If you can match it, I'll start looking for an office rental next week.' I had an idea where we could get the 'office employees' to provide background, too, but I kept it to myself. 'I'll count on you to be able to get the word out and attract new customers once we're ready.'

'Sure, I can get ten grand, and the clients will come rolling in as soon as the rumours start to fly. Let's do it.' Her eyes were bright, with excitement plus something . . . strange, but I didn't worry about what it was. This project would almost certainly provide me with ten grand worth of entertainment, plus I figured I could probably use the office as an additional dope-dealing front if nothing else.

But I couldn't get busy on the idea right away. I had a personal engagement set up for the following night. For my date with Possum Girl, I prepped the Econoline's interior with repro Lions Speedway drag race flyers, Surfaris posters, and other 60s-vintage surfer crap, borrowed a couple of boards from my surfer cousin, Robo, then fine-tuned the ambience more toward Possum Girl's most hated Surfer visions by adding some Anthrax and Napalm Death album covers and a sprinkling of 9mm shell casings scattered around the floor. I hung a few leis and shark-tooth necklaces here and there, then sprinkled a bag of sand around for that extra bit of realism. For my costume, some shopping at the crackhead thrift-stores of Santa Ana scored me a blinding red-and-white striped shirt that combined Jan & Dean with the Ice Cream Man, a pair of godawful mid-80s OP neon baggy shorts, and some ratty-ass Mexican huarache sandals (just like in the famous Beach Boys song, which I included on the soundtrack tape for the evening's festivities). Two fists full of gnarly biker rings, with the classic chrome skull-and-eagle iconography of the genre, and a fresh Huntington Beach skinhead shave job completed the look. I hummed 'Dead Man's Curve' happily as I finished the razor work. I felt like an evil Don Ho. I thought about maybe a phony skinhead tatt, maybe a Palmdale Peckerwoods prison job executed in crude blue Sharpie pen, but figured that would muddy up the image to the extent that even Possum Girl would become confused. No need to overpaint, I figured, and anyway the idea that tattooed white supremacists were fuckhead losers may have penetrated even her thick skull. Provided I had a bewildering enough mix of what she believed were icons of the Surf World, she'd be off-balance and filled with loathing for a world she knew only vaguely but hated the way John Birch hated Zhou Enlai's nutsack.

The plan called for a generous helping of reefer smoke and groaning Econoline springs. In order to avoid the embarrassment of Johnny Law intruding on our festivities, I needed a private venue. I rigged the garage up to simulate a beachified environment: Slide projectors beaming shots of waves and sky on all four walls, with an 'Ocean Vibes' environment CD playing on the boombox. Kind of half-assed, but I planned to have Possum Girl's attention focused elsewhere.

She rolled up late, of course, in her piece-a-shit '82 Tercel, and climbed through the window to exit, the doors being permanently mashed shut after an unfortunate incident involving a rum-fuelled after-work demolition derby in the Colonel Sausage parking lot. Unfurling the bag, allowing it to unroll in a masterly Dope Kingpin fashion, I whiffed the open end beneath her nose as she huffed into the van. Trying to avoid making any mood-wrecking possum-nosing-trashcan comments, I couldn't help but notice the primitive gleam of marsupial lust in her eyes as she scoped the red-haired buds, the pure THC crystals clinging to the bag. I wiggled it enticingly, first up and down and then side to side. 'All you have to do is let me love you up in true surfer style, and I'll give you this *whole sack*!' We're talking about a half-ounce of Northern Lights hydro-weed; worth maybe $450 retail but only about $100 cost to me.

Eyes locked on the dope bag and giving me a nice phony Porn Face, she reached under her skirt in what she probably figured was a devastingly seductive manner and did a slow peel-down of her panties. Pink, of course, but conservative cotton Old Lady™ Brand rather than the white-trash lace job I'd expected. She tossed them out the van's side window. Flopping back on the mattress and spreading 'em wide, she smiled coldly. 'Let's do it.' Oh, yeah. What man could resist such a line, eh? The legendary World's Tightest Pussy was looking right at me. Hmmm, I thought, it looks like any other. Standard Orange County swimsuit shave job on the pubes, pink, well-scrubbed labia, but no sign of the man-trap inside. She wriggled around a bit, preparing to endure the accustomed 30 seconds of humping before her deadly beartrap squeezed me dry.

Not today. 'Ah, my sweet beach bunny, *that's* not ocean love!' I sighed, making sure she noticed the distinct lack of hard-on beneath my OP shorts. This was going to be *my* show. The Maestro of Surf Passion doesn't just *do* it.' I made a big show of reaching into the ice chest for a fresh bottle of Primo, cracked it with the shark's-tooth opener around my neck, then eased back into my beanbag chair while pocketing the weed. 'When you accept the embrace of a true Hombre de la Playa, you must *be the ocean.*' I had no idea what that meant, but the surfer rebop seemed to come naturally, so I went with it. Patting the beanbag next to me, I gestured for her to sit.

'What a buncha bullshit!' she hissed, but I could see the confusion setting in. The seagulls screeched on the soundtrack; waves crashed on the film loop. A soothing Don Ho love song crooned from the sound system. She was weakening; getting *into* it. She got up and slumped into the seat with an annoyed grunt. Her flank against mine was taut and warm – very pleasant – but we had some business to transact before I took my pleasure. Reaching into a surfer bag (actually a standard-issue gym bag, but I'd put a few Sex Wax stickers on it beforehand), I produced a classy mahogany rolling tray, some organic hemp rolling papes, and a film can sporting an ominous-looking skull-and-crossbones symbol. She leaned into me, her heart rate revving up fast, as I spread the gear across our laps. 'To *love* the surfer way, you must get *high* the surfer way,' I intoned in my best Jim Jones manner.

'You really *are* a freak,' she whispered, her focus zoned down on the film can. I could see it filling her awareness . . . what kind of shit was she dealing with here? 'I hear what they say about you.' Hate, fear, and need slugged it out inside her little head. I savoured my power, but I could feel my grip on control getting a bit shaky as I caught the scent of her sweat and took a peek down the v-neck of her blouse: a sensible white cotton bra and small perspiration beads forming in the cleavage. And it wasn't supposed to be about power, I reminded myself. The *experience* was the thing, for her as well as me.

In light of what happened later on with (company name) and Charlene, I suppose alarm bells should have been going off in my head as I let myself taste sexual power over a woman I disliked, but at the time it all seemed pretty harmless. *A weird fuck in a van that temporarily scrambles Possum Girl's brain . . . no big deal.*

Her brain was indeed whirling as I popped the lid on the film can. The word had been going around the (pizza joint) kitchen that I wasn't able to get high on regular weed any more, that my tolerance had become so awesome that I required some sort of *super dope* to get me off. While 90% bullshit, it was true that I reserved a special product for my own personal use. Known as *Mota Malvada*, its manufacture involved the extraction by tweezers of the finest red hairs from the top colas of Michoacan Connoisseur-Grade *Cannabis sativa* plants (your *indica* varieties, with their mellow high, having all but replaced *sativa* in recent years due to its superior indoor-growing properties), followed by the careful blending with the sticky flower resin of the same plants and a sprinkling of the very rare but seriously stony *male* flowers from the same field. Explaining this to Possum Girl as I casually sprinkled some *Malvada* into a rolling paper, I noted her pupils dilate with fear and excitement.

'You fuckin' *fuck*,' she gritted, watching the joint form between my fingers. 'You . . . *surfer puke*! You think I'm gonna smoke *that*?' She was putting up a fight, but I saw her toes tapping along with the Don Ho beat and I *knew*. Beach magic, baby.

I stretched out a lazy finger and touched her neck, feeling the pulse jump. She didn't pull away. 'This is the finest reefer in the Free World. Next to this, you've been smoking *weasel* piss your whole life. I think you're ready to get *high* for the first time.' I sparked the dube and sucked in a big hit. 'Ten million volts of pure THC,' I hissed, holding it in, then slid my hand behind her neck and drew her mouth to mine. She knew just what to do, sucking the smoke from my lungs as I shotgunned her. The rampaging tide of *high* hit her instantly; she slipped me some tongue as she took in the last of the hit.

'Ohhhh, shit,' she mumbled, overwhelmed. Fried. Hell, I smoked the *Malvada* all the time and *I* was roasted. I handed her the jernt and urged her to help herself while I reached into the surf bag. Producing an Annette Funicello circa-1961 polka-dot beach-party dress, I draped it across her lap.

'Here, put this on. I'm wearing my baggies and huarache sandals too, so you need to dress the part.' Huge waves of confusion surged in her skull. What the hell was *this*? Surfer shit? Surfer *clothes*?

'Uh . . . I gotta *wear special clothes*? Can't we just, like *fuck*?'

'Do it my way and you'll get this half-ounce of Humboldt Bud, plus I'll throw in the rest of this super-weed here. This is no discount fifty-buck *pizza schtup*.' I made the dope sack do a little dance, made it look attractive. I had her. She stood, shaky, and began to strip. Remembering my role, I popped a Jan & Dean tape in the deck and ripped into what I believed to be a 60s style surfer dance, shaking my limbs and rolling my eyes like a drunken chimp. I capered around the van while she changed into the dress. Horror . . . self-loathing . . . disgust . . . all visible in her eyes, but there was no hiding the goosebumps, the erect nipples, the way she let her stoned fingers linger on her sex as she adjusted the goofy dress. I allowed myself a small ration of lust;

just enough to fuel me for what was to come. She looked pretty damn good naked, I had to admit; it was almost a shame that the routine required the Gidget getup.

I grabbed a surfboard and sighted down its length like I knew what the hell I was doing. Seagulls screeched outside. Waves crashed. Ah, the mighty ocean speaks to us. We ride the ocean, and we listen to its words. The dolphins, the jellyfish, the sharks. They speak to us. I rambled some more spacy surfer gibberish. I was getting into it. Spaced out, she stared through the van's bubble window at the ocean slide show outside. Easing behind her, I threaded my palms around her sides and across her belly, drawing our bodies together. She was sweaty. I liked it. Her pizza-whore instincts kicked in and she tried to grind her ass on my parts, obviously hoping I'd go blue-ball crazy, jab it in and pop my rocks 15 seconds later. No dice. I pulled her hard against me, stifling the ass-grinding ploy but letting her feel that she'd got me sporting some major wood in my baggies. Holding her still with my left, I permitted my right to take a leisurely inventory of her goodies: long, fine hair, nice babyfat neck with hammering pulse . . . I drew a line through the perspiration beads in her cleavage, followed the curve of a breast, then across the belly. She was digging it – the sense-enhancing effects of the weed winning out over her normal tight-ass attitude; I kept up the surfer gibberish stream as my wandering hand moved south. The sweat really pouring off her, the dress sticking to her flesh . . . not making the effort to hide her panting now. I peeled the dress hem away from her thigh and placed my palm just above the knee. Her brain was boiling . . . she wanted it to stop, this goddamn *surfer boy* getting her all stirred up, but . . . I felt her thighs twitch slightly in a parting motion and obligingly curved my fingers around to the inner thigh's softer flesh. Her sweat was firing me up in a big way – I hadn't counted on some oddball lust trigger like that jangling my concentration – so I rationed myself the touch of a tongue tip on the back of her neck. Just a taste, I figured, but the jolt was huge for both of us. I was hovering around the downward spiral that terminated in a squalid doggy-style stab job and a victory for Possum Girl. Time for the next step, I figured. With the lightest possible touch of my fingertips, I traced the outline of her coochie-lips, careful not to give any overstimulating touch to the clit area. The lips were swollen but still mostly closed; I knew without parting them that she was wet enough inside for what I had in store. This wasn't so much about getting her off, but I figured the man-draining powers of the Tightest Pussy In the Whole World would be less effective when fully charged with Poozle Juice.

'This way,' I commanded, guiding her to a vinyl folding beach chair. I took a seat and gazed up at her, trying to look frostier than I felt. I unbuttoned the baggies and let my schlong grab some air. She reached for it, but I caught her wrist.

'Uh-*uh*' I chided. 'There won't be any premature-ejaculation-inducing tactic in *this* surfer's van.' Guiding her with both hands, I gently arranged her into a position facing me, legs on either side of mine. She figured it would be your standard-issue straddle grind-bang deal, but she figured wrong. From the surfer bag I whipped out a hose clamp and adjusting tool. Not any ordinary hose clamp, mind you – this was a special teflon-padded deal, used for attaching super-delicate coolant hoses on million-dollar semiconductor-extrusion machinery. Slipping it lovingly over my crank, I tightened the screw just enough to clamp it just below the head, firmly in place but not uncomfortably so. She stared, transfixed. What now, she wondered? *A hoseclamp on a dick?* Holy shit!

'This is the extent of man-root I can allow you at this moment,' I intoned in my best phony-prophet voice – sort of a mix of Jim Jones and David Koresh, 'for this is the way of the Surfer Man.' Hands on hips, I eased her down toward me. With her cooch poised an inch from the stingy portion of cock protruding from the clamp, I lovingly arranged the blonde wisps of her pubic hair away from the labia, then parted them with a fingertip. That was fucking *it*. She was ready to just give up and *go with the flow*, as we groovy hodaddies say right before catching a wave. She put her weight on me and pushed down to the limit of the clamp. The head slipped in smoothly, and at this point her cunt just felt like the usual thing – no hint of the man-sapping grip I'd heard so much about. She tried to work it a bit, within the limits of the clamp, but I held her still.

'No, no,' I cooed, as she strained against the clamp. A milky bead of pussy-juice and sweat rolled over the adjusting screw – good thing it was stainless steel or I'd have a rust problem. She groaned, her face red and framed by sweat-plastered hair: 'God *damn* you and your sick shit! Take that fucking thing off! What the fuck?'

I knew I was in the driver's seat, driving with a full tank of *cool* now. Putting my palm on her pubes and curling my thumb softly over her clit, I gave her a little circular polish job. She liked it, but it jacked up the temperature another few degrees and didn't do a damn thing about the torment of the prick-limiting hoseclamp. 'Here's the deal,' I stated with firm, businesslike resolve. 'You have to *enjoy* fucking a surfer in his surfer van, with surfer music playing and actual surfboards all around you. You have to *get off* on it, not just *endure* it.' I continued to tease her clit with my thumb, while my free hand guided her fingers to the area. 'You *will* diddle yourself to climax with the fingers of this hand, while I enjoy the pleasant sensations in my depth-controlled penis, and you will *not* indulge yourself in any thrusting or otherwise penetrative motions.'

'Fuck that!' she spat, but her eyes closed and her fingers probed around my thumb and began a practised rubbing of her little button. I eased my thumb out of the way and rested my hands on her hips, to minimise her attempts at side-to-side and hula-hula-girl motions.

Tapping the clamp-adjusting tool on her calf, I continued: 'With each orgasm you experience, I will loosen the hoseclamp and slip it down a bit more, permitting a greater degree of penetration. If I doubt the authenticity of the climax, based on the strength of vaginal muscle contractions, I will move the hoseclamp back *up* and we will start the process over.'

So far I had a good grip on myself – my own jizz-o-meter was reading on the low range. Meanwhile, she was climbing the mountain fast, and I wasn't sure she was in any condition to soak in my instructions. 'Do you understand?' I barked.

'. . . *Yes* . . .' she squeaked, and crested the mountaintop at that moment, her cooch muscles working some serious voodoo on my cockhead, bringing a flush to my face and sending me scrambling for some reserves of cool, '. . . you *asshole*!'

I chuckled indulgently, giving a few turns of the clamp adjuster and sliding it down about an inch. She took up the slack immediately, and I got my first taste of her mean grip. It didn't seem *possible* for a woman's *panoche* to be so restrictive, but there it was. I could tell I'd bust a nut instantly if the clamp were removed and I could bottom out in her. Just the sensation of her fingers working her clit was causing me great consternation, the way the movements were transmitted to my most sensitive nerve endings. Did I dare loosen the clamp at her next peak?

I dared. I was grateful for the privacy my van-in-garage simu-beach setup gave us; all the noise she was making would have attracted a great deal of unwanted attention, particularly of the cop variety, had I simply parked it at the beach. She was fully into it, though still clinging to a few threads of hope that I would spooge quickly and give her bragging rights in the pizza kitchen tomorrow ('Yeah, he thought he could *handle* it, but I showed him different,' she'd tell her giggling cadre of pizza-slut companions). I needed to slash those threads, make her see the truth and *like* it. Flipping the release latch on the hoseclamp, I whipped it off and jammed her down on my wang as hard as possible, to minimise the friction time. Now, I'll be the first to admit that I don't have brutally huge tackle, but it felt like she'd stripped the top few layers of skin off during my rash thrust. Only the pain kept me from spritzing instantly.

'Come *on*, let me *move*!' she whined, still self-polluting up a storm. Movement? Far from it. Executing Step Two of my plan, I zipped the nylon strap of a trucker-quality ratcheted tie-down across her lap, then winched it down good and tight. Now she was locked into position, leaving me free to discuss serious business. She struggled hard, but the only way she could apply any real motion on my goods was to keep diddling and contracting.

'Ahhhh,' I sighed, gently dabbing facial sweat with a 'LIFE'S A BEACH' towel. 'Now we can begin down the path to true Surf Oneness.'

'. . . wha-*whaaaaat*? Beg*in*?' She tried to screw up her face into the old hateful Possum Girl expression, but her bitterness engine was running on fumes. Repeated orgasm while stoned-to-the-bejesus will do that. The key here was to make the change *permanent*. 'I . . . I can't *take* any more of this . . .'

Again, I want to emphasise to those readers who look at what Charlene did later on and equate my benevolent behaviour with her sociopathic excesses, or to blame Possum Girl's subsequent involvement in the financial misunderstandings on Chicom-style brainwashing – well, you're reading my intentions all wrong. While my surfer-dude fuck-scene was indeed supposed to change Possum Girl forever, I was doing it because I felt *sorry* for her. I *liked* her, and I still do in spite of her mendacious testimony against me after the walls came down at Sux-M-Owt.com. Of course, there was an element of surrealist head-fuckery happening, but I had to get *my* pleasure as well.

So, back to the van: 'Of *course* you can take more of this. In fact, you *should* take more of this.' I handed her a fresh bottle of Primo. 'If I had just given you the standard $50 fuck, would you have *learned* anything? Would you have *gained* anything other than a brief tickle of pleasure for yourself and a snatch full of *fresh spunk*?' She twitched like I'd slapped her with the last two words. Holding still now, strapped to me, her heartbeat worked on my unit.

Without her noticing, the soundtrack I'd devised for our little get-together was evolving into something a little less musical and a bit more edgy. Subsonic sine-wave vibrations became louder, causing confusion, while a subliminal voiceover, much like the ones at shopping malls that tell the suckers to *buy . . . buy . . . buy . . .* but a mix of my own devising alternating bits of Harry S Truman's 1949 Inaugural Address with an 80s-vintage AT&T telephone-operator training tape:

Communism . . . is a system that b'lieves people are incapable of governing themselves
Large Charge Coin Calls . . . the drop tone indicates
and requires the rule of strong masters . . . strong masters . . . strong masters
Consult with your supervisor for long distance chargebacks

It was making *me* feel weird, and I knew what was going on. The effect on Possum Girl definitely involved some spun bearings in her worldview. She plucked uselessly at the straps locking us together and whimpered. Her hands went back to her parts, figuring she might be able to get me off by repeated vaginal contractions. Not a bad idea, but a very time-consuming one, given the extreme levels of lubrication she'd produced inside – even with the Tight Possum Snatch of pizza-employee legend, I couldn't feel much from her slippery grip. She tried to wiggle her body from side to side, but I had her strapped too tightly for that, and I kept my arms tight around her to ensure a fully motionless posture.

This went on for quite a while; not to seem unduly cruel, but I had her locked up in that masturbatory embrace for a good 90 minutes. Tears down her cheeks, but completely hypnotised by the confusing soundtrack and unable to stop the endless series of climaxes, Possum Girl would be a *changed woman* when she set her first shaky foot outside of my van. Finally, I decided it was time for the last act of this drama. Reaching for a switch in the van's roof, I triggered flashing red strobes and sirens, apparently coming from outside the van. Like a cop had just rolled up on us.

'Oh, *shit*!' I wailed. 'We're getting *busted*!'

Her eyes widened. Where *were* we? My garage, she thought, but reality had taken a turn for the indistinct for her. I released the tie-downs binding her to me and lifted her off my prong in a shockingly rapid motion.

'Quick, get your clothes on!' I barked. 'You wanna go to *jail*?' I stuck my leg in the baggies and slipped them on – it was a trick bending my woody enough to get the things on, and I had a gooey coating of pussy-juice on every surface of my lower body from navel to kneecaps. The van reeked of reefer smoke and pussy; we'd be totally fucked if The Man really had stumbled on this scene. She was puzzled and unsatisfied, but game about it and staggered to her heap of clothes by the spare tyre. I willed some softness into my hard-on and summoned up a fresh load of *cool*.

She was still pulling on her socks when I hustled her out the van's side door and out of the garage. Stuffing her into her Tercel, I slapped the promised bag of dope into her hand. She was spaced oh-you-tee *out*. Dry and not-so-dry sweat and girl-spooge all over her, her hair glued into a standard-issue Crazy-Woman do, and a thousand-yard stare playing over the landscape, she looked gratifyingly dazed by her experience. 'See you at work tomorrow!' I said happily, like the kind of co-worker who keeps inspirational 'Friday's Coming' posters in his cubicle. On automatic, she slipped the key into the ignition and fired up the Toyota. Southern Californians can *always* drive, no matter how weird things get. The Tercel shrank into the Orange County haze as she drove off. Other than a feeling like I had a gallon of semen backed up into my nuts, I felt great.

Eight

Next day, I found myself hitting scuzzy office buildings and strip malls in the Anaheim/Santa Ana area, looking for something with the right combination of cheap rent, uninquisitive landlords, and depressing fluorescent-lit American Office ambience. Ideally, I was shooting for one of those grim three-story 70s buildings favoured by on-the-skids attorneys and bloody-handprints-on-the-walls alcoholic dentists. Walls made of sagging sheetrock and every surface encrusted with an adobe-like layer of cheap paint. I'd thought of all the pizza deliveries I'd made to office-zombies before I'd really gotten the dope business flourishing, and the one common denominator that really gave me the jeebers about an office was the unpleasantness of the Break Room. The place where employees spent their ostensibly free time, while praying hopelessly for a painless death and end of the grim treadmill of their working lives. I was quite picky about the Break Room for the Office of Torment; it would have to be simultaneously dingy yet brightly illuminated with a pitiless will-to-live-leaching glare. It needed cupboards with crooked, squeaky-hinged doors, an undersized microwave oven caked with years of pork-based Instant Lunch schmutz, and a buzzing refrigerator.

Finally, I found the ideal place. An entire floor of a small office building near John Wayne Airport. A pretty expensive area, but the proximity of the General Electric jet-engine repair facility, with its screaming turbofans and keronese jet-fuel smell, kept the high-rent tenants away from this particular building, which meant it had never been renovated. In fact, the entire place was empty; I talked the landlord into a cheap one-year lease for the top floor; I figured we'd want to minimise interactions with the other tenants – if any ever showed up. The landlord was a greedy little bastard who took one look at the wad of hundreds I whipped out and became quite agreeable about giving us the privacy we needed for our up-and-coming business and skipping all of that unpleasant paperwork.

'And what's the name of your company, sir?' he oozed, at least trying to get that much out of me.

Oh, shit – I hadn't even thought of the 'legitimate' name for our front. Dredging in a forgotten recess of my mind, I came up with 'Sux-M-Owt Home Stomach Pumps, Inc.' I had created the idea of the Sux-M-Owt years ago, as a stoned riff on those late-night infomercials. Cracked up all my friends with my rants about the Sux-M-Owt:

> Say goodbye to old-fashioned finger-down-the-throat remedies, folks! No more harsh emetics or costly trips to the emergency room when your child drinks a bottle of iodine or eats the roach poison! Just plug in the Sux-M-Owt and let the hissing chrome probe suck your troubles away!

The office came furnished with just about everything we needed: squeaky-wheeled desk chairs, workstations, humming/flickering fluorescents overhead in the crumbly acoustic-foam ceilings, and every colour taken directly from the puke-green/monkeyshit-brown palette. I picked up a couple of vending machines stocked with stale snack food, put some angry-secretary-style 'CLEAN UP AFTER YOURSELF' notes on the break room fridge, and rigged up a device on the phone switchboard to randomly ring extensions every few minutes. A few obsolete computers on the desks, some heaps of paper in various In/Out boxes, paper clips and pens, all that good shit, and the place was ready.

The next couple days were spent doing various equipment- and infrastructure-related work; I left the obtainment of Charlene's special tools up to her, though I insisted that she get top-quality torture gear: 'Nothing but the best for Torment, Incorporated!' But we still needed 'employees' to provide that final flourish of realism, so I headed straight for Colonel Sausage.

I figured a half-dozen French Pizza Slaves would be just about ideal for our purposes. Ten bucks an hour and we'd let them sleep in the 'office' after business hours – that was four times Pizza Slave wages and better accommodations to boot. Their utter lack of English skills and lack of experience in the American work environment was a great combo for our purposes – they'd probably figure the wealthy businessmen getting humiliated by Charlene was just SOP; a typical day in the American workplace, and there would be no danger of them trying to blackmail clients or screw up their experience. In any case, I figured they'd be so grateful to escape indentured servitude at the hands of Colonel Sausage and his French slavemasters that they'd be quite willing to overlook the strange behaviour in the offices of Sux-M-Owt, Incorporated. Once it was time to ship them back to France, we could just hire actual office temps – by that time, we'd either be rolling in cash or totally broke, anyway.

Naturally, I couldn't steal six Pizza Slaves without burning my bridges at Colonel Sausage, which meant the end for my pizza-man/dope-dealer business. But I figured it was time for me to try something different, and I figured the Office of Torment scheme had real potential. We could get a chain of them going . . . franchises . . . international licensing deals . . . we'd be bigger than McDonald's. In any case, I figured I was big-time enough to make my way in the weed-slangin' world without the crutch of the cover job. Even if the office dungeon fell through, I felt sure I'd manage to get by on my dealer-man skills.

I wheeled the van into the Colonel Sausage lot and fishtailed to a smoky halt next to the Evil Twins' red Trans Am. Truth be told, I was somewhat afraid of the Twins, and was dreading this day of reckoning. But I had a plan. I'd wait until the Twins were out of the restaurant on their daily afternoon trip to the bank with the morning receipts (they were too suspicious of skimmin' employees to entrust the task to any underlings), and I'd use a channel-lock pliers to bust the lock off the door to their locked office. Then I'd grab the FSPs' passports and return plane tickets. Following that, I'd head out and explain the situation to the FSPs: meet me outside in my van and I'll free you from Involuntary American Pizza Servitude. I figured I'd give them the choice of working for Sux-M-Owt as phony office employees – just sit at a desk wearing officy clothes and look busy when clients were in the place and otherwise do whatever they wanted, for good pay, unlimited free weed, and a place to crash – and anyone who didn't like that deal would get dropped off at the airport with passport and ticket in hand, free to return to France. That would be my way of turning in my notice of resignation. The Twins would be too stunned and humiliated to do anything and I'd have a clean break with Colonel Sausage.

The plan went fine up to a point; I busted the lock on the door to the Evil Twins' office, grabbed the passports and tickets, and did my Abe Lincoln routine with the FSPs, who understood my gist immediately in spite of the language impediment, were overjoyed, and just about crushed each other in the stampede out to the van. Explaining the deal with Sux-M-Owt, I recruited seven of them, three male, four female, to spend the rest of the summer as proud Sux-M-Owt employees; the rest waved happily as they burned shoe leather sprinting into the International Terminal at LAX. We drove away into a glorious chocolate-coloured Inglewood sunset.

Getting back to the new offices of Sux-M-Owt, Incorporated, I set up the staff on cots in a pair of server rooms toward the rear of the office. I pointed out their 'uniforms', a closet full of Dockers, polo shirts, frumpy skirts, and the usual depressing shit office drones wear as they trudge forward to their jobs, praying for a quick, painless death that will never be granted them. They had a refrigerator full of beer and microwave cuisine, a brand-new US Bong and an ounce of Commercial Grade Green, and I'd even scrounged up a TV and pool table for them. Advancing them each a week's pay, I handed them the keys to a primer-red '74 Chrysler New Yorker I'd obtained in exchange for several grams of hash oil and gave them directions to the nearest taqueria and the beach. Transportation, dope, beer, entertainment, and food. What else would they need? I could think of nothing. As for dick and/or pussy, I figured they could just hump each other or troll for fresh meat at the beach. It was getting late, so I headed out.

Next stop, Charlene's place. We'd need to get rolling in a serious way, now that I'd hired employees and the money was pouring through the hourglass. I felt pretty good after my free-the-slaves routine; yes sir, they'd been treated right for the first time since stepping off the plane onto American soil. I was a decent fellow, all right. Then I saw the red-and-blue lights in the rear-view mirror as I cruised down Bristol Street, humming 'Kumbaya' to myself. I pulled over, figuring I'd just get some cop rebop about my taillights being dim or something. Every cop in the area knew my van from years of pizza driving; the vehicle had become a normal part of the background, like smog, and I was usually able to maintain a pleasant cloak of invisibility while behind its wheel. After I came to a stop, the cop strolled up and leaned against the van, his 9-cell Mag-Lite pointed straight into my eyes. He seemed angry.

'This the guy, ma'am?' he asked someone standing in the shadows behind him. I was blinded by the flashlight beam and couldn't make out who it was.

'Yes, officer, that's the one.' Mimi's voice. Oh, *shit*!

Then I noticed that the cop wasn't even a real cop – it was one of the thugs from the notorious Extreme Response Protective Services, the rent-a-cop company used by strikebreakers, bill-collection agencies, and bookie joints. Its employees were mostly prison guards who had been fired for excessive use of force, which is quite an accomplishment given the 'beat the shit out of the fucking scumbag with a sock full of ball bearings first, ask questions later' philosophy espoused by prison guards in the California penal system. This particular ERPS goon looked like he scaled in at about 300 pounds of doughnut-fed brutality, and that baseball-bat-size Mag-Lite (of the type called a 'tonk' because of the sound it makes when whacked on somebody's dome) seemed to have a coat of dried blood and scalp on its business end. 'Listen, officer,' I suggested in my most reasonable voice, 'perhaps you might be interested in receiving a small bonus to, say, forget about this whole business?'

No, he wasn't interested. No doubt he'd been paid off real sweet by the Twins. So, I submitted docilely to a cuff-and-stuff into the backseat of the ERPS Chevy Caprice, with Mimi sliding into the passenger seat with Officer Thugg (that being the text on his plastic ERPS nametag). Sitting on my cuffed hands, I fumed as Mimi smiled ominously at me through the wire-mesh screen separating the back seat from the front. 'Hey, Mimi, does this mean I don't get my Christmas bonus?'

'Oh, we have a *bo*nus for you. Just wait!' Mimi didn't have much of an accent. She fired up a Marlboro and blew a streamer of smoke out the window as we roared away from my van. Fortunately, my cash and travelling weed stash was safely hidden in a sniffdog-proof compartment under the Econoline's dash, so Mimi and Officer Thugg wouldn't be able to get at it. I figured I was in for a hard time, but they couldn't push it too far – it was rumoured at Colonel Sausage that I had connections with the local chapter of the Vagos motorcycle club and could bring their wrath down upon my enemies at will (all bullshit, of course – I sold schmoke to the Vagos like anybody else, but that was the extent of the relationship). At least, I *hoped* the Twins believed in the Vagos connection.

The Caprice blasted into the Colonel Sausage parking lot. The place was closed for the night; the neon sign featuring a huge sausage sporting a handlebar moustache and a Confederate uniform was out and the dumpsters were locked tight to prevent the homeless from scrounging a free pizza meal. Officer Thugg popped the back door, grabbed my collar, and hauled me out of the car. 'Shit, man, take it fuckin' easy! I'm walking!' I protested as he half-dragged, half-carried me to the Colonel Sausage front door. I thought about kicking him in the balls and running off, but I'd surely get beat to snakeshit if I didn't succeed. Through the glass door, I could see Corinne inside the darkened store. Smiling in her evil way.

They hustled me through the restaurant and into the walk-in freezer. Officer Thugg hulked in the doorway, flexing his muscles and fondling the Mag-Lite like he really wanted to beat me into a fine red mist with it. His walkie-talkie crackled, sputtered. Mimi and Corinne leaned against crates of frozen cheese substitute, smoking.

'Fucking rent-a-cop,' I spat. 'I'll see you in fucking court. You too, Mimi.' They all laughed. 'I'm serious. My lawyer will grind you up like diseased hamburger.' More laughter. 'Not only that, I've got seven of your former slaves stashed away where you'll never get them, and one fucking phone call to the fucking State Labor Board and you'll be getting cavity-searched by the 275-pound bull-dyke matrons at fucking Tehachapi State Prison before you can say "Multiple criminal violations of labour practice regulations." '

That seemed to have some effect. Corinne whispered to Mimi, who nodded. I was already starting to shiver from the 25-degree temperature, but they didn't seem to notice the cold.

'Should I smack him around a little, ma'am?' asked Officer Thugg hopefully. 'Just to teach him some manners?'

Corinne shook her head. 'No, Mr Thugg, I think we know the best way to teach our friend a lesson.' She flipped her smoke to the floor, ground it out with the toe of her stylish Italian shoe, reached into her pocket and came up with a boxcutter knife. Before I could object, she had me by the shirt front and was slicing my shirt away. 'I think you will like this, so do not struggle,' she said softly, her eyes bright and scary as she carefully slit down the sleeves so the shirt wouldn't snag on the handcuffs. 'And even if *you* don't like it, *we* will like it.' She gestured to Mimi, who was handing a camera to Officer Thugg. 'And these photographs, they will show your friends how you like Mimi and Corinne, no?' Thugg grinned and took a couple of flash shots as Corinne cut my new pair of Soviet Navy officer pants away, leaving me goosebumped and clad only in my boxers as the Twins appraised my physique. Apparently they approved of what they saw.

'We have an arrangement, yes?' Mimi demanded. 'You be nice to us, we let you go.' She gestured to Thugg, who was twiddling with the controls of the camera. 'You go running to The Man about the slaves, all your friends see what you have done with the Evil Twins. They will hate you for it.'

It was true. And the whole thing made a bitter sort of sense – the Evil Twins were the type to get off on such a system of Mutually Assured Destruction; they'd be in jail or at least tremendously inconvenienced, and I'd be shunned by my peers. Seeing no response from me, Corinne took my silence as assent. 'Good, so we are agreed. Please, Mr Thugg, if you will take the photographs.' She lifted her designer skirt and wiggled gracefully out of her panties. Had to admit, the Twins had style. Always dressed with class, always pure evil. I steeled myself for whatever was coming next with what I hoped looked like grim resignation, but ol' Demon Lust, he started howling away in my groin and my thoughts got slower, sludgier as I caught sight of Corinne's girl-parts. The hairs carefully trimmed and plucked, each in its place, and the labia pink and positively *glowing* with good hygiene. Class. I willed my rod to stay quiescent, but to no avail; *damn*, I thought, *I'm poppin' a diamond cutter over Evil Corinne*. The Twins saw the bulge and nodded. Mimi unlocked the handcuffs and we were ready to go:

The camera flashes and flashes. Me freezing, on my knees, steam eddying off the heat of her pooz as she straddled my face and leaned into me. My palms on her ass. My tongue probing along the line of pink folds, arranging them and working in to the sweet inner flesh. The coppery taste of her classy, hygienic juice. The camera flashing some more. Dizziness. Working a couple of fingers in. Cold air, hot cunt. The only warmth in the place. A dreamlike sense of unreality. Corinne's climax. Another one. Now Mimi's turn. The camera flashes. I feel drugged and wrong, but continue.

Next Mimi arranges herself on a low stack of flour sacks, lying on her back. She has stripped off the rest of her clothes and stacked them neatly. Her body is trim and gym-conditioned, her breasts medium-size but obviously natural. Corinne guides me over to her so I stand over Mimi's nude body. More flashes; Officer Thugg has not been stingy with the film. Corinne strips off my shorts and begins to stroke my stuff. Her face is neutral, businesslike, no indication that she's just been on the receiving end of high-intensity rug-munching. Stroke, stroke. She's good. I'm getting ready to bust. She stops and steps back. Mimi looks up expectantly. I just stand there, confused.

'Now you finish! By yourself!' She makes jerking-off motions. I get it – the ultimate blackmail photo, me self-polluting over the icy flesh of Evil Mimi.

'Better do it, boy,' growls Officer Thugg, readying the camera.

I'm gonna have a record-breaking set of blue balls if I don't bust a nut after all this. No point in asking for a reach-around from the Evil Twins. I reach down and take a few strokes. Nothing to it. Beneath me, Mimi starts to writhe a bit – she's trying to stay cool but is getting seriously bothered and can't hold still with this action. I am suddenly consumed with the need to get down there and *throw it in*, but that would be even more humiliating than a self-induced jizz so I keep working it. Flash, flash. Finally, I make it, shooting a thick rope of semen onto Mimi's stomach and chest. I try to make no sound, but the load measures about a 7 on the Richter Scale and I can't hold back a gasp.

After that, it was all over. Mimi and Corinne dressed, lit up Marlboros and left. Thugg hauled me out to the Caprice, still in my cum-spattered boxers, and shoved me into the back seat. Dumped me onto the pavement next to my van and burned rubber into the night. On the face of it, a dreadful experience that left me shaken and angry . . . but a price that had to be paid to get Sux-M-Owt, otherwise known as Torment, Incorporated, off the ground. And a rebel nerve ending somewhere in my gut told me I'd be tempted to pay another visit to the Evil Twins someday . . . something weird for me to chew on later on, on a sleepless night with the roar of distant freeways in the air . . .

I steered the van back to the office and parked it in the CEO's spot (I'd made some nice stencils and marked out our reserved chunk of the parking lot; in addition to my special space, with its gold lettering, I'd marked off spaces for 'Controller', 'Head of Discipline', among others and, of course, 'Worst Employee of the Month'), feeling a surge of pride as head man of an up-and-coming business venture. In fact, I felt positively entrepreneurial, the bad taste of my shameful experience in the Colonel Sausage walk-in freezer fading from my mouth. I saw Charlene's car, a hipster-centric 1970 Chrysler 300H Hurst Edition sporting a candy-apple flame job, red velvet interior, the works, parked in the spot I'd stencilled 'Warlord' – I'd have to let her know that her official position of President outranked the VP-level Warlord, Strongman, and Bossman positions, and that she was entitled to the gold-painted PRESIDENT space right next to mine, at the front door. In fact, I'd produced a complicated organisation chart, something we could put on one of the big dry-erase whiteboards in the conference room. I wasn't too familiar with actual corporate terminology, but I figured every company had its warlords and strongmen, in spirit if not in name. The clients would see it and feel immediately that they were on familiar ground . . . familiar, up until the point Charlene's riding crop whistled through the air . . . and they *confessed their crimes*!

I'd gone ahead and ordered a *Sux-M-Owt Home Stomach Pumps, Inc.* sign (featuring the image of a smiley-faced industrial vacuum cleaner with an ominous-looking chrome hose) for the front of the building, so as not to confuse the landlord, but as far as the clients were concerned we were officially Torment, Incorporated, with a logo incorporating crossed bullwhips superimposed over an ornate stock certificate. I'd given up on the animated businessman-getting-whipped neon-sign idea after scoping out the cost, but I thought we might get one made later if the venture proved profitable. I'd had Torment, Inc. business cards made up for Charlene to hand out to the clients and we had a single active phone line coming into the office to take appointment requests.

Entering the building's lobby, I noticed that the Building Guide sign didn't have our company name (note to self: get those little white plastic letters and put Torment, Inc. on the sign). In the elevator, I observed with approval the oppressive, threatening ambience of its dim green fluorescent bulb, which flickered and buzzed as the decrepit elevator wheezed and lurched its way up to our floor. A client would doubtless feel a delicious sense of foreboding as he ascended toward his fate at the hands of Charlene, President of Torment, Incorporated.

I hit the reception office of Torment, Inc. and heard laughing French voices. The smell of Mexican chow and reefer wafted from the break room as ex-FPSs whooped it up on their first night of freedom from the clutches of Colonel Sausage and the Evil Twins. I headed over to the breakroom and poked my head in the doorway. A huge pyramid of empty beer cans was stacked on the break room table; several ex-FSPs were passed out on the linoleum from burrito-and-beer overindulgence. I could see that staff morale was high. 'Carry on, troops,' I called out to them.

Inspecting the premises, I felt that we'd covered everything in terms of creating a believable office environment; the whole effect was so real that I was starting to get that days-blurring-into-years sense that office lifers feel. I realised that I'd have to get a diseased-looking Xmas tree for the break room, and some postcards from exotic locales such as Branson, Missouri and Mazatlan, the kind of thing that lifer officeworkers send to coworkers on their brief respites from work; hang the postcards on the refrigerator door and cubicle walls and the fantasy would be that much more realistic. Sure, I could skip all those little details, rely on the clients' willingness to suspend disbelief to get the job done, but true competence was so rare in this day and age that I felt an *obligation* to the American work ethic to make Torment, Incorporated as perfect as I could.

I saw a light on in the President's office and assumed Charlene was inside. Sure enough, she was sitting behind the big oak boss-quality desk, applying purple polish to her toenails and nipping at a glass of red wine.

She smiled pleasantly as I entered the room. 'I see you got some employees. I've already had a talk with them and they know the score.'

'What, you speak French?' I asked, fishing my one-hitter out of my watch pocket and poking a load of exotic Chinese bud into the business end. 'Got a light?'

She handed me her Zippo (another one of her many hipster-chick conceits) and I filled my lungs with the Shanghai Smoke. 'Sure, I took a few years of French class in college,' she said, waiting for me to pack her a bowl. I had forgotten that she was a college graduate, unlike me (I'd dropped out from sheer boredom after two years at CSU Northridge and had pursued my own course of independent study afterward). 'How did things go at Colonel Sausage?' She stared intently at me.

I paused. She *knew* something had happened with Mimi and Corinne; I'm sure something about my bearing must have given it away that I'd undergone some kind of traumatic experience. She had an unerring sense for such things. 'Well . . . I had a little trouble with them after I dropped off the Pizza Slaves – I mean, Torment, Incorporated staff members.'

Her eyes locked with mine. She looked eager, excited. 'What happened?' she demanded, leaning forward in her leather office chair and setting down the one-hitter. 'Tell me what they did to you!'

So I told her about Officer Thugg and his rent-a-cop Caprice, and the walk-in freezer, and the sleazy mutual-blackmail deal, and being forced to service Mimi and Corinne. I figured I might as well give her the whole story, so I included the part about spilling my seed on Mimi's naked body and all the photographs of the act they'd taken.

She loved it. 'Oh, man, they played it *per*fectly! You'll feel stained and humiliated for months, if not a lifetime!' she crowed admiringly. 'Not saying I wouldn't have done a better job, of course,' this accompanied by a knowing wink. I admit, I felt a chill and a bit of warmth in the ol' package at the thought of performing sexual services on her lushly upholstered figure. 'Think we could hire them to work here?'

Oh, hell *no*! I thought, but kept my cool. 'Don't you think the presence of the Evil Twins might be a bit intimidating for our loyal employees, given that Mimi and Corinne were their former slavemasters and everything? Those poor fuckers are scared shitless of the Twins.'

'I don't think that's the reason, but we'll pass on the Twins. I'd rather work solo, anyway.' She got a thoughtful look. I was imagining her naked, of course, but I would never let her know that. It seemed important to maintain my sexual distance from Charlene, for reasons that went well beyond sheer professionalism. 'So, tell me, do the Evil Twins have nice bodies?'

'Yes, they do. No doubt about that.' Damn, she would have me heading back to the Twins if she kept up this line of talk. I wondered what I'd have to do to hose Corinne doggy-style? Tattoo her name across my ass? I was uncomfortably aware of a semi-hard-on stretching my jeans a bit, and a slight scent of the Twins' pooze-juice was still noticeable under my nose. I hoped Charlene didn't notice the bulge.

No chance of that – her eyes dropped to my crotch for a long, significant moment, and then back up to my eyes. 'Looks like the Twins got a hook in you, hey? Thinking it might not cost you too much to head back there?' She shifted in her chair and I realised her nipples were erect, just noticeable through her Bettie Page vintage sweater. Pupils dilated, too. She was getting hot-n-bothered over my little adventure with the Twins.

'What part was the most exciting?' she asked eagerly, 'Licking their pussies or masturbating over Mimi's naked body? Seeing your fresh semen on her breasts?' She wasn't trying very hard to hide her arousal. 'Or was it something else, something small and special that'll stick with you for a lifetime? Damn, I wish I could get copies of those pictures they took!' A look of raw lust at me. The air over her seemed to shimmer slightly, like the air over a hot asphalt parking lot.

Charlene was a freak, all right. I realised that she was smarter and crueller than I'd given her credit for. I'd better keep my distance or she'd eat me up. 'What would you do with those pictures? Frame them in your office?' I asked, trying to pretend this was just a playful conversation, like so many we'd had over the months.

She smiled. 'Maybe I'd have to play with myself, looking at them,' she purred, not really joking.

'Maybe I'd think about a man pleasuring me according to my orders, just like you did for the Twins.' She stretched her arms up and back, showcasing her full, high boobs in their tight 50s sweater, then got out of the chair and reclined across the desk on her back, hands over her head, entwined in her black curls. 'Maybe even think about you doing it.'

'Not like that,' I assured her. 'I only did that stuff for the Twins because that rent-a-cop would have pounded me into cat food if I hadn't,' I lied. 'I didn't get off on it.'

She wiggled and stretched a bit on the desk, like a cat cozy in a sunbeam. Unlike most of her Southern California hipster-chick peers who strutted like latter-day reincarnations of Bettie Page, she really did look like the pinup queen. 'Really? It was just a mechanical act, like taking out the trash or flossing your teeth? You won't dream about the beautiful naked bodies of the Evil Twins, how they made you their *house*boy, made you *love* it?'

'Just like taking out the trash, yeah. I even had a tough time getting a boner so I could come on Mimi,' I sneered, Bogart-like. 'You should have seen me – I was ice fuckin' cold.' Still in a joking tone, but with an edge.

'Well, since it doesn't *mean* anything to you, how about showing me how you did it?' She peeled off her sweater and tossed it aside; underneath she had a tasteful off-white bra, lacy and feminine. I would have expected some kind of Elvira-style black studded job, to be honest. 'I'll lie here like Mimi did, and you can demonstrate your ice-cold masturbation technique and come on my body.' She kicked off her shoes and started peeling off her stockings – the old-fashioned kind with a garter belt, naturally. 'I won't say anything or touch you – just lie here naked beneath you. Since it didn't mean anything with the Evil Twins, how could it with me?' Now the skirt came off. She stretched out on the desk, clad in her bra and panties. She was gorgeous and knew it. Pleasant surprise, no tattoos or body piercings – none of that stupid Modern Primitives shit for her. Just smooth pale female flesh. She hooked her thumbs under the waistline of her panties and looked at me expectantly. 'Well?'

I knew I'd regret it if I gave her anything. She was getting stronger, more sure of herself. The dilettante trustifarian I had known just weeks ago was starting to live the dream of being Mistress Carlotta for real. I backed toward the office door and turned to go. 'No, not like this.' I walked coolly away, crossed the office and to the elevator. Once I got downstairs, I sprinted to the Econoline. As I roared out of the lot and toward Gennifyr's place for some quick, lightweight release, I saw Charlene standing in the office window, waving. She wanted me, I wanted her. Any coupling between us would mean surrender for the one who broke down first, and it wasn't going to be me. Thus began the circling, wary dance we would do around each other for the next year.

Nine

Even with the new tension between us, Charlene and I proved skilled and efficient managers of our new business. There was no hoked-up 'dungeon' anywhere in the place; except for the ex-FPSs' living quarters, the offices of Torment, Incorporated were indistinguishable from a million other offices in the area. A glance around and you'd see about what you expected: people looking grim and typing away in cubicles or talking on phones. The smell of microwave popcorn. Cans of Diet Coke on desks. Photos of children and pets.

There was one crucial difference, however. When a client came to 'work' at Torment, Incorporated, his experience was a little different than what he got in the similar-looking confines of his real office. At Torment, Incorporated, the tough-minded manager, so used to asserting his will over the poor saps below him, would be working for an even tougher boss: Charlene Cabrillo, President of the Torment, Incorporated empire (I persuaded her to ditch the stupid Mistress Carlotta name and go with her real one). And, for that privilege, he would pay us $250 per hour, cash, or $1,800 for a full eight-hour workday.

She got a couple of her regulars from the Mistress Carlotta days to come in, they told their friends, and within two weeks we had dozens of the bastards clamouring to be part of the Torment, Incorporated team; it got so we had to turn potential clients away because the office was full. The business was a huge financial success almost immediately, and Charlene and I enjoyed each workday thoroughly. I took to dressing the part of CEO, wearing custom-tailored Italian suits that made our clients' Men's Wearhouse outfits look tattered and dumpy by comparison. Charlene dumped all her cheeseball vinyl and leather wear in the trash and came to the office clad in classy designer suits and Manolo Blahnik shoes.

I was part of the act, of course, in addition to handling all the nuts and bolts of maintaining the appearance of a genuine office environment. As CEO, I would drop in on the cubes or offices where our clients 'worked' and give them disapproving glares, drop fifty-pound stacks of busywork into their In-boxes, and so on. After the first week, I got really *into* it, with harsh fitness reports and lengthy verbal-abuse sessions. Charlene would be working over one of the clients by the copy machine, really laying into him with a swagger stick, and I'd stroll over:

Charlene would have the fucker cringing before her wrath: 'Jones, I *told* you we needed that report done by *yesterday morning*!' She'd rear back and let him have a mean shot across the mouth with the stick. *Crack!* 'And here it is noon and you have accomplished *nothing*!' A couple of ex-FPSs nearby would giggle, pointing at the spectacle, then get back to pretending to type memos. We found it added a lot to the client's experience if the low-ranking personnel witnessed his humiliation.

'Oh, I know, Ms Cabrillo,' he'd weep, 'I'm really, *really* sorry . . . it won't happen again . . .' A trickle of blood running from his split lip, he'd wait eagerly for the next blow.

'Jones, you dis*gust* me,' she'd hiss. 'I've got a mind to make you drink your own *piss*! Yes, that's an idea – strip down to your underwear and wait here while I get a glass.'

Jones would be peeling off his pants, trembling with excitement, and I'd step over to him with my confident, manly stride. Prodded him with the point of my shoe. 'Jones, I'm afraid I have bad news for you,' I'd say solemnly, like it was a common sight in *every* office to see a man huddled against the copy machine in his underwear awaiting the chance to drink a glass of his own piss. 'We've just lost the Toxium Electroplating account, and from what I understand we lost it because you had some strange do-gooder impulse and told them they couldn't dump 60,000 gallons of radioactive electroplating solution into the Los Angeles Aqueduct. What were you *thinking*, Jones? Are we here to save the world or are we here to *do business*?' Then Charlene would return and we'd talk about what a girly-man Jones was while the word processors and secretaries tittered.

And so it went, day after day. The money poured in and I stopped selling retail marijuana. Then I replaced the Econoline with a brand-new BMW sedan. Moved into a nicer apartment. There were only a couple of things wrong with the setup, from my point of view. First, I really wanted to show off our setup as a massive performance/installation art piece, to get credit for its brilliance from an audience that could really appreciate it for aesthetic reasons (especially considering I no longer had time to play with Randy Kraft & the Dead Marines or build projects like the WWI Santa or the Vacuum Nixon). Second, I had a constant case of swollen nuts from my 24/7 desire to fuck the stuffing out of Charlene; the fact that she felt the same way for me didn't mitigate matters much. In fact, she'd become so obsessed with reenacting the final masturbation sequence in the Evil Twins Freezer Incident that she'd taken to forcing clients who resembled me to perform the act with her. She'd catch my eye while lying naked beneath some youngish blond client wanking over her while another took photos, and I'd know she was imagining me as the guy choking his chicken over her while Officer Thugg kept order. Of course, she never permitted any client's semen to touch her skin – that was a privilege apparently reserved for me alone – but the hair-raising abuse she'd heap on him afterward served as a warning to me *never* to engage in any sort of sexual activity on Charlene's terms.

Naturally, I didn't give a shit about busting my nut *on* her; I wanted to bust the bedsprings with a straight-down-the-middle copulation, ending with my jism pumped into her cervix with maximum flow. But she had to *beg* for it, which seemed unlikely. Stalemate.

For the first couple months of business at Torment, Incorporated, we had an exclusively male clientele. Not just male, but most of them were of a type: 30 to 50 years old, white or Asian, mid-to-high-level managers with a fair amount of power in their offices. But it had to happen; one day we had a female client come in for a taste of that special Torment, Incorporated feeling. Janet was a hard-edged customer, a ball-bustin' sales VP from a big LA software company, in her late forties and looking for a new thrill. $500 haircut, even nicer designer suit than what Charlene wore, begging for a broken spirit courtesy of Torment, Incorporated.

We were happy to oblige . . . for our usual fee, of course. Charlene took it as a special challenge and devoted quite a bit of time preparing for Janet's appointment. I'm not quite sure what transpired in Janet's office at her new 'job' at Torment, Incorporated, but by the middle of the day Charlene had made Janet her bitch. She'd been stripped of her fancy threads and was wearing a mismatched outfit from the ex-FPS uniform closet – a really hideous combo of stained red-checked skirt, clunky scoliosis-correcting shoes, and one of those three-dimensional sweaters made by old ladies with glitter and glue-guns; this one featured plastic teddy-bear heads with jiggly eyeballs and a map of Texas in purple glitter across the chest. I could see fresh welts on her face from a few of Charlene's trademark backhands (she'd been taking martial-arts classes to improve her corporal-punishment skills and could deliver a slap that felt like something issued by Mike Tyson). She cringed just as whimperingly as any of her male counterparts, but Charlene wasn't satisfied. She left Janet trying to 'fix the printer' (one of my brainstorms had been to get a broken laser printer, into which I'd packed about 500 sheets of crumpled paper using a hammer and punch and then poured toner over the whole mess; it was a Torment, Incorporated favourite to force a client to spend a few miserable, toner-and-sweat-drenched hours hopelessly tearing little bits of jammed paper out of the printer with a letter opener) and came to my office, where I'd been savouring my midday joint.

'I've got Janet pretty well humiliated, but I can tell she's not really *satisfied*,' Charlene told me. I passed her the joint and she took a polite toke. She preferred a clear head while on the job, while I performed my duties better while cruising on a healthy cannabis buzz. 'I feel my professional pride is at stake here. Janet needs to feel like her employees feel after a full day of slaving for her; anything short of that means we haven't done our job.'

'I hear ya,' I said, 'But what can we *do*? You've given her the full treatment and then some. Maybe it's just impossible for our setup to work properly on a female client . . .'

'No, the Torment, Incorporated plan should work fine with both genders,' she mused. 'But in this case I'm unable to make much headway with Janet because *I'm* female. And that's where you come in. We need a bit more . . . *active* participation from you in this case.'

'Whaddya mean?' I objected, stung by her suggestion that I wasn't pulling my weight. 'I'm doing my part! I've already given her straight failing marks in her fitness report and raked her sorry ass over the coals about it, and it's not even 2:00 yet.'

Charlene sighed. 'Janet experiences a sense of sexual conquest from imposing her will on the men beneath her on the job,' she reasoned, sounding more like a shrink than a dom. 'So, to turn the tables and scramble all those ideas around in the way she needs, we must get a man with sufficient, uh, stamina to participate in a little drama I've cooked up for her.'

Stamina? 'You mean I've got to fool around with a Torment, Incorporated *client*, like in a sex-type way?' I asked, shocked. 'You *know* that's not part of the deal.'

But she wasn't paying much attention to my whining. All business. 'This is what we do. It's time for you to give Janet a little help with her *needs*.' She turned to leave, obviously heading out to fetch Janet. 'Just follow my lead. Anyway, I think you'll *enjoy* this.'

She returned to my office a minute later with Janet in tow. 'Close the door, Ed,' she told me, sounding

Very Disappointed with Janet. 'We need to have a closed conference about Janet's future with the organisation.'

Janet slumped into one of the office chairs; she seemed beaten down, but I could detect a spark of contempt in her, like we were amateurs and this was all silly playacting, not like the psychological paces she put her victims through in *her* office. Worse yet, that she wasn't getting her money's worth. That made me mad.

'Did I *say* you could sit down?' Charlene snapped, grabbing a handful of Janet's costly hairdo and hauling her to her feet. 'I don't know how they do it where *you* come from, but here at Torment, Incorporated we show respect for company officers such as Mr Kelvin!' Janet whimpered and squirmed a bit; she was beaten down but she wasn't *convinced*.

Much to my shame, I was starting to get somewhat aroused by Janet's grovelling. Knowing that Charlene had some kind of action in mind for us, I felt a bit of an anticipatory thrill. Janet was quite attractive, in spite of the goofball outfit and slap marks; tall, slender, with the good muscle tone that comes from years of workouts with a top-line personal trainer. She was pure class. And I'd never laid lustful hands on a woman nearly twice my age; the prospect of doing so had me developing some wood. Worse yet, I could tell Janet was getting a bit hot herself. Left to our own devices, I'd probably have her on my office's couch after maybe five minutes of persuasion.

But that wasn't how Charlene wanted to play it, and it probably wasn't how Janet wanted to play it either. 'We have some new technology we use for these special conferences,' Charlene explained, gently smoothing Janet's hair where she'd been close to tearing it out by the roots a second before. Charlene picked up my desk phone and dialled an extension. 'Marie,' she began, then some brief instructions in French. The ex-FPSs had all come to love Charlene, especially Marie.

Moments later, the door flew open and Marie entered pushing a cart full of electronic gear. It looked a bit like an automotive smog-test machine, with lots of probes and wires and readouts. Marie began attaching electrodes to Janet's wrists and forehead, smearing each spot with conductive jelly before applying the adhesive-backed pickup to her skin. Then I recognised the machine as a polygraph device, aka lie detector. A spring-loaded device wrapped around Janet's chest to measure breathing frequency and depth, and various other detectors were attached here and there about Janet's body. One strange device was a collar with a little plastic box attached, from which protruded a short antenna. It looked like one of those tracking devices scientists put on polar bears to track them.

'Picked it up at an FBI auction last week,' Charlene whispered to me while Janet submitted to the hookups with wide, confused eyes. 'Marie is a natural with the thing – I suspect she's had lie-detector training back home.'

There was no doubt about it, Janet was getting aroused by the activities, partly because she knew I was sporting some big pants-lumber over her and partly because of strange office-world impulses I knew nothing about. Charlene was getting worked up, too, and probably Marie as well; the room smelled *funky*.

Marie seated herself at the helm of the polygraph and started twiddling knobs. Moving quickly, Charlene knelt behind Janet. Reaching up, she grabbed Janet's panties and whipped them down her legs.

Janet helpfully lifted one foot and then the other so Charlene could remove the panties. *What now?* I wondered.

Now it was my turn. Charlene approached me and laid her palm gently on the bulge in my suit pants. 'Looks like I won't have to give you any help getting ready,' she whispered, 'How disappointing.' She pushed me toward the battered couch I kept against one wall of the office. I resisted at first.

She shoved harder, trying not to look obvious about it. 'Goddamnit, get your ass on the couch and *do your job*!' she hissed angrily in my ear. My professional pride was wounded and, besides, she seemed to know what she was doing. I went to the couch, staggering slightly, and sat down. I felt uncomfortable but pleasantly dizzy; a line I'd drawn when we started Torment, Incorporated was now being crossed at high speed, like a dynamite truck with brakes on fire hitting a 10% downgrade.

Charlene walked Janet over to me, Marie wheeling the polygraph cart behind. 'Now, Janet, you've proven yourself pretty much worthless as a Torment, Incorporated employee, but we're going to give you one more chance to show you've got what it takes to join the team.' Janet looked befuddled. Charlene gestured at the the polygraph. 'Our machine can tell us not only if you're lying, but certain other crucial facts about your mental state as well. Are you ready to start?'

'Y-yes?' Janet answered, hesitating. She was trying, and failing, to keep her eyes off my obvious erection. What I *really* wanted was to take Charlene out to her Chrysler and cover the upholstery with California Potato Chips, but I was ready to do a bit of grappling with Janet on the couch. I couldn't fathom what weirdness Charlene had in mind for us, especially with a polygraph involved, but anything requiring Janet to shed her panties probably meant there'd be some executive poontang involved.

Charlene stood behind Marie at the controls of the polygraph. 'We'll start you off with a few simple questions. If you lie, I'll know it.' She produced a little remote-control device. 'And I will administer a harmless correction for each lie using the Obedience Collar, like this.' She hit a button and Janet twitched, yelping. Charlene had rigged her up with one of those electric-shock collars, like the kind dog trainers use to stop dogs from barking inappropriately. This was a side of our business I didn't feel real comfortable about, but then I recalled that Janet had *paid* for this and was in fact getting off on it better than she'd ever gotten off in her life.

Charlene continued. 'OK, first question.' Consulting a list of questions on a clipboard. 'Have you ever felt sexually stimulated by the men working under you at your regular job?'

Janet swallowed, hesitated. Then, 'Yes.'

Marie looked at the polygraph readout and nodded. No shock for Janet . . . this time.

'Next question.' Charlene readied her thumb on the shock-collar remote. 'Have you ever used your authority to procure sexual favours from the men working under you?'

'No!' Janet barked. 'Never!'

Marie consulted the machine, shook her head. BZZZAP! 'Auuuuuugh!' Janet's body twitched uncontrollably as Charlene gave her a ten-second jolt. I could see blue sparks crackling on her neck. The room started to smell of hot electronics.

'We'll write that answer down as a yes,' said Charlene, jotting a few notes on the clipboard. Janet moaned slightly. 'Next question: Were any of those male employees upon whom you glutted your depraved and ungovernable lusts young, well-formed specimens of wholesome American manhood?'

Janet sniffled a bit. 'Yes.'

'Were those young, attractive men entirely enthusiastic about sexually servicing their cold-hearted, power-abusing supervisor?' Charlene got ready with the zapper. 'Those young studs who knew they'd lose their jobs if they didn't ring your fucking chimes?'

'Yes! Yes! They *wanted* me!'

Glancing at the readout. 'Wrong answer, Janet.' I watched in horror as Charlene gave her a full minute of zapping. But I was feeling something darker: the desire to glut my *own* depraved and ungovernable lusts in the orifices of Janet, Evil Power-Abusing Boss. Janet was looking somewhat crazy by this point; tears in her eyes but squirming like a teenage girl frustrated after six hours of unconsummated dry-humping in the backseat of the high-school football hero's Trans Am.

Charlene consulted the clipboard. 'Here's another one: Are you sexually attracted to our own Edward Kelvin, CEO of Torment, Incorporated?'

Janet swallowed, said nothing. Charlene gestured menacingly with the zapper. 'Come on, Janet, it's OK to get your panties all soaked over *him* – after all, he outranks you in this organisation, unlike the underlings you took advantage of at your previous job. So let's try it again. Do you want to fuck the attractive young man sitting on that couch? The one with the big bulge in the pants of his Armani suit?'

Actually, it wasn't an Armani suit – I found them too car-salesman-like for my taste. But I kept silent. 'Yes . . .' Janet whispered. Marie checked the dials, nodded.

'Well, why don't you take a look at what he's got in that package,' Charlene suggested, 'Maybe it's something *all* us girls would like to see.' Janet knelt in front of the couch, careful not to break the polygraph wires leading to the cart. As she reached for my zipper, I was able to catch a nice view of her small, elegant breasts. Charlene and Marie watched intently as Janet worked through my schlong out into the open. I was a little uneasy about those two seeing my gear, for different reasons, but the rollercoaster had started on the downhill slope and there was no stopping it. Janet kept her fingertips lightly on my shaft, careful not to touch the head, and stroked it lightly. She was good.

Janet touched her tongue-tip to the tip of my cock. I tried to keep cool but couldn't prevent a sharp intake of breath. Marie nudged Charlene and whispered something to her; they giggled. Marie held her hands apart, apparently indicating the length of my stuff. I have nothing record-breaking in the measurement department, mind you, but Marie and Charlene seemed to approve. Janet's teasing, feathery touch was getting me riled up in a major way; she had plenty of experience and knew her way around the male anatomy like no 20-year-old honey ever could.

Charlene approached us. 'I think Ed's had enough of *that*, Janet.' She pulled Janet's hands and mouth off me – much to my disappointment – and hauled her to a standing position, facing me. 'I bet you've got a *better* place to put the CEO's penis, don't you?'

Janet nodded. Trancelike, she allowed herself to be arranged as Charlene saw fit; in moments, Janet's knees were on the couch on either side of my thighs, her palms on the wall behind my head, and her breasts pressed against my face. Charlene lifted Janet's skirt out of the way, then placed my hands on her ass. I slid my fingers around the curves of her cheeks and rested their tips on her labia, keeping my touch as light as possible – just as she'd done to me. She was wet; I felt a drop land on my nads as I centred her a few inches above my stuff. I couldn't push her down on it because Charlene had her knee wedged against Janet's tailbone, preventing just such an action.

Charlene laughed. 'Now, Janet, this isn't going to be quite like the other times you had some randy young stallion in your office.' Janet strained against Charlene, wanting to get busy on some hot man-action. No dice. 'This time, it's going to be all about *his* pleasure, not yours.' She removed her knee suddenly, and Janet promptly ground her ass down onto me, my wood slipping effortlessly into her well-lubed cooch, her ass slapping on my thighs as she bottomed out. Janet wasn't wasting any time; she got rolling with a vigorous up-and-down on me, spicing it up with some hip-gyrations and little flourishes.

Janet moaned. I moaned. Even Marie moaned, ditching her duties at the polygraph and sitting in one of the office chairs with her bare foot tucked under her crotch, rocking her weight on the heel (the oldest surreptitious girly-masturbation trick in the book, but Marie probably thought nobody noticed). Charlene, however, stayed very businesslike. At that point, I wouldn't have complained if Charlene had traded places with Janet, but that wasn't part of the programme.

Charlene went out into the hallway. I thought I heard glass breaking, but didn't care; I was on the receiving end of some of the most skilful coochie action I'd ever had. I heard Charlene come back into the room, but I was too busy pulling Janet's sweater over her head to pay much attention.

Janet kept at it, and I could tell from the tension in her body that she was getting close to a big climax.

I decided to hold back, in order to prolong my enjoyment of a quality schtup. But my enjoyment was cut off sharply by a blast of water that knocked Janet off me and to the other side of the room. What the *fuck*?

Charlene stood over Janet's half-naked form with a firehose nozzle in her hands. The hose trailed out the door. She'd busted the glass on the EMERGENCY firehose compartment in the hallway and now she was using it to tumble Janet end-over-end across my office. Already the floor was several inches deep in water.

She cut off the flow. Janet huddled in the corner, stunned from the force of the water. 'I *told* you, Janet, this wasn't about *your* pleasure.' We'd need a serious carpet cleaning for this mess. 'The polygraph tells all, Janet, and it told me you were fixing to come in a few seconds.' Janet sobbed, beaten. I snapped to a realisation: this was exactly what Janet *needed* from Torment, Incorporated. 'Now, drag your soaking-wet ass back to Mr Kelvin and get to work. Only this time, no orgasms for *you*.'

Janet crept back to the couch, which was wringing wet and would have to be tossed straight into the dumpster if we didn't want a mildew nightmare. I was freezing cold but still had a ragin' hard going. Janet crawled back into position on the couch, her knees squooshing a couple gallons of water out of the couch cushions, and gingerly slid her cooch back onto my unit. Her heat was most welcome after the chilly firehose bath.

Charlene stood at the polygraph, the firehose nozzle trained straight at Janet. 'If you even get *shouting* distance from climax, I'll let you have it with the hose again,' she threatened. 'And next time I'm washing you right down the fire stairs.' Marie had fled, either out of horror or a need to masturbate in private.

Janet started working on me again, this time with noticeably less enthusiasm. I was crazy with lust madness after her rowdy humping prior to Charlene's rude interruption – planted my hands on Janet's shoulders and pressed her down with all my might, thrusting upward at the same time. I was gonna split her in two. It would be best for both of us if I came quickly, so I didn't hold back. Janet did her best to avoid getting another soaking, as Charlene's eyes were locked on the polygraph dials, but she was heating up fast.

'Pull out, Janet!' Charlene ordered, 'Finish him off with your hands!' Obediently, Janet struggled free of my grip and got busy stroking me two-handed; no subtlety this time. She'd been so wet my schlong was plenty slippery, and she went right for the kill. After what seemed like a few seconds, I busted a nut, my semen squirting between her knuckles. I played it cool, just closing my eyes and holding my breath as I shot.

Silence. I hoped it was worth destroying my office with a few thousand gallons of water for this – Janet's fee for the day wouldn't begin to pay for the cleanup. Quickly, so that Janet didn't notice, Charlene dipped her finger in a droplet of spooge on my thigh and carefully licked it off her finger, eyes locked with mine. Damn. She knew I'd keep that mental picture for a while.

After Janet left, first having reserved two 'work-days' for the following week, I sat silently in another office, trying to put some kind of interpretation on the day's events. I was learning things about myself I wasn't wholly happy knowing. I'd gotten aroused by the walk-in-freezer episode with Mimi and Corinne, and now I was fantasising about the demeaning acts I'd have Janet perform for me when she returned. I felt a loss of sexual innocence; before Torment, Incorporated I had fucked for the pure California-style sensual joy of the act – oh, sure, maybe spiced up with a little taste of evil here and there – and for a sense of closeness with my partners. But now I was becoming more Old World, more cynical. More like Charlene, in fact.

We got the water pumped out and the carpets replaced in my office. Business at Torment, Incorporated continued as usual; with a backlogged waiting list of six weeks to 'work' at our company, we were raking in truckloads of money. The ex-FPSs weren't sufficient manpower to keep the operation going at the proper level, so we took to hiring actual office temps to sit at the desks and go through the motions of typing spreadsheets and answering phones.

After a few more months, a strange transformation started becoming evident around the offices of Torment, Incorporated. Actually, it was *two* transformations, one inside and one outside: we started becoming more like a real business and the dot-com/high-tech boom got rolling in true, supercharged, irrational-exuberant glory.

The process inside the office was the direct offshoot of having so many temps now punching time clocks; we didn't bother to tell them the score about what Torment, Incorporated was all about. In fact, we'd started using the Sux-M-Owt Home Stomach Pumps name more frequently; it seemed a wiser move to use that name when dealing with temp agencies and other non-client contacts. All our bills and 'legit' correspondence came to Sux-M-Owt, that's what the temps called it, and we started *thinking* it as well. The temps seemed to sense that something was odd about the office, but not enough so that they complained about it.

The clients kept showing up and glorying under the cruel lash of Charlene's punishments, I kept playing the bastard-CEO role, and so on, but now it seemed that actual *work* was taking place. The temps were grinding on God-knows-what busywork that the clients handed to them; meetings took place that had nothing to do with our office-themed sexually overtoned humiliation schtick. 'Business Plans' and 'Progress Reports' and a whole deck of memos started showing up in my In basket. Everyone in the place was so familiar with the office environment that they automatically started doing whatever it is people in offices *do*. Never mind that they weren't told what our office *did*, other than scratch the itch that all the quasi-Inquisition phony-ass 'dungeons' never could reach. Never mind that Charlene and I never made the slightest attempt to provide any information about the Sux-M-Owt Home Stomach Pump other than the name. Never mind that the clients were doing all this stuff in between taking cattle-prod shots to the nuts and cat-o-nine-tails beatings. I was learning the core truth about Office Land – people went to the office and accomplished . . . *nothing*! They didn't care if the eight hours they shot through the head every weekday were pissed down a rathole. This realisation was making me very, very depressed.

Charlene just laughed when I explained the problem to her one night after business hours. We were hanging around at her place, knocking back a couple of cold ones, just like in the old days. 'This *surprises* you?' she asked when she'd stopped busting up enough to speak. 'Oh, Eddie. I hate to tell you this, but a pretty good case could be made that Office Life is the *normal condition* for *Homo Americanus Suburbanus.*' She swigged her beer, burped. 'You need to go with the flow, dude. We're gonna ride this tide of scum to glory!'

But it got weirder, fast. We'd been abusing and humiliating the very *cream* of Southern California corporate manhood. Some of our clients were highly-placed officials in companies that were viewed by investors as being in the forefront of . . . some kind of futuristic shit. Computers. Phones. Jet-powered backpacks. I had no idea, and frankly my vision of their 'real' jobs was pretty much what I saw going on all day at Sux-M-Owt/Torment, Incorporated: a bunch of waste motion, digging and refilling the same holes all day, and soul-destroying pecking-order games that ground up the low-rankers like meat in a sausage grinder. How they could actually *accomplish* anything in such an environment was beyond me.

But it wasn't beyond the venture-capital companies. Within weeks of the startup of Torment, Incorporated, the more savvy VC wizards took notice of the constant traffic of hotshot execs from a virtual *Who's Who* of California high-tech corporations. The way they made money was by having the inside information on all the hot companies, and Torment, Incorporated showed up on their radar like a fleet of Libyan Mig-29s heading straight toward the Lincoln Memorial at Mach 3. They had platoons of private detectives following the major players, and more and more of them were coming to our office. They'd see the VP of Product Development from the #1 maker of computer disk-drives in the Western Hemisphere heading out to this unknown company near John Wayne Airport . . . he'd park his Porsche in the 'Worst Employee of the Month' spot and disappear inside for the whole day. While the VC snoop was taking telephoto shots of the guy's licence plates, the

CFO of a multinational satellite-TV corporation would show up, followed by another half-dozen 'Persons of Interest'. They knew that the whole Sux-M-Owt cover had to be a sham, a front, and they couldn't make any sense out of the info they picked up about the goings-on inside the Torment, Incorpated office. But they knew it had to be *big*.

At first, we had no idea that we were the focus of so much attention. Anyone attempting to enter the office without an ironclad appointment was promptly shown the door – we assumed they were just chisellers trying to get a Charlene beating without paying – and incoming telephone calls not coming to the secret clients-only number were funnelled into an endless maze of phone trees and faulty voicemail boxes. It never occurred to me or Charlene that we might attract outside attention; in fact, we tried to keep a low profile so as to avoid difficulties with Johnny Law and/or the Tax Man. But the curiosity from the VC firms was such that we finally started noticing it. Our little gold mine wasn't so secret any more.

At the same time, the internet bubble, the dot-com boom, the stock-market runup – whatever you want to call it – was in full motherfucking effect. It was centred 400 miles to the north, in Silicon Valley and San Francisco, but there was plenty of cash from the waves of investment washing over Southern California as well. The office-parks near our office started to fill up with flaky-looking high-tech businesses, many of them sporting *.com* in their names and every one of them showering a rain of stock options on packs of newly-minted millionaires. Lexus and Mercedes dealers couldn't keep cars on the lots. Even the once-vacant floors of our building started to fill up with bright-eyed entrepreneurs, their snazzy logos on the sign with Sux-M-Owt. Now we had to deal with the *real* Office World right under our noses. The outfit in the floor beneath ours, known as iStalker.com, provided tools for stalkers of all stripes; their pop-up website ads proclaimed 'Restraining order? Change of address? Unlisted phone number? YOU KNOW SHE STILL LOVES YOU!' That bunch was sure to get rich.

We already *were* rich, or felt like it, anyway. Charlene and I were clearing $50,000 a month cash between us, even after paying the rent and bills and hiring all the temps. So the first VC weasel who managed to worm his way into the office and offered to make us rich got Tazered in the solar plexus by Charlene, who then shoved him into the elevator with a Bruno Magli in the ass. 'Whatever you're selling, we ain't buying!' she screamed after him. That just spurred them on; with most up-and-coming young business types willing to offer an unlubed crack at their bungholes to any and all comers promising suitcases full of investment cash, a company that violently ejected such suitors must really *have* something. They kept showing up; I couldn't hit the taqueria for a carne asada super burrito without some guy with five cellphones wanting to have a sit-down about his great 'opportunity' for my company.

Once Charlene and I got it through our heads what was really going on, however, we knew we'd be able to take the Torment, Incorporated concept to undreamed-of levels. All we needed to do was hit the venture capitalists like the biggest ATM machine in the world, take their free money, and insist on retaining full decision-making control over our destiny. Charlene would have the opportunity to do her thing on an unprecedented number of willing victims, and I would get to build the largest and most brain-rattling performance/installation art piece the world had ever seen – the WWI Santa piece writ fifty million times larger. So, dear reader, there was never any talk about defrauding anybody, or doing the venture-capital equivalent of the dine-n-dash. We actually made *more* money, in terms of actual take-home pay, during the early pre-VC days of Torment, Incorporated, than we ever did during the period for which we were prosecuted.

But what's done is done; I'm almost finished paying my debt to society now, so no hard feelings. Back to the story: Once we'd figured out the story behind the VC types we picked the greediest, most gullible one and arranged a meeting with his Board of Directors up near San Jose. It was a laugh riot at every stage; Charlene and I both dressed up like movie stars, made a dramatic entrance at the VC firm's Sand Hill Road HQ, shook everyone's hands, and then made like fucking clams when pressed about the philosophy, goals, or plans of Sux-M-Owt.com, Incorporated (we'd jumped on the dot-com bandwagon with our new name; we ditched the 'Home Stomach Pump' part and we thought what was left had an edgy, hip sound). In fact, we refused to talk about *anything* having to do with our business, other than the fact that we wanted a few thousand acre-feet of cash, to spend as we pleased, and a full management team to turn our every whim, no matter how deranged, into full, rampaging reality. What did we *do*? Ain't saying.

And it worked. We had a deal. Sux-M-Owt.com was sure to be bigger than Pets.com, bigger than Webvan. Handshakes all around. They even held a press conference, just to rub it into the VC firms that had missed the boat on Sux-M-Owt.com.

Once we were flush with effectively unlimited cash, courtesy of our trusting investors in Palo Alto, we no longer had to charge our clients for our services. Now we just *hired* our favourites (including Janet, of course) and made Sux-M-Owt.com their day job. Nothing much changed as far as our day-to-day operations, of course; Charlene still operated the place according to her principles of sadism and humiliation, the temps still punched their time clocks and did whatever it was they did, and I still had fun playing with the icons and archetypes of Office World.

The difference now was the scale; not only could I now commission the custom neon-sign I'd always wanted for the building, the investors suggested that we get a whole new building. As a matter of fact, they were downright insistent on it. They would have preferred a location in Mountain View or Milpitas, but Charlene and I held firm on an Orange County office. The investors kicked down the money for a beautiful mirrored-glass postmodern monolith in Irvine, complete with positive-pressure server room, technical-support call centre, and so on, plus a whole raft of employee-coddling frills and perks: A rock-climbing wall. A gourmet kitchen, in which we could (and would) install a full staff of world-class culinary professionals to cook five-star meals. A private garden with turf seats and exotic birds. A video-game arcade, with everything from Space Invaders through an Israeli Air Force fighter-bomber simulator. A 'nap room' complete with velour couches in edgy, late-90s colours (I knew where I'd take Janet for a little lunchtime get-together). And the furniture: Aeron chairs for everyone. Plasma displays on the walls. NSA-grade computer hardware. Money was no object – in fact, we were often hassled for not spending *enough*.

So the money was just the background, the sea through which we all swam, not the prize Charlene and I were striving for. Once in the new office, we had room for hundreds more employees than we actually had, even with the eager new hires culled from the pool of former clients. The task of filling our ritzy new facility seemed daunting, but the management team put in place by the investors handled that. We realised that we couldn't have a company 100% staffed by Torment, Incorporated clients, as enjoyable as that might seem, so we had the management team whomp up a Human Resources Department and told them to hire whatever we needed. It seemed that such things were accomplished using a just-add-water kit thrown in a shopping cart in a huge Personnel Warehouse outlet; I'd mention that we ought to have a 'Sales Team', for example (although we didn't have anything to sell), and, within a day or so, we'd have a whole wing of the office swarming with hard-charging sales hotrods, sporting Power Ties and shouting into telephones.

You'd think there would have been a jarring incongruity between the sight of Charlene hog-tying a $150,000-a-year VP on his desk, using zip-ties cutting viciously into his wrists and ankles and his head completely wrapped in duct tape (a toilet-paper tube sticking out for an airhole) and a brainstorm session conducted by a dozen eager young strategists in the next room. But nobody seemed to think it unusual, thus lending weight to my grim theory about the true nature of Office World.

Meanwhile, the time I poured into the job had taken its toll on my social life. Randy Kraft and the Dead Marines had disbanded. No more cruising with my buddies in the Econoline, or drinking beer after beer while debating the relative qualities of Fear versus the Suicidal Tendencies. I felt vaguely guilty about leaving my friends behind, but the new,

VC-turbocharged version of Sux-M-Owt.com was proving to be great fun for me. Total freedom to indulge my budding artistic sensibilities, with less need to provide sexual gratification to power-obsessed torture clients and no accountability whatsoever for me when I whipped out the company checkbook. One night, after most of the Sux-M-Owters had gone home, I kicked my feet up on my desk, sparked up a bowl of White Widow, and let my mind wander. Of all the folks outside the company, Violet Tran was the one I missed most. We talked on the phone now and then, but I always told her I was 'too busy at my new job' to see her. Which was true, in a sense, but her shy, oblique references to how excited she'd been by my brief penetration of her a few months back worked on my mind. She wasn't too upset about it, as she was pleased that I now had a career and wore a suit to work, etc. I still didn't think it would be right for me to gratify my maddening, Visigoth-style lust on her prostrate form – the way I had done earlier that day with Janet on the futuristic stainless-steel table of Conference Room #4 (Janet had become a valuable addition to the Sux-M-Owt.com team, not just for her eagerness to spread her legs for me anywhere in the building I happened to find her, but for her management skills in building Sux-M-Owt.com into an *empire*).

I thought it might be good for my soul to have a good ole-fashioned high-school-style makeout session with Violet, just like we used to do before slipping over the line into something a bit more home-run than second-base (to use the appropriate high-school terminology); although I told myself we hadn't technically fucked, since it was just a bit of insertion and my spunk had ended up in her mouth rather than her vagina. Having taken the edge off my lust with Janet a few hours earlier, I felt that I'd have sufficient self-control to avoid Going Too Far with her even after a couple of hours roaming my hands over her taut, economical curves and feeling her dry-hump my leg while sucking my tongue. Yeah, great idea, I though, dialling her number. My end of the conversation:

'Hey, Vi! Yeah, I've been busy here at the office. The new one, in Irvine. Sure, I want to see you. Why don't you head on down here and I'll show you around. Yeah, I think we could find someplace private to work on your homework.'

Oh, yeah. I'd work on her homework, all right. So she was hopping into her sensible Geo Metro and zipping down the 405 to the offices of Sux-M-Owt.com. Seconds later, a rapping at my office door. Charlene, also working late. She looked mighty fine; if anything, the rigours of keeping her thumb pressed firmly on the spirits of hundreds of potentially rebellious employees had made her even sexier, given her more spirit, a musky glow to her skin and a traffic-stopping pride in her stride. She yearned for me to break down and love her up according to her strict specifications, but we were still locked in the same old you-blink-first battle of wills.

'I watched you and Janet in the conference room,' she said. 'You know all the conference rooms are wired up for holographic teleconferencing; no such thing as privacy in this place.'

So she caught the action with Janet – not like I was trying to keep it a secret. 'So you've come here to offer a critique on my technique?'

She laughed. 'Well, I *was* disappointed that you came inside her this time, instead of giving me a nice money shot. I prefer to *see* a man climax, if you know what I mean. But I'm glad you're doing Janet regularly; I like to think about it when she's going down on me during our morning conferences.'

Well, *that* was new; Charlene had always swung only hetero as far as I knew. She caught my questioning look. 'Oh, I've had to become more broad*minded* in my position as President of the company,' she said. 'I'm only half as effective a boss if I can only use my *full* repertoire of, um, managerial techniques on the male employees. And female flesh *feels* good, which I hadn't realised before – I get hot just thinking about how that curvy first-floor receptionist will feel while I'm having an employee review session with her.' She licked her lips. 'I bet she'll do whatever I say, right away. I can tell. I'll have her naked and blindfolded within five minutes.'

Ah, Charlene's infamous employee reviews; they were the subject of much hushed, fearful/stimulated talk around the water cooler. I'd cautioned her to limit her dominance games to employees who clearly desired them, suggesting that we might face an onslaught of employee lawsuits if she got out of control with the wrong Sux-M-Owter. But Charlene was becoming more self-absorbed every day, more sociopathically concerned with her own hungers and giving less of a shit about possible consequences. Such concerns were meaningless to her – she accused me of 'wimping out' when I brought them up.

'Hey, maybe you could help me with her review,' she said, leering. 'We could *share* the duties.'

I hesitated. That *did* sound intriguing, although it edged far into the darker shades of grey on my personal morality scale. That scale had become less distinct during my association with Charlene, I knew. But it would be a chance to nibble around the edges of our desire for each other, while having the first-floor receptionist to satisfy our carnal cravings –

her name was some kind of Middle Eastern thing, Neda or Nada, and she was a looker (wolf whistle, etc.). Except for my several-times-a-day trysts with Janet, I'd steered clear of boss-on-employee so-called 'inappropriate contact', but the reasons for this seemed hazier than they once had. The reasons for a *lot* of things seemed hazier, these days.

'No, you go ahead and review her yourself. Just don't do it in the conference room if you don't want me watching on the hologram,' I said. And I *meant* it, too. 'Hey, I have a visitor coming over, so I need to, you know, get going.' Trying to get Charlene out before Violet showed up, of course; I didn't need anyone cramping my style while I gave Violet a case of blue ovaries from an evening of petting.

Too late; the security guard called from the lobby to let me know my authorised visitor, Ms Tran, was being brought up to my office. 'Ms Tran, eh?' pouted Charlene. 'It saddens me that you don't want me to meet your *lady friend*, Eddie.' She made *lady friend* sound like *colostomy bag*.

'Not at all, Charlene. I'll introduce you.' Violet showed up with the security guard, who made me sign a complicated authorisation form, part of the institutional paranoia Charlene and I had decided to put in place, as part of our keep-the-employees-off-guard strategy. The investors dug it.

'Hey, I had to get a *retinal scan* before they'd let me in,' Violet complained. She looked cute in her tight Chapman College Volleyball sweatshirt and sensible shorts. Her volleyball-enhanced leg muscles looked sleek. I knew she'd be itching for some roaming hands and heavy breathing. I felt a few heartbeats in my dick and shifted a bit to allow it a more comfortable arrangement in my pants. Charlene caught the movement and knew it for what it meant.

Her eyes narrowed slightly and she gave Violet a cool once-over.

'Yeah, we have tight security here at Sux-M-Owt.com. You're lucky they didn't strip-search you – they're supposed to do that with non-employees, but I told them to skip it in your case,' I said. Then, introducing them: 'Violet, this is Charlene Cabrillo, President of Sux-M-Owt.com. Charlene, this is Violet Tran, my girlfriend from Garden Grove.'

'Oh, yes, Edward has told me all about you, Violet,' Charlene said graciously. It was almost hard to imagine her pouring molten wax on a man's balls when she used that voice. And I *had* told her all about Violet, I realised with a shock; Charlene knew the whole story, told to her one drunken night back in my dope-dealin' days. Oh, shit . . .

They shook hands. 'I'm really impressed by how *big* your company has become,' Violet said. 'Wasn't it just a couple months ago that you were in that little building by the airport? And didn't it have a different name back then?'

'Well, the New Economy and all, you know,' I said. 'Say, Charlene, I was thinking Violet and I wanted to have a little chat, you know –'

'Oh, don't let *me* stand in the way of your private discussion,' Charlene said, 'I'll be running along.' She turned to go, then whirled around. I did a slow simmer. What was she up to? 'But where are our manners? We haven't even offered our visitor any of our customary, time-tested Sux-M-Owt.com re*fresh*-ments!' Refreshments? What the *hell*?

'Oh, sure, I'd *love* some refreshments,' Violet gushed, looking very much the part of the wholesome college student. 'That would be fun!'

Charlene went straight for my Intoxicants Cabinet, an ornate Chinese armoire next to the plasma-screen wall display. I groaned inwardly, but went with it and invited Violet to take a seat on the plush couch facing the window; as CEO, I got a glorious view of the Pacific. In fact, the whole office was top-shelf all the way, with that squander-iffic Saudi-sheik brand of excess: about 3,000 square feet, Persian rugs on an inlaid ebony floor, the works. So far all I'd done to put my personal touch on it was the Intoxicants Cabinet, a necessity for any hard-working chief executive.

And from that cabinet Charlene was selecting some choice refreshments. Hashish-infused baklava straight from Lebanon. 100-year-old New Orleans absinthe. And, of course, an ornate Turkish hookah packed with the deadly Gulag Gunjah and topped with a fat ball of Burmese opium. Obtaining the legendary Gulag Gunjah had been a minor triumph for me; the result of decades of careful breeding and selection of the cough-worthy Russian *Cannabis ruderalis* plant by exiled Soviet botanists in Siberia, the stuff was so stony that supposedly even Jerry Garcia had freaked out after smoking a single joint.

I was horrified. 'Uh, Charlene, I don't think these are the right kind of refreshments, if you know what I mean . . . maybe we should just grab a few Cokes out of the break room . . .'

'Oh, come *on*, Eddie,' Violet said, annoyed. 'You must think I'm some kind of *sheltered* little girl or something. I know how to *party*. I'm feeling a little crazy tonight!'

You'll be feeling more than a little *crazy if you touch the Gulag Gunjah*, I thought, but said nothing. Her idea of crazy was drinking three wine coolers to her head and mock-dirty dancing at a dorm party. I'd offered her some training-wheels-potency weed once or twice and she'd turned it down. Well, she was a grown-up. 'All right. Charlene, if you'll do the honours?'

Charlene poured us each a shot of the absinthe. I was proud of the vintage 1920s shotglasses; it was said that Dutch Schultz had once owned them. 'To madness!' I toasted, and we clicked glasses and knocked 'em back. Ah, demon wormwood.

'Whooo!' Violet gasped. 'This stuff is strong!'

Charlene handed her a slab of hash baklava. 'Here, this will cut the bitter taste.'

'Aren't you having any yourself, Charlotte?' I asked, cutting off a huge bar of baklava with a jewelled confectioner's knife and offering it to her. 'It's real Lebanese.' I jammed a wedge of the stuff into my own mouth and chewed. I'd had a pecan-sized piece the day before and had felt pleasantly high for most of the day. Given the amount we'd just consumed, they'd be pouring all three of us down the sink by about midnight . . . and we hadn't even touched the Gunjah yet. But I was having a good time – nothing like that *here we go* feeling of making the decision to get truly hammered on quality dope. And it wasn't like I needed to get up early for work.

The wormwood was warming me nicely, but it would take about half an hour before the hash we'd eaten would take effect. I poured another round of absinthe shots and belted mine down, then took a swig straight from the bottle. Violet giggled, already buzzed from the first shot.

Charlene was using a small butane torch to toast the opium ball crowning the bowl of Gulag Gunjah. The hookah was a beauty, with amber carvings depicting Turkish village scenes; the eyes of the horses were tiny emeralds. It cost Sux-M-Owt.com $8,000 but it was all deductible for 'entertainment expenses' or some such (yes, dear reader, this was the famous '$80,000 Bong' that everyone heard about during my trial; amazing how legends build – the thing was hyped with the outrage reserved for thousand-dollar Army toilet seats). Once the opium was prepared (it being crass to just fire up a cold opium ball), she put one of the delicate hookah tubes in her mouth and directed the flame downward, sucking down a big hit of opium-enhanced Gunjah.

I handed Violet one of the tubes. She giggled and put it in her mouth. 'When Charlene lights the bowl with the torch, suck gently on that tube,' I told her.

'Oh, I *like* to suck,' she said, looking me dead in the eye. Had I really *heard* that?

Charlene laughed out a lungful of smoke, then lit the bowl. 'That's right, honey,' she said, 'What girl doesn't? Especially with a hunky guy like Eddie here? You're lucky – he won't even *look* at me!' Violet's eyes bulged as she took a pretty good hit, for a beginner.

Hunky? Shee-it. I'd show her hunky. I grabbed a hookah tube and had a toke. 'Hold it in as long as you can,' I told Violet in that stoner grunt/squeak voice you use when holding in a hit. Violet started to cough and reached for the absinthe bottle.

Just like that, we were higher than the bejesus. Uncontrollable laughing jags, and so on. I staggered over to the stereo (a custom-built audiophile tube amp feeding speakers built into the room) and looked for the stoniest album I could find; I considered Muddy Waters' psychedelic effort 'Electric Mud' or maybe some early Beck, but settled on Cypress Hill's first album. As 'Pigs' thumped through the subwoofers, I saw that Charlene was leaning over to Violet and whispering something to her. Charlene's hand rested on Violet's thigh. Violet was either too loaded to notice or was enjoying it; her dazed smile could be interpreted either way.

I didn't care. 'More dope! Louder music!' I shouted, doing a little white-boy dancing to the pounding Cypress Hill beat. Worked my way back to the couch and flopped down between the two women. A curl of smoke rose from the hookah; they'd killed the bowl while I was fooling with the CD collection. Even Charlene, who had quite a tolerance, was visibly reeling. The hash was coming on hard, too; the room seemed to be pulsing, bending a little. You know you're high when you're getting psilocybin-style visual hallucinations. Violet was holding up well, all things considered.

Suddenly, I loved my job. I was getting higher than Cheech and Chong put together, on the company tab, with two beautiful women, in my private office, with a view of the ocean out my floor-to-ceiling observation window.This beat the shit out of a quick toke behind the dumpsters at the pizza joint. Violet leaned over me to whisper something to Charlene. Her breast mashed against my arm and her sweatshirt pulled up in pack, revealing the spot at the base of her spine I loved to kiss. A wave of sweaty, desperate lust rushed through my system, the way it sneaks up on you when you're high. I slipped my hand down Violet's back and let my palm come to rest just under the waistband of her shorts.

She and Charlene were giggling over something, some kind of girl-talk stuff. When she pulled back from Charlene, I was left with my hand in place and my arm around her. She was a little sweaty; I could sense she was getting turned on. 'Aren't you hot in that sweatshirt, Vi?' asked Charlotte sweetly. 'We're casual here at Sux-M-Owt.com – you can get *comfortable.*'

'That's a good idea,' said Violet, peeling the sweatshirt over her head. Underneath, she had on a tight wifebeater shirt. Her tiny, dark nipples were erect, clearly visible through the thin fabric. Her arm and shoulder muscles were small and sharply defined, the way female athletes' bodies get. I was smitten. I tried not to paw her, but it took just about all my self-control. I realised that I wasn't going to be able to get out of the office without fucking the taste out of Violet's mouth; there was no alternative. My balls would swell up like huge boils and explode otherwise. I'd deal with the fallout later on. The one thing that worried me was the presence of Charlene; I might end up slipping it to her as well, and I was saving that for the moment she'd let me take charge of the act.

'I'm feeling pretty casual myself,' said Charlene, shedding her jacket and stripping off her blouse. She wore a sheer pink brassiere, the kind that snaps in the front. I leaned back on the couch and chugged another rip of absinthe. I felt like Hugh Hefner. 'Violet, you have such a *nice* body,' she said. 'I'm envious of those muscles. And such great boobs!'

'Oh, no,' said Violet, pleased. 'Your body is *much* better. I'm just sort of . . . plain.' The hash was coming on full strength now; Violet was struggling to retain focus. She giggled some more. 'Wow, this stuff makes me feel, uh . . . *funny*!' She started unbuttoning my shirt, became fascinated by one of the buttons, started studying it intently.

Charlotte reached over, finished unbuttoning my shirt and tossed it aside. Now they could see how hard my heart was pounding; there was no hiding my tungsten-hard erection. 'It's sweet of you to say that, Violet, but I need to face facts – these days men want women with petite, firm breasts, like little apples, and good muscle definition. Like you. I would have been considered attractive back in the fifties, but these days . . .' She gestured helplessly at her Marilyn

Monroe physique. Poor Charlene. 'I could never catch a handsome man like Eddie here with *this* body.'

Oh, for Christ sake. *I* didn't feel sorry for her, but Violet fell for it. 'I always wanted boobs like yours.' She cupped her own. I quivered, wanting the taste of her nipples under my tongue *now*! 'I always wondered what it would feel like to have big ones, like the white and Mexican girls at school,' she said, wistfully.

Charlene got up, walked around me, and knelt in front of Violet. 'You can feel mine if you'd like,' she said, slurring a little. Charlene was too blitzed to hide her lust now. Violet looked confused, hesitating. 'It's OK, we're just being casual here,' said Charlene. Violet leaned forward, not sure what to do. Charlene unsnapped her bra and let it drop, then took Violet's hands and placed them gingerly on her breasts. She closed her eyes, sighed. I felt an unreal, distant sensation, like I was watching the whole thing on TV.

I thought Violet would just give Charlene's breasts a little squeeze and pull back, but instead she traced them with her fingertips, letting the nipples brush her palms, curious about their texture. I started packing another bowl in the hookah, just to have something to do with my hands. Charlene kept her eyes closed as Violet leaned in closer, letting her bangs tickle Charlene's face. Charlene moaned. I couldn't look away. Violet worked her face closer to Charlene's, careful not to touch. Her hands moved up, over the flawless white skin of Charlene's shoulders, then her neck, finally coming to rest with fingers twined in her thick curls. Charlene placed her palm on Violet's inner thigh and slipped her fingers under the fabric of her shorts. She moved closer, their lips touched. Violet's tongue traced the outline of Charlene's lips, then eased between them. They kissed deeply, calmly. I finished packing the bowl and sparked it. Now I *really* felt like Hugh Hefner.

They finished their kiss. Charlene went back to her seat on the couch. Violet was panting, sweaty, obviously shaken by what she'd done but heated up as hell and wanting more. From my makeout experience with her, I knew her cooch would be literally dripping wet by now, her labia swollen and dark-pink. The question was: how was I going to get into it without Charlene poisoning the whole experience?

'Violet, can I ask you something a little bit personal?' Charlene asked. Violet nodded. 'Have you ever given a man a blowjob?'

'Oh, of *course*,' Violet said. 'Only once, though. With Eddie.' She laughed, thinking about it. 'I *loved* it. But I didn't really do the whole thing that way. With my mouth, I mean. He was in me . . . somewhere else, you know, and then he pulled out and I just did the last part with my mouth.' She looked a little sad. 'You don't think there's something *wrong* with me, do you? That I'm 20 and only did it once?'

'No, not at all. In fact, the reason I brought it up is that I thought I could maybe give you some pointers. Maybe then Eddie would be nicer to you, give you what a man *should* give a woman. Eddie can sometimes be a little mean.'

'Would you? Then I might be able to convince him to make love to me all the way. Here, let's get started.' She ducked over me, heading toward my crotch like a duck after a junebug. Her fingers were shaky from lust and her head was full of enough THC to disable a platoon of Marines, and she had a lot of trouble with my pants.

Charlene leaned over and helped her get my pants unzipped, then took my shoes off and yanked my pants off completely. My rod stood at attention, poking out the pee-flap of my undies. What the hell – I pulled them off and flung them away. Charlene: 'I think this won't be a *complete* lesson, though – we need to make sure Eddie has enough lead in his pencil to satisfy you later on.'

Charlene got up, stripped off the rest of her clothes, tossed them across the office. Stretched her arms over her head and wriggled a bit, then sat down next to me on the couch. *¡Ay, Chihuahua!* What a body! Giggling, Violet followed her lead, stonedly struggling her way out of her clothes. She looked even *better*. 'First of all, a good blowjob should be performed by a *nude* woman,' Charlene said. 'OK, we got that part done. Now, first thing you need to do is let him know how *good* it's going to feel when you really get to work on him. So get in there and give him a few little kisses – on the shaft, not the head – and hold his balls a bit while you're at it . . .'

Violet followed instructions well. Charlene talked her through the full range of teasing hoover-job trickery. I knew what was going on: Charlene was giving me a blowjob through Violet. I knew it and Charlene knew I knew. We locked eyes and stayed that way as Violet got down to some serious tongue work. 'All right, Violet,' Charlene said, 'go ahead and suck on it a little bit.' Violet did as ordered. I was delirious but nowhere near coming. I was saving that.

Charlene made Violet stop. 'I think that's enough for now. It's easy to give a man oral pleasure – no great secrets to it. But a *real* lover can please a woman as well, and that's harder.'

Violet blushed, knowing what Charlene had in mind. After the kiss they'd had, though, she was ready. After all, she could blame it on the absinthe later on, if she had regrets. 'Yes, I can do . . . that, too. You can show me.'

Charlene splayed out against the corner of the couch and gestured for Violet to come to her. They kissed some more, with Charlene working a couple of fingers inside Violet; when she pulled her fingers away a string of Violet's juice came with them, stretching and finally snapping as Violet inched her mouth down Charlene's body. Charlene guided her down to her goodies and whispered instructions. Violet was on her knees, her ass held high. Her parts were swollen and her inner thighs were glistening with pussy juice. A light bulb went on over my head at the sight.

I positioned myself behind Violet and gently nudged her legs wider apart. She knew what was going on; even as her tongue probed our corporate president's secret folds, she reached back and grasped my wang, guiding it into her.

As our three-way conference continued, the massive overload of THC in my system seemed to bestow hyperacute sensitivity of touch on me, so every one of Violet's vaginal ridges rasped on my nerve endings like a wire brush – not to say I wasn't enjoying it, but the stimulation was a bit too intense. I figured she was probably orbiting Neptune about now, thanks to her sudden introduction to reefer and lesbian sex in the same evening; no doubt she'd prefer to recall the evening's events as a really weird sex dream, once she sobered up in the morning.

Charlene was really making an O Face, having long since given up any hope of keeping up a cool, reserved appearance. Violet's tongue seemed to be hitting all the right spots; compared to my first time eating pussy, an embarrassing failure at age 15 – I lapped aimlessly like a cow at a salt lick – performed in the back seat of my 16-year-old partner's '81 Pontiac Phoenix under the influence of parent-filched gin and vodka mixed together in plastic bags (clear liquors can be watered down to hide evidence of pilfering), Violet was a tongue-lashing *natural*. Charlene's breath rasped, her head whipping from side to side, spraying sweat droplets in a fine rain over me. 'Shit . . . yeah . . . you bitch . . . Christ . . .' she gritted in classic dirty-talk mode, grinding Violet's head into her.

Violet was getting off, too, judging by the mean, pulsing grip I kept feeling on my Johnson from her panoche contractions, but her mouth was buried too deeply in girlflesh for much sound to escape her. I caught myself syncing my thrusts not with the peak-and-plateau rhythm's of Violet's orgasms, but with Charlene's building one. Just as Charlene had used Violet to go down on me, so was I doing Violet to go down on Charlene. In fact, Violet sort of faded from my awareness; I zeroed in on Charlene's face and made her react to *my* actions, not Violet's. Charlene didn't seem to have climaxed yet; she was more of the one-or-two-big-explosions type than the Violet style lots-of-little-peaks sort. I focused on Charlene's sounds and facial expressions; when she finally did pop I was going to join her, doing my best to squirt my load all the way through Violet and into her.

Finally, the moment came. There was no missing the warning that Charlene was about to come; she announced it to both of us in an escalating wail: 'Oh, fuck, I'm gonna come! Oh. Fuck. Coming!' Her stop-the-presses approach was amusing under the circumstances, but later on her self-absorption would be the key factor in bringing us both down. I geared down for some good leverage and pumped on Violet with everything I had. When Charlene made it, she literally *screamed*, like a schizophrenic confronted with CIA agents brandishing a mind-control transmitter. I came at that moment, grasping Violet's hard little ass and emptying what felt like the entire contents of my body shell into her, leaving me empty like an insect's exoskeleton.

The three of us collapsed in an exhausted, stoned heap. Charlene shakily pulled her sweaty hair out of her face while Violet rested her face on her belly. And somewhere The Great Scorekeeper debited my karmic account an unknown amount. The tally was building up.

Ten

Our Board of Directors felt that we needed to have our own 'product' in addition to our 'services', whatever those were, so we got several million to set up an Engineering Department, with the promise of more cash when we ran out. 'When you have an IPO, a products company gets more than a services company,' they said, mentally tallying up the ten-figure number every board member's stock options would be worth, post-IPO. I figured it would be nice to get some programmers writing software that would automate the generation of my Daily Memos, permitting both quality and quantity to increase while leaving me more time to expand the range of my organisational responsibilities. Charlene and I started interviewing applicants, me peppering them with non sequiturs while she paced behind the poor bastards, swagger stick tapping. And poor bastards they were – I'd never seen such a pathetic bunch of Monty Python-quoting, Star Trek-watching, no-sex-getting weenies in my life. Charlene was like a cat who stumbles across a room full of confused, crippled mice – plenty of games to play, no need to work hard. Lazily bat a few mice around, enjoy their fear. After the first few interviews, we had our system down: bright spotlights aimed at the interviewees eyes, both of us wearing mirror shades and dangling cigarettes from mouths, gun bulges, etc., *a la* Contra torture room. Absurd, yes, but effective (and, as things later turned out, an ominous portent of the uglier corners of Charlene's mental architecture). We'd hammer the sorry-ass sap with an onslaught of hostile, insulting questions in the proper General Stroessner mode, and anyone who showed the slightest hint of backbone or spirit got shown the door immediately. After a few days we'd culled the herd down to a couple dozen ideal candidates, mostly male but a few females as well, and got to work setting up the Engineering Annex at the headquarters. Charlene was in a frenzy to get busy on her new crew – she'd insisted on being Chief of Engineering Operations – and make them her personal stable of eager slaves. 'I'm taking the whole mistress/slave relationship to the *next level*!' she crowed, squirming in her new threads. No more fashionable designer-label outfits for her; she'd ditched them just like she'd ditched her tacky vinyl/leather wardrobe earlier. Her new look called for harsh Teutonic custom-tailored suits that looked like what Eva Braun would have worn had she been CEO of a particularly sleazy home-foreclosure corporation.

I was getting into it as well; designing the most unpleasant, soul-crushing work environment would require the hand of a master. I told Charlene to give me a week and I'd have her team slaving in the ideal setting. First order of business was the Annex. I sketched out some plans and rang up some contractors, paying triple-time for fast building. We set the place up in the basement, for that gloomy, oppressive ambience. Since the existing basement was a bit too cheery for our needs, some major remodelling was in order; I obtained several boilers from a shuttered Detroit asbestos factory and had them rigged up to leak steam and heat the place to a miserable, humid 100 degrees. The fluorescent lighting was ripped out and replaced with several 500-watt mercury-vapour floodlights, chosen for their unearthly pinkish-orange light and dismal hum. We rigged up a couple of telephones in a locked office next to the work area and had them set up to ring for hours on end. Scratchy Chinese pop music played on lo-fi PA speakers, punctuated by blaring commands in incomprehensible tongues like Urdu, Basque, and Miwok. The 'work stations' really gave me the satisfied feeling of a job well done: I modelled them on the primate-behaviour-testing cubicles used by the army to train chimpanzees to find land mines, down to the banana-pellet dispensers and shock-electrode ankle clamps. Each cubicle had a Soviet-era terminal, complete with 9″ monochrome monitor and Cyrillic keyboard; the whole mess served by an ENIAC 500 mechanical-relay computer of late-50s vintage. Each programmer would be hooked up to a catheter for urination; each 18-hour shift would have one 'defecation minute', during which the employee would be permitted to shit into a hole in the concrete floor, finishing up with a traditional corncob wipe. They'd sleep in tattered Cub Scout folding bunks and awaken to a bugle call for morning calisthenics, as the rats scurried around their feet, snouting hungrily for banana-pellet crumbs.

Money was no object, of course. An endless torrent of free money washed over us, courtesy of the VCs – just hold out a bucket and I'd pull it back full of $100 bills. For the millionth time, dear reader, we never thought of it as stealing or even improper use of funds, as we never tried to hide what we were doing or why. In fact, when I was honest at meetings ('. . . actually, I have no idea what we're trying to do, but we should do it twice as big!') I just got blank looks. Gibberish made them happier, and I just wanted everyone to be happy.

Since I had, or at least tried to have, a fundamental set of moral values appropriate to my time and place, I did my best to exempt the low-level Sux-M-Owt.com employees from the soul-eroding bullshit the white-collar types underwent. Naturally, all the temps, secretaries, copy-machine personnel, file clerks, janitors, and so on got full access to the recreational facilities, and I enforced an unprecedentedly liberal policy of slackness when it came to working-hours-versus-break-time for support-staff employees. If a word processor temp felt like taking two hours over his Patagonian Toothfish pesto kebabs down in the employee cafeteria, followed by a couple of highballs in the employee bar – hey, no problem; good morale means higher productivity. And if the entire IT Department ditched their jobs in the Server Room to engage in a high-stakes World Championship of Asteroids video-game competition in the employee arcade – again, *no problemo*.

The employee 'nap room', an innovation I'd read about in *Wired* magazine and immediately insisted we incorporate into our master plan, didn't really work out the way it did for Marimba and Excite.com's offices, where exhausted employees sawed a little wood in between 16-hour stints banging away at their jobs; the Sux-M-Owters promptly turned it into a semen-and-reefer-scented party pit, replete with purple shag carpeting, strobe lights, disco balls, and every Jimi Hendrix Day-Glo poster ever made. Illumination came from a couple of dim beer signs hanging over the Anchor Steam kegs in the corner. Cheap incense burned day and night and an endless loop of hypnotic dub music thumped out of 50,000 watts of dance-club-quality sound equipment. The place looked like the inside of the world's largest Kustom Van; all we needed was a big airbrush mural of a Norse god hurling lightning bolts into a seagull-studded sunset. Bongs and pipes were placed on every horizontal surface. Carnal grunts and groans issued from the beanbag chairs and fluffy couches, as the employees explored each other's mucus membranes. A few middle managers, thinking they'd ring up some brownie points with the Big Boss, handed me reports – exposés, really – detailing the excesses of the Nap Room in pornographic detail. Names were named. One guy hired a private detective to take infrared photos: '. . . and this one shows Aaron Chang – *your file clerk* – engaging in an act of *anal sex* with Joseph McMillon, mailroom boy!' I hate a rat – first I had Charlene give the snitch a working over that he'd remember every time his piles ached during rainy weather, then, in recognition of their initiative, I promoted Chang and McMillon to Recreation Directors, in charge of the mandatory 'team-building' exercises for managerial employees (they came up with some good ones; my favourite was a sort of boot camp involving equal parts pushups-in-the-mud-with-full-pack-and-rifle and Helium Karaoke).

But my finest innovation as CEO, the one I hope rises from the ashes of Sux-M-Owt.com, was to give all office temps the power to fire one manager per month apiece. It really made life better for the poor fucks, who'd accepted temp life as one that involved having one foot in a puddle of cold urine and the other poised over a punji pit. The pleasure of putting some powermad boss at the top of the 'Yer Fuckin' Fired List' (my official name), and then rearranging the list as the days dragged by to the much-anticipated firing date . . . those pleasures made temp life *worthwhile*.

Naturally, Charlene and I were exempt from such nonsense – a good thing for her, too, because it took a helluva lot of work to keep her from making life hell for the lower-ranking employees. I gave her carte blanche to do her worst with white-collar staff, but her slide into ever-more-brutal modes of dictatorship made her hungry to fill the camps with *everyone*. After a while, it didn't matter what I told her she couldn't do; she had her empire and I couldn't touch it.

Eleven

Charlene pushed the geek-basement concept too far right away, naturally. I had thought we should have 'trusties', like in prison, to get the geeks to police themselves, but Charlene didn't want her authority diluted. By that time, I'd done a bit of research on what the real dominatrix world was all about and it seemed that Charlene hadn't read *The Dom's Handbook* or anything else; she just assumed that her inborn sociopathy, admiration of two-bit dictators, and a vague sense that sex and fear ought to be connected all gave her a 33rd-degree Black Belt in Dom-hood. The real pros would have staggered away in horror if they'd seen what Charlene was doing in the name of their profession.

But, as I've said, I didn't know shit about this stuff. Thanks to double jeopardy and the settlement of all the civil suits, I have no motivation to lie about my non-involvement in the suicide of Willy Nguyen and the institutionalisation of those three other poor geeks. I figured Charlene knew where the line was and wouldn't be crossing it.

I was wrong as hell, of course. A couple weeks after the Engineering Annex was in full effect, I went down there to see how MemoCranker® Beta was going. Cubicle after cubicle of 'software developers', the

Engineering Department, pounding keyboards, pissing into catheters. The boiler hissed and sputtered. One poor geek was curled up in a corner, chained to a water heater, with a doggie dish full of kibble and the words 'BAD DOG' scrawled across his pimply back in purple marker. On closer inspection, it turned out he'd been crudely tattooed with a linoleum knife and purple price-marking ink. Already getting infected. A few geeks glanced up briefly, recognised me as a company VIP, and increased their frenzied typing with real fear in their eyes. Christ. This sorry bunch was as spineless as they come, but *this* scene looked like Exhibits A through ZZZ of the biggest lawsuit in California history if one of them managed to escape and crawled into some shyster's office. Where the hell was Charlene? I'd have to try to get her to turn the volume down on this noise. Way down.

Grabbing one Code-Monkey's shoulder, I asked him where I might find Charlene. 'Gmph?' he asked, his mouth full of banana pellets from the chimp-food dispenser. A sack of Koko Brand Primate Pellets leaned against his cube wall. These freaks were *literally* code monkeys. 'Dude, this is some disgusting-ass shit!' I wailed at him. 'Now *where* the fuck is Charlene, so I can get outta here?'

He swallowed his kibble. Apparently this guy was the most productive Code Monkeys, since he was permitted unlimited banana pellets. I noticed the cigarette burns on his neck, the T-shirt sticking to blood-crusted lash marks. He sported a nametag reading 'HI! MY NAME IS WILLY THE CHIMP!' He'd somehow lost about 30 pounds since I'd interviewed him a couple weeks back. Jesus. His parents had hauled him across the Gulf of Tonkin, Commie bullets zipping across the waves after them, to start a new life in America, and he'd found a job as Willy the Chimp. Streets paved with gold. 'You mean our Dear Leader?' he stammered. 'She's in the Quality Control Office, doing some bug testing with a couple of programmers.' He cringed from me, expecting a blow. 'I mean, with a couple of *Monkeys*! Worthless Monkeys! Like me!' He pointed a shaky finger at a closed door at the end of the row of cubes.

'Dude, take 'em easy. You want to go upstairs and, like, take a break or something?' But he was back to his keyboard, pounding out code. Leave his cube? No way! For the first time, I felt uneasy about our foray into the corporate world. My discomfort level increased as I approached the so-called Quality Control Office; *maybe if I don't see any more of this stuff I can claim I didn't know about it*, I thought. Sure. *I vas only followink orders, mein herr!*

But I was getting pissed off as well. Charlene was gonna fuck up my fun, just to satisfy her unnatural cravings. Deciding to make a dramatic entrance, I lifted my boot and gave the flimsy door a good kick, right below the knob. The door splintered, just like the movies, and I roared through it like an 18-wheeler through a Hyundai.

The room sterile, full of medical-looking gear. Bright under high-end halogen lighting. Soothing classical music playing from hidden speakers. Charlene nude, on her belly and oiled up on a massage table, with a female Code Monkey in pink hospital scrubs rubbing her shoulders. Behind her, a naked male Code Monkey, blindfolded and clamped to some sort of huge exercise machine, pushing him forward, back, undulating like a slow-motion mechanical bull. Squinting against the bright light, I realised he was fucking her, or rather, the machine was *making* him fuck her. Pinned to the naked flesh of his chest was a name tag reading 'I. M. Iggorant'.

In that moment, Charlene smiled sweetly and glanced back toward the hapless fuck-monkey servicing her, and I followed her gaze to his package. A hose clamp was screwed cruelly onto his shaft, keeping him hard as long as Charlene desired (and from the slick of pussy juice on her hindquarters and the raw look of his schlong, that looked to be quite a while already).

'You evil *bitch*!' I hissed. 'I never should have told you about the hoseclamp trick! Or the Vacuum Nixon!' I felt betrayed – she'd taken my brilliant idea of a gently applied hoseclamp as a simple tantalising limiter of penetration and changed it to a painful means of glutting her own cruelty. But, I must admit, she always looked damn good naked, complete with heart-shaped ass, and the whole situation was so wrong and foul that my defences weakened fast. She knew – she could probably *smell* my hard-on, and she luxuriated in the upper hand it gave her. She turned to the female Code Monkey, a petite blonde white girl (who, as I recalled from her interview, had a name like 'Bootsy' and was from some upscale place like La Jolla), and whispered something to her, never breaking eye contact with me.

'Mr Kelvin is *CEO* of our company, Bitsy,' she purred, as Bitsy peeled off her surgical garb and approached me, smiling. Bitsy must have been a special pet of Charlene's, as she seemed freshly scrubbed and well-fed, with no sores or whip marks. A stark contrast to the rest of the Monkeys. Her #1 toadie. The medical outfit was surely part of some unpleasant torture game of Charlene's. 'He's *my* boss, so we need to treat him right or he'll give me a bad report when Employee Review time rolls around.'

Oh yes, Employee Review. I had only myself to blame for that one, having instituted an incredibly complicated system of mutual backstabbing and rat-rewarding. I actually laughed hard enough to spew beer out my nose while writing the Employee Review Handbook. Now the spewed beer was a rising ocean of piss, climbing up around my grille. Charlene and I had been circling each other for months now; we both *wanted* to X each other, with a maddening and nearly ungovernable lust in our boiling brains, but the whole thing had become a monstrous battle for supremacy. Sux-M-Owt.com and the endless torrent of money that was destroying us. My harmless fucking-with-heads games had become more malignant, and Charlene was getting scarier by the minute. Still, we would only fuck on my terms, no matter what it cost me. And she felt the same way.

I locked eyes with Charlene. The only sound was the squeaking of the mechanical fuck-bull as it jabbed her with I. M. Iggorant's insensate rod, the soft schlupping of her pampered, executive-grade poozle being serviced. The monkey seemed unconscious, or maybe just ordered to act that way. I leaped, shocked, when Bitsy grabbed my zipper and started to work it down – it felt like a shock to the nuts from a torturer's cattle prod. I had forgotten about Bitsy. Maybe I should order the Code Monkeys out of the room and pour Charlene some pork on the spot, fuck the stupid power games. Pop my load into her and then cruise back to the office for a well-deserved bongload. Get on the phone and fire her ass. A coup d'état, dot-com style. Send her back to powerless obscurity.

No. We were trapped in the Sux-M-Owt.com downward spiral together, and I planned to be the one to emerge unscathed, even victorious, when we hit bottom. It felt good to have a destiny – that bottom was rushing up at us at an ever-increasing rate. I was the mighty, mighty CEO of the Sux-M-

Owt.com Corporation, $220 million in capitalisation, with more money pouring in every day! I would crush my opponents and stand triumphant atop a pyramid of broken, defeated bodies. First on the To Do list: Have my way with the naked underling even now working the wood out of my pants.

I had passed up on numerous chances to slip some execu-sausage to the pneumatic females working upstairs in the nice office – it just seemed wrong, especially with the temps I had crushing the balls of various middle-management types – but here in Charlene's turf the rules seemed somehow *different*. A pleasant, unmoored feeling lightened my head as I slid my palms down Bitsy's back and onto her ass, noting the pearly feel of skin treated with a lifetime of top-shelf skin-care products, La Jolla style, then lifted her up and looked for a convenient horizontal surface to set her on. Bitsy was a delicate, slender item, couldn't have scaled over 90 pounds, with dark brown hair in an expensive-but-geeky asymmetrical style, straight out of 1986, in true unironic rich-girl-turned-tech-nerd fashion. Small breasts, pink nipples; sight of her wisps of dark pubic hair turning the siren up real loud in my head. Charlene, seeing my search for a nice place for a nice romantic interlude with her assistant, obligingly pivoted on the massage table, disengaging her pooz from the mechanical fuck-machine, and patted the spot she'd vacated. Oh *hell* yeah! I thought, plopping Bitsy down in the wet spot. Charlene dangled her legs over the edge of the padded table. I. M. Iggorant's hose-clamped dick continued to thrust, retreat, thrust, retreat. A strand of gooey liquid dangled from the head. The Monkey's expression didn't change; I noted needle tracks on his arm and figured she'd jacked him on some med-grade downers.

Charlene arranged Bitsy on the table, with the gentleness reserved for her pet, as I stood there meekly with the pulse in my schlong pounding at 150 per. 'My gift to you,' Charlene mouthed, gesturing toward Bitsy, whose tang was now lined up on the crotch-height table's edge with convenient orientation to my tackle. Charlene adjusted Bitsy's labia and smoothed the hairs, making it look attractive. Bitsy seemed to have slipped into some kind of zombified state, staring past Charlene at the acoustic ceiling tiles. *Last chance to stop*, I thought in the microsecond before contact between Tab A and Slot B.

No. Too late. On autopilot, I worked an inch or so into Bitsy. She kept staring straight up, seemingly tuned out, but I felt her pushing back a bit as I felt the various folds and surfaces of her pussy doing their thing. Not very wet, but enough V-juice to keep things slipping smoothly enough. Charlene was in charge; Bitsy and I were in the same boat as the Code Monkey pumping air at the other end of the table. Charlene smiled as I bottomed out in Bitsy's panoche. Straddling Bitsy, Charlene faced me, lacing her hands behind my neck and pulling her face close to mind. Her eyes opened wide; I believed at that moment that I could see pure insanity and evil in them, a concept I'd always scoffed at when I read it in accounts of interviews with serial killers. *This is what Hitler's eyes probably looked like*, I remember thinking as she pulled me to her for a kiss.

It was a good, juicy, *wrong* kiss. I knew I would be paying for it for quite a while, if not the rest of my life. Charlene had turned from half-assed slacker to full-on dictator sociopath, I had been the catalyst for the transformation, and nuclear fire would soon rain from the sky to smite the guilty and innocent together. Without noticing, I had begun really grinding into Bitsy, who was now pinned under Charlene and taking all my action with no sign other than a few clenched-teeth squeaks. Just about all of my attention was on Charlene, who mercifully was unable to keep her death-squad eyes open and had to break our mouth seal a bit to breathe around our tongues. Panting, then moaning. I glanced down to her candy and saw she had a couple fingers plowing the ol' potato patch. Then she made her mistake; figuring she'd throw in a little something to keep her stranglehold on the Code Monkeys, she let go a fat stream of piss all over Bitsy's belly. I'm sure it was something she read about in *Dom Digest* magazine, back in the pre-corporate-kingpin days. When the yellow river started rolling its way down to my work area, it jolted me out of my trance – I felt my control rushing back. I disengaged my tongue from Charlene's and pulled my head back enough to give her an appraising, superior look. I *ea-a-a-a-ased* my wick out of Bitsy and watched the pee roll down her parts and onto the table. Got her off *good*; Bitsy squealed and flipped around beneath Charlene, but I summoned the ice to repackage my tackle and zip up, ignoring the pecker-tracks Bitsy's fluids left on my $800 Armani silk trousers. Charlene stared, stunned, defeated. I. M. Iggorant chose this moment to snap to life, struggling in his bonds and howling: 'AAAAIIIEEEEEE!'

'Come on up to *my* office if you'd like to finish this conference,' I said, striding in my most managerial style toward the door, like we'd just had a proactive meeting about 'rebranding' the corporate image or something. Were she to take me up on the offer, I'd wrestle her straight to the luxurious Italian leather sofa (which cost more than my total earnings as a weed dealer last year) and give her a crude missionary-position redneck fuck, after which there'd be no more nonsense about who was *really* in charge. Sure.

By this time I'd become a quasi-famous person among certain business circles, my name being brought up in breathless articles hyping the 'New Economy' in various business publications. Sort of a rags-to-riches deal, with my supposed shrewdness cloaked in a mysterious veil of cryptic statements. In truth, the cryptic statements were what I was actually all about, and the Sux-M-Owt.com juggernaut had taken on so much momentum from the Mississippi-like flow of cash pouring into its coffers that I couldn't help but look like some sort of business genius. After all, the name of the game was 'building market share' and 'synergistic coordination', and we sure had plenty of that stuff. Profits would come later, everyone agreed. And, contrary to the venomous press I got later on when I became White Collar Crime Poster Boy, I wasn't stashing away massive sums in Bahamian accounts, or pallets full of gold bar in a secret compound in Montana; no, we squandered all our investors' money fair and square, on good old foolishness and sky's-the-limit growth.

I wasn't all that comfortable with the newfound attention. While I enjoyed an audience, the national scale of the latest round of press scrutiny on Sux-M-Owt.com seemed likely to blow up in my face if I got too weird with it. Incredibly, the most absurd gibberish seemed to result in a huge cloud of cash erupting from the investors, like hornets from a hive poked with a stick, but I didn't want to push it. I set up a Press Centre in a tiny, overheated concrete room near the air-conditioning equipment on the roof of our building, and held the occasional press conference at which my answers to most questions were 'that's a company secret' and 'no comment'. This served to enhance my reputation as a mysterioso-type wizard of business acumen. I'd grant the occasional one-on-one interview now and then, and I learned that nobody ever wanted to ask the hard questions, that the Ponzi scheme of the current overheated economy was based on investors never looking too closely at what they were actually pouring their bucks into.

One interview stood out from the others. Soon after we'd hit the 500-employee mark at the new office, *Jolted* magazine from up in San Francisco sent down a reporter and photographer to do a story about me. *Jolted* was sort of a lifestyle/gadgets/business publication, hugely fat with about 1,100 pages of ads and 50 pages of content, and featured headache-inducing layouts with lots of white-on-yellow text, hip-hop slang, and so forth. It was apparently quite a coup to have a special feature in the rag, but I blew them off at first. Finally Charlene talked me into granting them an hour or so. 'We'll get even more recruits of the special type I like,' she said, winking. 'They all read *Jolted*.'

The *Jolted* team turned out to be a couple of 20-something hipster chicks, complete with Pynchon quotes and facial piercings. They brought their own dope stash, obviously hoping their San Francisco Geekoid-Hipster-Grade supply would knock me on my Southern California ass and loosen my tongue up enough to give them some sort of scoop (God knows there was no business secret for me to give up, and I never tried very hard to fake any expertise, preferring to jabber on with a bunch of jarring non sequiturs during interviews). Their stuff was all right, I judged after taking a few hits off their lumpily rolled joint, but I had a better idea.

'How about we smoke some of *my* pot, eh? This stuff is OK, but . . .' They were all for it, not realising that I used to be in the dope-slinging business and knew something on the subject, so I broke out my latest blend, known in the trade as 'Atom Smasher'. Atom Smasher was quality Moroccan hash fed through a particle accelerator by stoner physics majors at a major California university (which will remain anonymous at the insistence of the publisher's attorneys) in order to extract the purest, high-THC substances. It looked like a very soft hash of a uniform tan hue, and tasted very clean when smoked. I usually saved the Atom Smasher for my late-night smoking pleasure, but this was a special occasion.

A couple hits of the Atom Smasher later, my interviewers couldn't even remember their own names, much less the big list of questions they'd planned on asking me about the day-to-day operation of Sux-M-Owt.com. Giggling fits. Cindy, the photographer, kept opening her camera to see if it still had film, which kept exposing and ruining the film. They thought that was a hoot. Rather than guide the interview back to something related to Sux-M-Owt.com, I filled their tape recorder with a 45-minute lecture on the subject of Silverfish Hashbrowns, which were like potato hashbrowns only made with thousands of mashed silverfish bugs. 'Mmmmm, nothing like a nice silverfish hashbrown breakfast, huh?' I kept cracking into the mike as they fell about. I'll bet their editors enjoyed that.

Carla, the reporter, still wanted that scoop, although she was way too baked to recall what she had been told to find out. 'What's in it for *me*?' I asked, passing her the bong. 'Why should I give up any hard-earned Sux-M-Owt.com insider stories?'

'How about I, uh, *do* something for you?' she suggested with a waggle of her pierced eyebrows. *Now* we were getting somewhere. Carla was a little on the skinny, nervous side, but had that waifish-hipster appeal that sometimes appealed to me.

'Oh, I get to watch!' piped in Cindy, looking up from her photography gear and still stonedly destroying a lot of expensive-looking film.

Surreptitiously palming the batteries in Carla's tape recorder, I pressed the Record button. 'All right, what are you going to do for me, in exchange for my double-dog-secret info?'

She went right for my zipper and proceeded with a noisy-but-effective head job. I watched her spiked inky-black dyed hair bob up and down as she gnawed on my stuff. I solemnly told the true story of Torment, Incorporated into the dead microphone, knowing neither one of them would remember any of it. Cindy laughed and offered helpful technical tips on the art of the blowjob, but Carla had her style down pretty well and quickly got me to pop my string in her mouth. They left thinking they'd captured some good stuff on the tape. 'Be sure to publish that recipe, 'kay?' I called after them, imagining Silverfish Hash-browns becoming all the rage in SF's South of Market area.

Twelve

As it turned out, the Code Monkeys produced some good tools to help me with my meeting schedule. Not just MemoCranker® 1.0 (which enabled me to concentrate on what I *really* loved: incomprehensible, eye-glazing PowerPoint presentations, for which I required my audience to strap into Jap grey-market virtual-reality goggles, so as to hit them with a Mississippi-esque torrent of crypto-meaningful data in full 3-D and Hyper-Dolby Surround Sound), but some extra-trick productivity-monitoring software, which I dubbed MistahOverseer® 2.6. MistahOverseer® provided a Great Leap Forward in technology-assisted management tools. In fact, the software coming from the Engineering Annex was so good that I was able to block out the reality of what was really going on down there.

MistahOverseer® enabled a take-charge, success-oriented managerial type to really keep the clamps down on his or her workers. Based on the principle that white-collar employees are thieving, lazy, incompetent turds floating in the toilet bowl of the office world, MistahOverseer® was built to my exacting specifications and QA-tested by a crack team of cathetered Code Monkeys under the lash of their ruthless supervisor, making it from concept to functioning, debugged application in a stunning nine days. I could see that Charlene had a real future in the software industry. Every keystroke and mouse click were monitored, of course, but it was the accompanying hardware that enabled the savvy manager to, say, get a real-time readout of the height of papers in a given employee's IN basket, or to time bathroom trips down to the millisecond that *really* set MistahOverseer™ apart from its competitors. I drew some inspiration from the no-eatum-pizza-toppings policy at Colonel Sausage, and more from Charlene's approach to management strategies. The results of the various sensors and counters could be displayed on the manager's own computer. I envisioned an advertising campaign showing a chiselled manager in a fine Italian suit beating a huge drum at the prow of a slave ship, while office workers pulled oars in submissive harmony, all heading toward a glowing sunrise symbolising corporate success, or maybe a happy costumed Simon Legree character to pitch the product at trade shows: 'Yess*iree*, folks, once you've got Sux-M-Owt.com's MistahOverseer™ software suite in place, your employees will do as they're told or *feel the lash*!' (he cracks a bullwhip to emphasise his point; onlooking execs applaud).

But that was nothing next to the glory of MemoCranker™. I scheduled mandatory meetings just about every day. Each one was organised via a lovely piece of software made to my strict specs down in the Geek Basement; rather than using the mundane, boring old calendar functions on your typical Microsoft Outlook or Lotus Notes application, LifeSentence™ 2.0 was patterned after the complementary psychologies of telemarketers and prison guards. When I created a meeting and entered its specifics into the LifeSentence™ administrator interface, an inexorable sequence of events got rolling: first, everyone on the invitation list had a popup message appear on top of everything else on his or her computer screen; the message required a 15-step procedure to confirm that, yes, the invitee would be attending the meeting and, no, he or she had never been a member of the Communist Party, and so on. But that was just the beginning. Reminders, each requiring multistep inputs, would continue to harry the employee on a randomly scheduled basis. At about three hours before the meeting, the invitee's phone would start ringing . . . louder and louder, faster and faster, the urgency reaching a maddening crescendo until the victim – I mean, invitee – picked up the phone, only to hear a dial tone. Car alarms, of the must-kill-the-asshole-who-owns-this-fucking-thing variety, would blare in the cubicles of the hapless invitees starting at about an hour before the meeting. You get the picture.

I had this system down pretty well, and the meetings themselves were a blast – godawful complicated rules of order (I had a judge's gavel and enjoyed shouting 'ORDER! ORDER!' when things got out of hand), rapidly shifting temperatures from 50 through 100 degrees (it's actually quite a challenge to get an office thermostat to order such absurd variation), clocks running backward, and so on. I'd make them go through one of my patented brain-twisting memos and answer questionnaires on them. The crowning glory was the PowerPoint slide shows; if any tool was ever devised for surrealism-minded bosses to reduce employees to whimpering blobs of protoplasm it had to be the evil product from the folks up in Redmond.

But the real drawback was that the memos and PowerPoint shows took me a lot of time to do properly, time that could be better spent designing

TormentLand, the waterslide theme park that Sux-M-Owt.com, now apparently designated a 'multi-modal activity portal experience provider' or some such, would be building at my request on 100 acres of land in Inyo County, or slipping the sausage into the young lady of my choice, or staring at the bubbles in my lunchtime champagne while staring blankly at the ocean out my office window. But my workman's pride *insisted* on keeping the quality level up to snuff on the meetings. Something had to be done, and that something was MemoCranker™.

MemoCranker™ was actually two separate applications, but both shared the core OfficeJive™ engine. The Code Monkeys had devised a series of clever algorithms to generate limitless volumes of running-in-place-style office 'content', and incorporated those algorithms into OfficeJive™. An intuitive interface, basically a plug-in that rode on top of the Microsoft products, made it possible to create a stultifying tedious document with a few clicks of the mouse; the manager who felt like making an incredibly complicated, brain-jarring presentation that shredded concentration and gave meeting participants a queasy, seasick feeling could do so with a little more effort. Features included the Meaningless Pie Graph Generator, a Jargon Enhancer, and a Tail-Chasing Argument Wizard. So, when I called a strategy meeting to discuss 'Reverse-Magneto Heuristic Modalities for the Current Five-Month Plan', a 100-page wiro-bound memo in 6-point font, with diagrams, maps, et cetera, was ready to slap down in front of the grimly determined participants with only a half-hour's work by me.

The PowerPoint presentations were even better. MemoCranker™ incorporated a massive database of sound, video, and image files and could generate on-the-fly animations that resembled a cross between Japanese TV commercials and Department of Health anti-VD cartoons. Gigantic flowcharts and command structure diagrams could be vomited forth with a couple of keystrokes, and the end result made the implosion calculations for advanced neutron fission devices look like kindergarten teaching materials. It was no sweat for me to create sufficient slides to fill a six-hour meeting. Sure, I got tired officiating over those meetings, but my pride as the creative force behind MemoCranker(TM) never got old.

During this time, Sux-M-Owt.com had its IPO. You may recall the hype that came with it, although we certainly got less attention than other soon-to-join-us-in-bankruptcy players in the futuristic New Economy. At that point, we had even more money coming in (and I had a stack of stock options I could foresee would be worthless at some point in the not-too-distant future) but also a lot more probing questions about what we were really doing with all the money. I figured we could fend them off for a time, but sooner or later the mess was likely to fall apart.

A couple weeks went by after the little incident in the basement without any sign of Charlene, and then I looked up from my pre-lunch joint to see Charlene let herself into my office and take a seat in a Liao Dynasty scholar's chair I'd had airfreighted straight from Guangzhou after I figured I had an image to uphold and replaced all the European designer office furniture with far more costly Chinese antiques. 'Care for a taste of the good stuff?' I asked, offering the exquisitely-formed dube. I now had a full-time joint-roller on the staff, a guy we'd imported from Arcata, in keeping with my high-roller image, and his skills actually came in handy when I met up with young, hip CEOs from other 'bleeding edge' corporations ('*Damn!* This is a *perfect* joint!' they'd whisper in awe as we kicked back during a 'partnering' conference – clearly I was a man who enjoyed his pleasures).

'Don't care if I do,' she said, taking the reefer and sucking down a hit. Just like the old days, sort of. I got on the intercom and ordered us up a light lunch from the in-house chef, complete with a couple bottles of our 'house brand' wine – we'd apparently bought a winery as part of our 'complete lifestyle portal' strategy.

'What's on your mind?' I asked, like we were a couple of normal suits having a sit-down. I knew what was on her mind, and she knew I knew. She'd dressed in a hard-looking business suit – very severe and appropriate to her management style, yet within acceptable limits for American Successful Business-women's Office Garb.

'This isn't a game for you any more, is it?' she asked, pointing the dube accusingly at me. 'An *installation-performance piece*, you called it? Look at this – you've *sold out*!'

Sold out? That was the best the mighty Mistress Carlotta could do? As far as I was concerned, everything except her crazy shit was going exactly according to plan; in fact, I was shocked I'd managed to ride this deal for so long. I had huge captive audiences *eager* to try to make sense out of my mind-scrambling works and a big crew of assistants to do the grunt work. And I got paid huge for it, from a seemingly endless money torrent spewing from a massive venture capital pipe. What was going to fuck it all up was her goddamn dictator game in the basement. I mimed taking an arrow to the heart: 'Oh, that's a cold shot!' I sneered. I was back in the saddle, as if our kiss had actually meant nothing.

She got up, strolled over to a monstrous flowchart I'd had etched on a 15-foot-wide slab of Lexan and gestured questioningly. A combination of organisational structure, pie chart, and timeline, it managed to combine several mutually incompatible measuring systems in a 7-dimensional package that redefined the meaning of *cryptic*. The junior management go-getters pored over it for days, like the thing was a Dead Sea Scroll. I'd fired one or two randomly in its presence, just to establish an aura of fear around it, and promoted others whose comments indicated a deep understanding. I considered it my masterpiece. Explaining this to her, I observed a deepening smirk on her face.

'You're no better than *me*. You're doing the exact same thing I'm doing down in the basement, only *worse*. These people will never recover from your head-fucking.' Seeing that she'd stuck me pretty good, she bored in close. The mellow high evaporated fast. 'In fact, *my* slaves *get off* on what *I* do. Look at the MistahOverseer® software you had the Code Monkeys make. I had I. M. Iggorant explain it to me –'

'What? That guy actually *functions*?' I was astonished. Last time I'd seen I. M. Iggorant it looked like he'd have trouble tying his shoes, much less write good code.

'Of *course* he functions. All my slaves do their job at maximum efficiency and are happy to do so. They *trust* me to lead them. Anyway, don't change the subject. MistahOverseer® is exactly the kind of thing your old, mellow-stoner-dude, pre-Sux-M-Owt.com self would have *spit* on as a tool of pure evil.'

'Oh, bullshit – MistahOverseer® is *funny*! I can still look myself in the mirror in the morning.' But there was an uncomfortable grain of truth in what she said.

'Face it, Eddie, you're *like me now.*' She smiled knowingly. 'There's no going back now. We're on the horse together and we need to ride it to the finish line.'

The *horse*? 'What finish line? We're gonna milk this thing as long as we can – I don't want to hear that kind of talk.'

'No, we're building up to something great here, Eddie. It would just be foolish if we didn't take it all the way. We've got the kind of setup I've always dreamed of . . . and you've always dreamed of as well.' She tapped my heart with a perfectly manicured fingernail. 'I know what's really in here, Eddie. It's not some kind of dreamy California world of *karma* and *kick-back party time*, or any of that stuff – you'd like to believe that stuff, but you're just fooling yourself. And it sure as hell isn't the desire to be an artist, sharing your vision with a willing audience; you haven't had a willing audience for *months*.'

'Yeah, what do I really want, then?'

'Slaves. Same as me. And you *have* them, only you won't admit it. In fact, you're even more of a natural than *I* am. If you'd just let go and go where your real desires would take you, there'd be no limit to what we could do here.'

I was getting pissed off. 'Bullshit! I'm just having a bit of harmless fun and making big cash while I do it! You're gonna fuck it all up with this crazy slave shit, and then where will we be? In fucking *jail*!' I shouted. What if she was right? More likely, she was just working one of her control games with me. 'We need to chill out a bit, keep this gravy train rolling for a while longer. Then you can cash out and start another slave joint, on your own.'

She stayed cool. 'No, Eddie. It's not going to be like that. We *need* each other, and this is the final stretch. We're going out in a blaze of glory, arm in arm. It'll be better than the Manson Family . . . better than Jonestown, even. And there's no stopping it. They'll never forget us.'

What . . . the . . . *fuck*? I thought. *Jonestown?* 'Sweet creepin' Jesus! What kinda crazy shit are you planning down there? You've been reading too many of those serial killer books! You think you're the next Charles Manson? Your loyal followers will bring down the evil, corrupt city and then roar off into the desert on dune buggies?'

She pulled me to her, kissed me hard. Her eyes looked passionate, bad crazy. 'I love you, Eddie. Don't betray me.' she whispered threateningly. Then she turned and left, no doubt headed down to her basement empire.

This scene smelled pretty bad. I was getting scared. She was no harmless flake playing at being a dominatrix in black vinyl. She was a *cult leader*. I was to realise soon enough that the reality was even worse than that. She was already too powerful to challenge directly through the Board of Directors. And the rancid cherry on top of the sundae was that she believed our destinies were linked, padlocked together – when she sank the ship I'd go down with her, along with a lot of other people . . . and I had a feeling the end result would be a lot worse than a trip to the Unemployment line.

I could quit, just hop in the car and disappear to Cleveland or Uzbekistan, but that would mean the end of the free dope, captive audience for my work, free quality poontang in new and interesting settings. Plus, Charlene had enough money and power to track me down wherever I fled, and her professed love for me wouldn't keep her from hooking me up to the catheters and banana-pellet dispensers in the Geek

Basement, servicing her with my poor callused member at a snap of her fingers, any time her girlparts had a little tickle – in fact, her loving me made such a hideous fate even *more* likely.

I'd been increasing the frequency and severity of my meetings as the weeks passed by; first weekly, then daily, then – thanks to the help of Janet, who had taken on the role of Special Assistant to the CEO – every few hours. Once I realised that I didn't actually have to *be* at the meetings, I was able to focus more and more on crafting the finest possible graphs, charts, posters, and other meeting accessories; in concert with MemoCranker®, I was creating some real meeting masterpieces. I had our chefs cook up a special variety of donuts for consumption by meeting participants; referred to as 'Meeting Sinkers', the donuts were all hockey-puck density and pumped full of jelly containing three times the normal amount of sugar. Meeting Sinkers, when washed down with our house-brand caffeine-enhanced coffee, caused meeting participants to become giddy and amped for about an hour, then sluggish and confused as their bodies attempted to process the massive overload of sugar and speed – the same effect you'd see with a bunch of 12-year-olds spaced on video games and 64-ounce tubs of Pepsi.

On my Thursday two o'clock HDES meeting (HDES was one of many meaningless acronyms I threw around; I had a whole deck of them, like a cardshark wielding extra aces), I was a bit shocked to find Charlene sitting at the table in Conference Room Four. By this time she rarely left her growing basement empire; it looked like she was ready to expand her territory upstairs, but I couldn't be sure. She was in her usual severe Harsh Businesswoman attire, with her hair styled into a cruel-looking

Marlene Dietrich perm. A notebook and a bottle of designer water sat primly in front of her. She smiled at me. We were in for an interesting meeting.

'All right, folks, this HDES meeting features a rare treat – a visit from our esteemed president, Ms Charlene Cabrillo,' I said. The group looked warily at her; her reputation was well-known upstairs, with some of the old-time ex-clients speaking of her with awe and the newcomers curious but intimidated. She *seemed* human enough, but word on the street was: don't fuck with Charlene.

'Please, Mr Kelvin, don't mind me,' she said. *Mr Kelvin*, eh? 'I'm just observing, keeping current with the work of other departments.'

And rightfully so. I got about five minutes into one of my signature presentations, this one featuring a cut-up version of Spiro Agnew's 'Nattering Nabobs of Negativism' speech intermixed with barking seals on the sound system, coupled with a Memo-Cranker®-generated PowerPoint presentation covering some inscrutable Basic Truths. I had a specially commissioned laser-pointer that had several randomly swivelling heads, resulting in a maddening display reminiscent of a Led Zeppelin laser show, circa 1979. Things were going well; I was just gearing up to switch to Spiro's fine 'Effete Corps of Impudent Snobs' speech when Charlene yanked the plug out of the LCD projector and switched on the room lights.

She slapped the guy sitting next to her, a harmless suit named Larry who had worked at some big computer manufacturer before hiring on as a 'Group Focus Facilitator' at Sux-M-Owt.com. 'This bastard just grabbed my LEG!' she screamed, giving him another wicked backhand across the chops. 'I hope you have a good *lawyer*, you weasel, because I'll take you for everything you got!'

Stunned silence. Larry's mouth just hung open. His face sported some nasty welts, already swelling in just seconds – he'd be feeling those Bruce Lee-style slaps for a while. Charlene pulled a tiny brushed-stainless-steel walkie-talkie from her purse and whispered into it. Moments later, two of her thugs kicked in the conference room door.

'That's the one,' she said, pointing to Larry. 'Larry, you and I need to have a little talk . . . downstairs.'

'NO!' Larry shrieked as the thugs put him in a hammerlock and lifted him out of his Aeron chair. 'NOOOOOOOO!'

As they hauled him off toward the elevator, Charlene paused at the door. 'Remember, folks, we do not tolerate *sexual harassment* at Sux-M-Owt.com headquarters. Let this serve as a gentle reminder.' Larry was in for a long, long night. The sound of his agonised screams cut off suddenly as the elevator doors slammed shut.

I plugged in the meeting gear and continued with my presentation. Better to look like this was all part of our plan; it wouldn't do to let my underlings know that I had no more control over Charlene's actions than they did. Their faces showed real fear. I felt a sickening, tingling surge of lust at my power; *I* could be doing the same kind of thing Charlene did, and nobody would say boo. I could demand that everyone in the room subject to a chunky peanut butter enema delivered with a grease gun and *they'd do it*. The sexual possibilities seemed endless. Would I bring four of the carefully made-up, MBA-packing businesswomen into my office for some sweat-semen-and-menstrual-blood-smeared action on my desk? Or perhaps take a walk on the queer side and get some smooth-muscled young stud to swab out my pipes? Or some combination of the above? I could do just about whatever I wanted, and nobody seemed to have the inclination or even the ability to stop me.

But I'd kept a lid on my darker desires up until this point, while Charlene had fed hers. And I knew she was thinking of the next step: her slaves' lives literally in her hands. Probably the evil, quickly-suppressed headrush of power I'd felt was the kind of fuel she kept hissing through her brain-pipes day after day. The tolerance builds up. Giving some poor bastard ten lashes yesterday doesn't satisfy today – give him twenty! More!

During the next couple weeks, the ethical dilemma of my position vis-à-vis my artistic predilections and swirling lustful impulses gnawed at me. Here I was, in a position to indulge my vilest appetites, and I was refraining from taking advantage of the position due to some sort of deeply-ingrained California-dude sense of right and wrong. What would Oscar Wilde have thought of me? The Marquis de Sade? How would I feel about myself when the whole Sux-M-Owt.com vehicle blew out the transmission and left me high and dry at the roadside, blinking confusedly in the smoke swirling from the burnt-out shell? Would I have tasted even a little bit of the forbidden fruit? Clearly Charlene was living on a 100% forbidden-fruit diet and was thriving.

Then too, I admit, I gave consideration to ideas of beating Charlene at her own game. Being a *take-charge* kind of guy. *Success-oriented. Proactive.* I'd be on top of her, both figuratively and literally. She'd finally beg me to be her man. I'd be victorious. The world would be my bitch.

Well, probably not. But I had an idea that I could get a little taste, *inoculate* myself with some of the madness. I had already arranged for the preparations for my experiment. I buzzed Janet on the intercom:

'Yes, Mr Kelvin?' she answered immediately, a hint of eagerness in her voice. Most of the time I was calling to get her to put a group of suits through the wringer of a six-hour dig-holes-and-fill-them-up-again meeting, or to invite her into my office for a quick hump on the Freud-style antique psychiatrist's couch I'd had placed in my office. She enjoyed both activities immensely, although I think she enjoyed the meetings more than me grinding her hips into the couch – it appealed to her mean streak.

'Janet, I'm getting jaded. Need a new thrill.' I sparked a kitchen match and fired up a meerschaum pipe packed with Kenyan flower tops. Blowing the smoke at the intercom, I continued: 'I think we could *both* use a little breather from this daily grind, if you know what I mean.'

'Oh, of course, Mr Kelvin. Would you like me to have the bar send us up some of those new Apricot Stingers? They're all the rage in the Nap Room.'

'No, I've got some tequila made by a 107-year-old *bruja* in Quintana Roo, which is far tastier than any trendy new drink.' I took another hit of the Kenyan. 'But this isn't about drinks, Janet. This is about the absolute corruption that comes with absolute power. I think we deserve a piece of that.'

I could hear her pause a moment at the other end of the intercom; I knew she was getting excited. She loved fooling around with power and corruption; mixing the two could only be a good thing. 'Well, that sounds good to me, Mr Kelvin. I'll be in there in just a second.'

'No, not yet, Janet. We're going to have a little meeting, but it won't be just the two of us. I need you to use your eye for weakness – I know it's a sharp one – and pick out a couple of assistants for this special closed-session meeting to take place in my office.'

'Assistants?'

'Roger. I want one male and one female. The male should be a young, lean beefcake type – you know, the sort you used to have your office adventures at your last job. Pick one that looks good, but weak. The type that you know will do as you say . . . and *like* it. I *know* you're familiar with the type.' For the next part I tried to think like a rockstar choosing my partner for the night from a crowd of squealing groupies. Jaded, like I'd told Janet. 'For the female, I'd like the same quality of eagerness to submit to authority, but with an edge of shame at her appalling self-discovery. She should be a slightly plump red-head, with a freckled, round face. Maybe with an ineffective attempt at harmless individuality, like a stud in her nose or a Gumby collection in her cubicle.' It was just like ordering a pizza, I thought.

'No problem, Mr Kelvin. I probably won't even have to leave our floor. We have over seven hundred employees now, and most of them are eager to please their CEO.' I knew she was licking her lips at the prospect of whatever weirdness I had in mind.

'All right, Janet, bring them back here when you're ready. Tell them they'll be interviewed for new positions in our Carson City office.' There was no Carson City office, but I could create one with a few phone calls if necessary. I pictured grizzled old prospectors scratching their heads at the sight of the Sux-M-Owt.com tower rising from the sand on the edge of town, their burro trains loaded down with high-grade ore . . .

I kicked up my feet and tapped out the ash from the pipe. The smoke had already been cleared from the room by silent, futuristic ventilators. I watched the Pacific waves break on the beach about a mile outside my view window.

Soon, Janet brought in our interviewees. The male was a lithe, athletic-looking Hispanic lad named Marco Rincón, who did some sort of sales-related job involving a lot of phone calls (in spite of what you may have read about my masterful con-man-style financial juggling and bottom-dealing scheming, I paid little or no attention to anything at Sux-M-Owt.com that had anything whatsoever to do with selling anything or making complex deals; that shit just took care of itself naturally, fuelled by the reflexive commercialist energy of our multiple layers of competing/overlapping staff). He wore a Hong Kong-tailored quality silk suit. His eyes darted around my office, nervous. The female was exactly as specified, a pale-skinned redhead named Heather Anderson; she had an alluring extra 25 pounds or so packed into her office-girly-girl-grade tight pink sweater and sensible black skirt. Heather shuffled paper in one of the many accounting offices where they ran like rats on an endless treadmill of cash funnelled into our laps by the Venture Capital Fairy.

I swung my feet off the desk and faced them. 'All right, soldiers, my assistant Janet has brought you here so's we can determine if you're made of the stuff we need for managerial positions in our soon-to-be-opened office located outside of Carson City, Nevada. Righteous *managerial* stuff.' Yeah, maybe we *would* put together a Carson City office. Why not?

I continued: 'So, my dear colleagues, we're going to head out to the Sux-M-Owt.com Proving Grounds out near Victorville – you know, the site of the future Sux-M-Owt.com Land theme park. Yes, a field trip!' I buzzed the motor pool to let them know we'd be leaving and hustled everybody to the elevator. I had a moment of nervousness that Charlene would want to stick her nose into this project, which I considered serious business, and mould it to the specifications of her own dream/nightmare. Another performance-installation art piece, if you will, but overlaid with some of Charlene's own concepts; a dip of the toe into her pool.

At the motor pool, my current favourite company car, a 1931 Isotta-Fraschini 8B, driven by one of the stable of Sux-M-Owt.com chauffeurs, purred up to my little group. This was the same type of car driven by Gloria Swanson in *Sunset Boulevard*, only the Sux-M-Owt.com model didn't have all the silly wicker bodywork and pimpin' leopardskin upholstery the movie version had. Marco and Heather seemed awed by the display of squandered wealth, and hesitantly entered the car. Janet and I joined them.

'Champagne?' I offered, pouring glasses for everyone as we rolled smoothly onto the 55 East. I'd had the motor pool replace the original antiquated Isotta-Fraschini straight-eight engine with a much quieter Cadillac 500 V8 and double mufflers – it ran a lot better than it had with the vintage wheezer, plus what was the good of having an outrageously valuable antique car if you weren't willing to destroy its value with such modifications? Janet was hardly able to contain herself – she sensed from my talk earlier that she'd be getting a crack at the handsome young Marco and the knowledge that I had some sort of strangeness cooked up gave her an intolerable tickle in her secret parts; I gave her a sharp glance when she got a little too fidgety. I was glad that I'd made her my own assistant rather than let Charlene glom her; with her twisted drives and urge to please her boss to the nth degree, she would have been Squeaky Fromme to Charlene's Manson down in the Geek Basement.

After a little over an hour of soundless cruising, during which I refilled the champagne glasses several times but otherwise spent staring contemplatively at the miles of sprawl interspersed with desert stretches rolling past the windows (Marco and Heather kept their lips zipped out of respect for the vips in the car), we arrived at a massive construction site on a patch of hardscrabble desert. This was the location of our flagship 'Entertainment Nexus', the soon-to-be Sux-M-Owt.com Land Theme Park and Resort. It had been a whim of mine at a meeting ('. . . as part of our Total Lifestyle Portal Strategy, I propose that we build an amusement park, like Disneyland but with that Sux-M-Owt.com *special feeling* . . .') and something about the throwaway idea touched the Board and the investors in their hearts and pocketbooks. Never one to throw cold water on a dream, I hired a crew of artists and architects, gave them a few hours of instructions, and sent them on their way with a seven-figure budget and heads full of my ideas of what a *real* theme park ought to be like. As I'm sure you know if you've been reading the newspapers, dear reader, a sanitised version of Sux-M-Owt.com Land has opened (I won't risk the wrath of the corporation that took it over by naming names), but it hardly remains true to my artistic vision.

I hadn't actually thought much about the place since, there being dozens of other money-down-a-rathole ideas that appealed to my whimsical side, but I'd received a bunch of photographs and models of the Sux-M-Owt.com Land site and figured I'd take advantage of the possibilities inherent in the setting. As we exited the Isotta-Fraschini, I pointed out some of the more advanced features of the park: 'That rollercoaster under construction over there –' I pointed to a tangle of tracks arcing around a gigantic fibreglass goat's-head-and-pentagram structure '– is the *Satanic Apocalypse of Terror and Agony*, which will be *the* scariest rollercoaster ever built. Now, you may ask yourself, what makes it so scary?'

'What makes it so scary, Mr Kelvin?' Janet asked, on cue.

'I'm glad you asked. See, you might think at first glance that it's the Satanic imagery, the references to the inferno below, witches at black masses, souls wailing in eternal punishment, et cetera, but that's just some window-dressing to make the rubes get all worked up in a Judaeo-Christian frenzy of indignation. Naturally, we'll have an all-black-metal soundtrack for the ride – I think the Venom song 'Welcome to Hell' will be the theme music – but the *real* scary part will be a surprise.'

We were walking past the SATA site and heading toward a completed-looking corner of the park. I continued speaking as we walked: 'See, what really scares people about a rollercoaster is the fear of death. Because death hardly ever actually occurs on a rollercoaster, it's not a significant fear.' I slammed my fist into my palm, startling the others. 'However, they're paying for *fear* and, by God, Sux-M-Owt.com is gonna give 'em fear. So what we'll do is give them the idea that death is not only a possibility but a *likelihood* on this ride.'

I pointed out some wrecked rollercoaster cars buried nose-down in the dirt beneath the tracks. They had apparently been pried open by Jaws-Of-Life-wielding paramedics and were caked in dried blood and bone fragments. 'We're going to have the remains of what appear to be dozens of grisly wrecks littering the ground beneath the ride, looking like they left the tracks and slammed into the earth at high speed, killing their shrieking passengers instantly. The passengers waiting in line will have plenty of time to study the wrecks and contemplate their own mortality. But they'll be distracted by other stuff, particularly the rickety appearance of the roller-coaster's structure itself. Crucial components will seem to be held together with duct tape and zip-ties – naturally, we'll build it quite strong, so as to avoid actual wrongful-death lawsuits, which are a real hassle in any business, but the *appearance* of ricketiness will be there. Sparks and smoke will issue from circuit boxes; frayed wires will dangle and arc. The smell of burning insulation and blood will be piped into the air, as sort of a ghoulish counterpoint to the Venom songs tearing at their souls.'

'Oh, that's a great touch,' said Janet approvingly. She was kissing ass, of course, but I could tell she liked the idea of scaring the living shit out of amusement-park patrons. Heather and Marco just seemed confused. Well, they'd be a helluva lot *more* confused in a few minutes.

'Then they'll get to the rollercoaster cars themselves. The attendants will look like hookwormy rednecks and gangsta'd-out ghetto thugs, grabassing and drinking from Mason jars of corn liquor, smoking blunts, staggering around helplessly. The seat belts in the cars will just be old ropes. Bloody handprints on the cars themselves. We'll have a priest giving the passengers the Last Rites.' I thought for a moment. 'Hmmm . . . it might be cheaper to just have a guy *dressed* like a priest – I bet the Catholic Church charges a lot for a rent-a-priest . . . since no one will really be killed, they won't need the real sacrament.'

I went on describing some of the other innovative, leading-edge ideas to be incorporated into Sux-M-Owt.com Land, including the gritty urban thrill of Barrio World, an exact replica of a three-square-block area of Boyle Heights, complete with evil-looking *eses* wrenching on primered-out '73 Pontiac

Grand Ams, crooked cops shaking residents down for cash, and so on. The futuristic world of Radiation Town, featuring a smouldering full-scale model of the core of Reactor #4 in Chernobyl ... Costumed characters dressed as Hiroshima A-bomb victims (complete with burned strips of flesh dangling from their arms) would stagger about, and all the rest of the park employees in the area would be sporting decontamination 'bunny suits' and would wield clicking Geiger counters in an anxious fashion. We'd also have the Red Light District for the grownups and a Sugar Binge Alley for the kids.

Finally, we reached the goal of our travels: Peckerwood Paradise. Sort of a riff on all the popular stereotypes of poor white folks in states with no front licence plates on cars, it was a nightmare trailer park built to speak to the deepest fears of the Southern California middle class. The fear of their own failure and slide into a world of cheap speed, Marlboro Reds, disability checks, and unidentifiable auto parts leaking oil into the gravel in front of the double-wide. The trailer park looked sort of like an 'after' picture of a tornado strike, with swaths of pink insulation bulging from tattered aluminum trailer bodies. Each trailer had a couple of cars up on blocks, real classics of the American automotive underclass, like an '81 Pontiac Phoenix full of beer cans, or the burned-out shell of a '72 Oldsmobile Delta 88, weeds growing up through the charred engine compartment. Fine-tuning detailed touches on projects such as this one really made my workdays feel *meaningful*. I had sent out a squad of car searchers to scour places like Bakersfield and Needles for the most wretched examples of the decrepit vehicles on my list; it's attention to detail that really separates the wannabes from the real deal. When the park got underway, we'd even have vicious dogs chained in front of the trailers, and the distinctive red-phosphate smell of a meth lab cooking. Lynyrd Skynyrd music would twang from lo-fi stereos and the sounds of domestic violence would wail and crash from speakers hidden in the trailers.

But now the place was deserted, on my orders; not even construction crews were in Peckerwood Paradise. We headed for a particularly squalid trailer, a 40' Roadrunner Dee-Luxion straight out of Slab City, a squatter's paradise out by the Salton Sea. Inside, the trailer was upholstered in a vile-looking coat of purple shag carpeting, with cat-piss-scented beanbag chairs scattered for furniture. A refrigerator full of retrograde beer and a couple of B&W TV sets showing high-static UHF broadcasts of NASCAR racing. The stench of Trailer Failure strong in our nostrils; I could see expressions of ill-concealed horror on the faces of Heather and Marco. Good. The question I'd make them answer was, how much distasteful experiences would they endure for those plum jobs in the future Carson City office? Would they have spines or would they serve as the passive instruments of our depraved whims in order to claw a little higher on the heap?

'All right, folks, we're here in this setting as part of our new Maximum Team Mighty Whoop-Ass Employee Screening Programme,' I said solemnly – I'd made that up on the spot, but I'd created an average of twelve such programmes a week during the 18 months I'd been the Great Helmsman of Sux-M-Owt.com and I figured nobody would know the difference if I felt like adding yet another one. 'The question Janet and I are here to answer is: do you have a sufficiently large tank of Whoop-Ass to be the calibre of manager we need to run the mission-critical Carson City office?'

'Yes, *sir*!' they chimed in unison. Jesus. This was too easy. Janet was still having a hard time containing herself; I was reluctant to let her alone with Marco, or me for that matter – she'd probably spin out of control at the first opportunity.

I reached into a cabinet (covered with Hustler centrefolds and a very dated 'Good Morning Mr Khadaffi – TERRORISE THIS!' bumpersticker featuring the faded image of an F–18 blasting camel-jockey caricatures to oblivion) and pulled out a couple of outfits specially created for the occasion by the seamstresses in our in-house ad agency's costume department. 'Put these clothes on and we'll start the process.'

They started to look for private rooms in which to change clothes. 'No, no – right here,' I admonished them. 'Don't you have *what it takes* to succeed in corporate America?' I tried to inject a Charlene-like snap to my voice as I issued orders. And I was getting into it; I felt contempt rising for these toadies, these ass-kissers.

They started stripping. I stared openly at Heather's body as the office-wear came off. She was on the plump side, with pale, almost translucent skin; the extra pounds on hips and belly looked very *womanly*. At the sight of her generous, high breasts with their delicate pink nipples, I fought the urge to have my way with her right on the spot – grab her by the extra flesh around the waste and wrestle her onto the nearest horizontal surface; I could picture the pleasant jiggling I'd see as I plowed that field. I knew I *could*, with no negative consequences, but I wasn't here for a crude, trailer-flavoured rut on the purple shag. Heather's outfit was a burlap dress made from potato-sack cloth. Holes for arms and head, and so short it barely covered her auburn pubic har. She kept smoothing it down over her hips in an attempt to cover up her privates.

Marco had a striped prison outfit straight out of 1910. I dragged out a set of vintage manacles and a genuine ball-and-chain rig. Clichéd, sure, but this was for Janet and her Subtlety-O-Meter usually registered pretty low. Janet watched his lean, sinewy body hungrily as he changed into his new outfit. I snapped the manacles on wrists and ankles, feeling like something of an evil bastard for encouraging Janet in her proclivities, but Marco could get out of everything by just calling bullshit on the proceedings. But neither he nor Heather objected. In fact, both of them seemed to be getting aroused by the situation, perhaps because of the kind of power-worshipping crap that right-wing/strongman politicians always ranted about. Marco was half-hard once the ball-and-chain assembly clinked into place and Heather had dilated pupils and pounding heart.

I grabbed his wrist chain and dragged him, clanking, through the trailer and to the grime-encrusted trailer bathroom. Shackling him firmly to the shower nozzle, I guided Janet over to him. 'OK, Marco, Janet's going to interview you now. If she says you're the man for the job, you'll be Nevada Regional Manager for the latest outpost of the Sux-M-Owt.com empire.' At this point, if he'd had a pair of real balls and demanded we stop this silly shit, I'd have promoted him to an even better position at the home Irvine office – maybe official Dope Taster or something. No way. I closed the door behind them, so Janet could work in private. Then I changed into my costume: grimy jeans soaked in diesel fuel and deer entrails, wifebeater shirt with coffee stains and cigarette burns. Rubber flip-flop sandals. Too bad my ancestors hadn't seen fit to give me the genes for a rancid mat of monkeylike body hair, but I tried to push out my gut for that 'Milwaukee Tumour' beer-belly look and put a Pabst Blue Ribbon sneer on my face.

Back to Heather. She was reclining on a stinky beanbag chair. She had given up trying to cover her girl-parts and her poozle-lips and silky red pubic hair were plainly visible. *Oh* yeah! I fished my one-hitter and lighter from my jacket pocket and sparked a hit of Lake County Locoweed. I thought to offer Heather a hit, but caught myself; I was here to get a taste of Charlene's world, not do the good-time-stoner-dude thing. Bogarting the dope, I studied Heather, looking for signs of fear. A swelling sense of power coursed through me. She was *mine*, to do with what I pleased.

'Let's go to the kitchen,' I ordered sternly. Dream-like, she got to her feet and headed to the trailer kitchen. The sound of Marco's chains jingling and Janet's strident voice penetrated the thin trailer walls. The whole trailer vibrated as Janet did her thing with/to Marco – I figured the ol' chain-gang fantasy would be right up her corporate alley.

The trailer kitchen was about what you'd expect – built and stocked to my explicit specs. Lots of canned meats, pork chops, flies. I decided that a class dame like Heather – what with her suburban roots, Business degree, and unlimited red-white-and-blue ambition, the office her natural habitat – would be most humiliated by a genuine dentally-challenged white-trash sexual experience, submitted to with gritted teeth to please the strange desires of the boss but, to her everlasting shame, feeding a previously-unknown hunger, blah blah blah. That seemed to be Charlene's gig – make 'em *like* it and hate themselves for it. I felt certain I could work this – a watered-down, less cruel version of what Charlene did all day and night. Stealing her magic, or *subverting* it as the eggheads would say.

Unfortunately for my heartlessly calculated plans, but fortunately for whatever shards of tattered karma remained in my possession, Heather was digging it from the git-go. 'Woman, fry me up some FLAP-JACKS!' I demanded, slamming my fist into one of the flimsy kitchen cabinets and knocking it off the wall in a shower of dirty coffee cups and roaches. I noted the baby-food jar of gold teeth in the wreckage and made a mental note to give a pay raise to the go-getter from the Sux-M-Owt.com design department responsible for that detail. 'You heard me, baby – get your ass a-cookin!' I felt like busting up laughing but maintained the act.

Heather had more of a sense of humour than I'd given her credit for – I'd pictured her sheltered upbringing in some place like West Covina or Corona del Mar and figured she'd be in shock by about now, the passive instrument of my beastliness and so on. Not at all; this was obviously way more fun for her than a typical day in the office, and I realised belatedly that she didn't find me repellent at all in spite of being the main lord high bossman honcho (in my worldview, the boss should *always* be loathed, no doubt the result of Commie programming by teachers who escaped the California State Loyalty Oath). She promptly dug out frying pan and pancake mix and popped a kitchen match with her thumbnail to light the pork-grease-caked stove. Bending over the stove, she lifted the potato sack over her hips and stuck her ass out invitingly. It was white and soft and round, dear reader, and I found an animal-like growling issuing involuntarily from my throat at the sight. No cottage cheese or folds or anything unsightly, just stuffed-to-bursting with healthy white-girl goodness. Goddamn!

'Oh, I got some *flapjacks* for you, Mr Kelvin,' she said, looking back at me with a wink. That ass filled my frame of vision like something on a widescreen Panavision screen. I stood, frozen for a minute. She wiggled it invitingly. This wasn't going according to plan – right about now she was supposed to be agonising over the maintain-integrity-versus-sell-out dilemma – but that wasn't a *bad* thing. I moved slowly toward her, robotlike, caught by the tractor beam of her mighty ass. I placed my right hand on her right hip. My left hand on her left hip. Grabbed a couple of handfuls and pulled her toward me. She ground her ass into my groin, hard. She reached around with one hand and worked my zipper down, then expertly extracted my tool through the various clothing flaps and slots – I had a momentary twinge when my phallic flesh made contact with the filthy cloth of the jeans (perhaps that detail had been done a little *too* accurately) and guided it unerringly to her poontang. No messing around for Heather – once she felt the head was in the right spot she shoved her ass backwards and took my full length in a heartbeat. I held on to her hips and braced against the floor, she gripped the countertop and spread her legs as wide as possible, and we got that trailer rocking in true Bakersfield style. She kept her fingertips on her parts, providing her own reach-around. This reminded me of my Econoline surf-fuck adventure with Possum Girl, less than two years ago but seemingly a lifetime, and I tried to sense the tugging of her fingers as they pulled the labia around my shaft.

I was pounding away, thankful I'd been using the exercise machines in the Sux-M-Owt.com Executive Gym, because I'd need all my wind for this schtup.

Heather had a reasonably tight cooch, about standard issue, but hyperactive pussy-juice glands that overlubed the action to the extent that I couldn't feel much. It would take a lot of oil-well-style pumping before I'd manage to get enough friction going to bust a nut. Heather breathed raggedly but didn't moan or cry out, even during orgasm. And she had quite a few, because I was on that jellyroll for what felt like hours while rivulets of juice trickled down her thighs and formed a little pool by her heels – I'd never noticed before that pussy juice has a *colour* – it's whitish, like watered-down spooge, not the clear colorless liquid I'd always seen when faced with lesser quantities of the stuff. It worked for her; even the most hair-trigger guy probably held on for at least a respectable amount of time with her slip-n-slide equipment.

Heather had her face jammed in the sinkful of dirty dishes and the potato sack up over her head. The trailer was lurching back and forth and stuff was falling out of cupboards and off shelves – God knows how Janet was dealing with the bouncing in the bathroom and I was practically frothing at the mouth from overexertion. Finally, Heather starting vocalising a bit, making some little mouselike squeaks to the rhythm of my thrusts. That was enough. I finally blasted off, saw stars, the works. A day in the life of the busy executive.

Stripping off my costume, I did my best to mop up some of the joy-juice from my body – stomach to kneecaps were pretty slimy – and gave a few futile dabs at Heather as well. I put my regular clothes back on, as did Heather. I wasn't sure what she'd make of all this – after all, if I'd just wanted a quick office hump there'd have been no need to go to a make-believe trailer park out in the desert. Note to self:

Make a few calls and get the Carson City office under construction.

I decided to check on Janet and Marco; a suspicious silence from the trailer bathroom had me a little uneasy. They were nowhere to be found. Checking around, I found she had him on the Corinthian Leather backseat of a '79 Chrysler Cordoba, he totally entangled in cast-iron chains and with a blue plastic tarp over most of his body, with a slit cut in it for his member to protrude, with Janet bucking on top of the whole mess. She was covered in spiderwebs, dirt, and sweat. With the tarp in place, it looked like she was fucking a heap of trash in an abandoned car; Marco seemed to have a mouthful of seat-stuffing foam rubber and was coughing and choking as Janet proved once more that Rank Has Its Privileges.

Later, on the drive back, I felt a smug satisfaction that I was incapable of sucking pleasure from the sick shit Charlene got off on . . . but I knew at a deeper level that I was more like her than I'd want to admit. I'd learn even more on this score as Sux-M-Owt.com headed into its death dive a little later on.

Thirteen

By mid-2000, all my most vivid fears about Charlene's ominous cult-type plans for her empire were blown away by what I found in the Geek Basement, soon enough; the reality made my most overheated imaginings seem like a Steven Spielberg happy-faced version. I'd been concerned that she wanted to be Charles Manson, or even Jim Jones, but we had bigger problems downstairs. The quickie 'Unauthorised Inside Story' paperback about Sux-M-Owt.com published by that hack journalist from the San Diego *Star* about nine minutes after my arrest claims that this was the beginning of the end.

Charlene's role models had shifted from the lovable/agonised Southern California iconic trio of Bettie Paige, Tura Satana, and Exene Cervenka and morphed into doomsday cult leaders and charismatic serial killers – scary, but plenty of goth-type SoCal chicks went that route and suffered no harm from it other than a really unfortunate fashion sense. From there, however, Charlene had shifted role models one more time: Third World dictators like Idi Amin, Papa Doc Duvalier, and Kim Il Sung. The geek basement had become a thugocracy, ruled by fear and awe of a single strongman (or, in this case, strong*woman*).

She'd hired a crew of musclebound goons to serve her as bodyguards and enforcers. Standard-issue

Death Squad types, straight out of the Contra playbook: wraparound mirror sunglasses (worn even at night, of course), bulging doughnut-fed guts straining the buttons of coffee- and blood-stained khaki uniform shirts, filterless cigarettes dangling from lips. Saddam-esque moustaches. Walkie-talkies squawking on utility belts bristling with cuffs, stun guns, beavertail saps, brass knucks, etc. All weighing in at 250 or more, with huge, bone-crushing hands, jacked on cheap amphetamines and suspicion. The floor creaked beneath their steel-toed boots. And they worshipped Charlene, of course; anyone who so much as looked at her funny would undoubtedly be blowing teeth out his nose seconds later, while being hustled straight to a holding cell where a confession would be extracted.

It was no joke about the holding cells. I went down to the Geek Basement a few weeks after our confrontation in my office, dreading what I'd see but needing to know what was going on. Charlene, who rarely showed her face upstairs by then, was decked out in a quasi-military uniform with Sux-M-Owt.com logos on shoulder patches and a Saddam-style beret cocked at a jaunty angle on her head. She was in her office, behind a majestic oak slab of a desk, seemingly the size of a football field. The desk and her chair sat up high, so a visitor would have to stare *up* at her during interviews. Her office walls sported displays of weaponry, including a sort of 'AK-47s of the World' exhibit, and portraits of Ceausescu, Enver Hoxha, and Marshal Tito (apparently she was on a Warsaw Pact Dictator kick at the time, although I supposed she might switch the portraits to Asian dictators the next day, African ones after that, and so on).

The photograph that really disturbed me, however, was the one on her desk. It was a shot of me, taken by her in the old days, on one of my deliveries to her house. I remembered her taking the shot – I'd been unrolling a big sack-o-weed when the shutter clicked, and I was concerned that such a photo was proof that I was a Dealer Man. I picked up the framed photo and studied it; I had a knowing, stoned smile and didn't give a shit.

Not like now. Replacing the photo, I looked at her questioningly.

'I keep it on my desk to remind me of the day, very soon I hope, when we'll be lovers,' she said, solemnly. 'When you finally let go of your debilitating illusions and claim the prize.'

That kind of spacey-ass talk would usually be cause for much eye-rolling on my part – the talk of some freak who'd read too many Ayn Rand books – but in this case, with her goon squad parked outside the office and dozens, if not hundreds of slaves, toiling for her, it scared the shit out of me.

'Well, shit, we can be lovers any time you want,' I said. 'Only we gotta cash out and quit this thing first. Go down to Ensenada and check into a nice beach hotel. Forget Sux-M-Owt.com ever existed. Then we can hump until our genitals look like overcooked pork.'

'There'd be no *point*, that way. We wouldn't be ourselves anymore. It's already gone too far to stop. We're taking this thing all the way to the end. The blaze of glory.'

There was no talking to her; every time I tried to get her to make sense she'd go on a lunatic tirade about the brick wall we were eagerly speeding toward, and the great fuck we'd have in the last few minutes before we went out in a gigantic explosion of bone chips and meat particles, taking several hundred souls with us. How we were ful*filling* our *dest*iny, blah fuckin' blah. The part about the Blaze Of Glory made me really edgy; it sounded very Jonestown-like. I had a sick, trapped feeling that got worse by the minute. Then Charlene suggested we view the holding cells, where 'the guilty confess their crimes' as she put it.

We headed out of her office. A couple of members of her personal goon corps glowered at me, until she put her arm in mine – the way you'd do to let an angry guard dog get the message: 'THIS PERSON=FRIEND! NO BITE FRIEND!' Then they went back to leaning against walls, kitchen matches and toothpicks in teeth, mirror shades opaque, huge slabs of biceps bulging as they crossed their arms, bored. One goon cracked his knuckles and muttered something into his walkie-talkie. A couple of them had lunging Rottweillers on leashes. We took off walking down the damp concrete hallway. She'd expanded the basement realm so that she seemed to have more floor space than the upper stories, and the whole place was lit by bare hundred-watt bulbs or buzzing high-intensity-discharge lighting fixtures. Our footsteps echoed off concrete as we sloshed through puddles. I saw some bloody handprints on one wall and saw what looked like a couple of teeth in the shadows. Seriously creepy scene.

But it got worse. We came to a row of steel doors, each with a little barred window. 'This is where we keep the Time Thieves.' Charlene said. Oh, shit, she learned about the concept of 'Time Theft' from my stories of Colonel Sausage – I should have kept my flapping gums firmly closed. I peered through one of the windows. Inside, a concrete cell about six feet square. A bucket for a toilet. Huddled in the corner, a naked Code Monkey. Female. She noticed my face at the window.

'No! No! No more!' she screamed, sobbing. 'I'll work hard! Please! No more interrogations!'

Charlene closed the little steel shutters over the window. 'We'll let Debra have some exercise in the yard tomorrow. For now, she needs to consider the error of her ways. Caught her sending a personal email on *company time*!' She sighed. 'It's for her own good, of course.'

'So what happens when one of your prisoners squawks to The Man about this kind of treatment? This has got to be illegal as hell. We'll be doing the *perp walk*!'

'Oh, no, that won't happen. My employees *love* being slaves. You'll see how far they'll go for us, when the time comes.'

I groaned. 'You mean when we go out in your blaze of glory?'

'You laugh now, but you'll be in my arms when the end comes. You'll see.'

Crazy as it may sound, I was still *warm for her form*, as my peers in junior high used to say. In fact, I wanted to bone her more than ever. Maybe I should just relax, give in to my so-called destiny, fuck her cross-eyed on top of a heap of chained-up Time Thieves and then head upstairs to convert the entire company into a gigantic Geek Basement. Hell, lock up the Board of Directors if they bitched about it. Then we'd dump a huge load of nitrous into the engine and keep the pedal pasted to the metal until we reached her goddamn Blaze Of Glory. I'd helped create this nightmare, of course, and now I couldn't escape it.

At the same time, things were falling apart fast outside the office. The New Economy had turned out to be a scam built on a lie built on a misunderstanding, and its financial underpinnings were being dissolved like sugarcubes in hot water. Investors suddenly wanted an accounting of where the money was going, who was spending it, and on what. The type of questions we sure as hell couldn't answer to anyone's satisfaction at Sux-M-Owt.com, even with our army of creative bookkeepers and smiley-faced lawyers. The hounds were starting to bay outside and the barking seemed to get louder by the hour.

Next thing I knew we had all kinds of government types sniffing around the office. I wasn't too worried about getting busted for stealing company funds, since my bank account held only cash I'd earned during the pre-Sux-M-Owt.com days (I never even bothered to take a salary, although as it turned out I might as well have paid myself millions a month), but I was getting the impression that the world was hardening against our type of operation. No longer were we to be indulged as geniuses *pushing the envelope* or *rewriting the rulebook* – now the gentlemen with the green eyeshades and ledger books wanted to take a hard look at a lot of columns of figures, and if they didn't come out right somebody was going to be in a lot of trouble. *Jail* trouble.

By late 2000 we were laying off employees left and right. Big layoffs, during which we'd chop a whole department and send them packing on the spot, and sporadic 'sniper fire' of individual employees. I tried to get everyone severance bonuses and told the rent-a-cops to look the other way when they took their laptops and coffee machines with them, but the red ink was rising around our ankles and showed no signs of abating.

I started getting disturbing phone calls from various law enforcement officials. 'We know you and that Cabrillo woman are up to *something*, Kelvin,' they'd say. 'She's already made it clear she'll give you up to save herself, so your only chance is to cooperate now.'

It was amazing how fast the walls crumbled; once Webvan went down it seemed to spark a chain reaction of panic throughout the state. Office parks emptied, FOR LEASE signs multiplied like corpses during a Black Death epidemic. And the calls continued. The SEC. The FBI. Orange County Sheriff. All of them saying Charlene was going to drop a dime on me.

Fourteen

I *knew* Charlene had been talking dealsky with The Man, and she suspected the same of me (in truth, I figured my best bet was to flee the state and start life over as a weed salesman/artist in some other city that would be receptive to my special talents; this option seemed a longshot due to the large amount of press exposure I'd received during Sux-M-Owt.com's meteoric rise and turdlike fall). Things were getting more than a little frightening for me, with Charlene on one side and The Man on the other . . . and the idea that they might be on the *same* side wasn't comforting at all. The fact that Charlene was at least looking to throw me to the wolves had one bright side: if she was thinking that way, she probably wasn't going to execute Operation Blaze of Glory, the End Times plan to have her slaves kill themselves and hop on board the passing comet and/or go out on a Mansonesque murder rampage throughout the Southern California area. But I didn't know.

I was considering setting up my own squad of protective thugs, maybe hiring the entire Santa Ana chapter of the Hangmen Motorcycle Club to lounge around my office twirling chains and tyre irons, with a rack of AR-15s on the wall and a panic button on my desk. The idea depressed me; that would mean the end of my carefree romp through a make-believe corporate world. I had bought a Patton-style chrome-plated .45 automatic and pulled the strings to get a concealed-weapons permit, but the very idea of living with a handgun under the pillow and one eye open seemed intolerable. The gun stayed in a file cabinet, gathering dust. What had happened to the reefer-scented world of seagulls screeching in front of an inspiring brown sunset?

An ominous silence from the Geek Basement. I tried to call Charlene, maybe try to work out some kind of deal, but the phone just rang and rang. The building's floor was suspiciously empty, with most of the employees who hadn't yet had their heads chopped off in layoffs calling in sick or just plain not showing up. The word was probably out that I was in big trouble, dripping with poison, and nobody wanted to be associated with me when the shit hit the fan. I called a few old friends and got the brush-off. Violet remained freaked out over the threesome with Charlene way back when. Even once-loyal Janet had headed for the hills, apparently starting up her own consulting business in Riverside. I hunkered down, feeling like Nixon in '74, when he was ready to start nailing 2x4s over the windows and doors of the White House. I realised that I hadn't heard any phones ring for a while; looking out the window at the parking lot, I noted an exodus of cars peeling rubber out of the lot.

It was probably my conscious urge to avoid undue paranoia that made me ignore the knockout gas hissing from my office's air-conditioning vents. *Just normal climate-control behaviour*, I thought, *and you don't really smell anything*. As it turned out, however, some paranoia might have been justified. The last thing I remember, as they say, was Charlene's smiling face in my doorway as a couple of her goons, sporting gasmasks, busted down the door. *It's unlocked, you dumbshits*, I tried to tell them, but I couldn't even dredge up the energy to get off the floor. Then, as is traditional when the bad guys gas you, blackness.

When I woke up, it was much like your standard hardboiled detective novel – face down on a concrete floor, hands cuffed behind my back. The requisite details were all there: Bad, chemical taste in my mouth? Check. Pounding headache? Check. The tiny cell illuminated by a single bulb, placed high enough that I wouldn't be able to break it and use the glass to slit my wrists and check out? Check. A sense of grim foreboding? Motherfucking check.

I wanted to switch novels, though. How did my dazzlingly successful stint as corporate VIP end up *here*? My disagreements with Charlene should be hashed out in a conference room, with lawyers and writs and shit, not in her private prison. As I contemplated my undeserved fate, feeling sorry for myself, I heard a key rattle in the cell door. I remembered Charlene's speech, in the early days of Sux-M-Owt.com when we were planning the building's setup, on the subject of old-fashioned key locks versus the more efficient solenoid-operated electrical locks:

'See, the key lock requires the active, nearby presence of a threatening personage. Working the key, turning it slowly, menacingly. Inside the cell, you *know* he or she is out there, the one you fear. The knock on the door at midnight. The unmarked van taking you to the Lubyanka. The remote-controlled lock is so *impersonal*; it makes the person in the cell feel less human, like a part of the machinery itself. No blame, no culpability, no good or evil. Makes the fear somehow less *personal*.'

I could see what she meant. The key grudgingly scraped the lock's tumblers to the open position and the deadbolt *clacked!* out of the slot. The door c . . . r . . . e . . . a . . . k . . . e . . . d open (I wondered how Charlene went about getting that hasn't-been-oiled-for-decades sound from 18-month-old door and lock hardware; she must have put the same kind of thought and energy into the question that I had into PowerPoint presentations and theme park design upstairs).

But it wasn't Charlene, as I'd expected. It was Mimi and Corinne, the Evil Twins. I should have expected it would come to this. No doubt Charlene was following the whole show on closed-circuit video, probably while a couple of her slaves waxed her legs and fed her grapes from a solid-gold bowl.

'Well, Eddie, long time no see, as you Americans say,' said Mimi. She looked good. Both of them looked good, dressed to the gills by Charlene's severe-clothing tailor and sporting matching designer accessories and top-shelf hairstyles.

'Ms Cabrillo gave us the jobs – how do you say, special consultants?' added Corinne. 'We have very much to speak about, Eddie.'

'I have often thought over our . . . meeting in the freezer at Colonel Sausage. When we saw you last,' said Mimi, a dreamy smile on her face at the recollection of having me coerced into stroking off over her nude body after satisfying their foul, pizza-store-manager lusts with my tongue. 'Ms Cabrillo tells me you talked of it often. Maybe you missed us?'

I sighed, feeling at a distinct negotiating disadvantage from my cuffed position face-down on the cell floor. 'This is about money, right? What's she paying you? You know I can pay more – Charlene never could save a buck,' I said. 'Do you have the keys to these cuffs?'

They tittered, razor-edged amusement in the old French style. I could picture them questioning Algerian or Indochinese prisoners, the old colonial scenario. The pride of France. 'Eddie, we are not here for money,' Corinne said, after nudging her sister with amusement. 'Money is nothing. We are here for *you*.'

I didn't much like the sound of that. Maybe the stick would work better than the carrot. 'Well, I hate to bring it up, but I might have to call in my favours with the Vagos if you don't let me go. They'll make you wish you'd never been born once they're done giving you the ball-bearings-in-a-sock treatment.'

More Evil Twin laughter. 'Eddie, your motorcycle friends cannot help you,' Corinne said. 'How will you call them?'

'There is no help, Eddie,' Mimi added. 'You are alone.' She lit up a Marlboro and stood there, smoking and watching me lie helpless on the concrete.

That sounded awfully final. Charlene's Blaze of Glory might be underway, in which case I was fucked. But what was the deal with Mimi and Corinne? Charlene had fantasised about reliving the walk-in-freezer event since I'd told her about it, but to bring in the real-life Evil Twins seemed to take Charlene herself out of the game. I couldn't picture her letting others have the pleasure of breaking me, which she felt entitled to. Unless they were there to play the old Good Cop/Bad Cop routine, with the Evil Twins cast in the Bad Cop role.

'So what's it gonna be?' I demanded. 'You gonna strap me onto some kind of jive-ass torture rack and make me submit to your demented will? Maybe see if that kind of setting gives a little extra zing to your empty sex lives?' Sad to say, I was getting hot for them – the strange subsurface miasma of lusts and motivations all mixed up inside me. My half-hard was uncomfortable against the cold concrete floor. In the distance I heard some shouting, probably some Code Monkeys undergoing their pre-Blaze-of-Glory indoctrination, or maybe just business as usual in the Geek Basement.

I continued trying to deal. 'Tell you what, gals – you unlock these cuffs and I promise on my honour I'll give you both my best lover-man treatment, here or on the horizontal surface of your choosing. You can flip a coin to see who goes first. Or arm-wrestle for it – hell, it doesn't matter to me. I guarantee not to come until you've climaxed three times each yourselves.'

At least they seemed to be thinking it over. 'Only three?' Mimi asked, amused.

'All right, four.' Silence. 'Five?' More silence. 'For God's sake, Mimi, there *are* physical limits!'

'No, Eddie. It will be our way,' Corinne said, in a chillingly final manner. Mimi snapped her fingers and a couple of Charlene's 350-pound glandular-case goons rushed in and lifted me to my feet by my shackled wrists. Hustled me out the door, like I was late for an appointment with Saddam Hussein. My feet never touched the ground. The Twins waved bye-bye, cheerfully.

The goons hauled me down what seemed like miles of damp concrete hallways, far longer than the basement footprint of the Sux-M-Owt.com headquarters building should have allowed for. Had Charlene blown off all zoning codes, property rights, and sanity in general and constructed underground tunnels and bunkers, Vietcong-style, under the entire neighbourhood? She could have paid for it all from the same bottomless pool of cash I drew from for my wild-ass schemes, and the bookkeeping wouldn't have revealed much of anything. Were there arms caches and stocks of freeze-dried food, so she and her acolytes could hold off The Man for months of siege warfare? Maybe that was what she meant by the Blaze of Glory crapola. I'd seen a few AK-7s in the hands of her security forces, but not enough to really give that Final Days impression; I had a sense they were just trying to create a Warsaw Pact atmosphere. I tried to talk the goons into accepting a cash payment (or better yet, from my point of view, Sux-M-Owt.com *stock options*) to let me go, but I might as well have been talking to myself; they probably didn't even hear me over the radios crackling in their earphones.

We arrived at an underground loading dock. It looked like the Sux-M-Owt.com building's docks – perhaps the warren of tunnels was just a big phony maze, like those zigzag lines you get at crowded amusement-park rides – but I couldn't be sure. A stretched Sedan de Ville limousine was waiting there, engine idling. The goons yanked open the door and shoved me in. The limo roared off, the door slamming from its acceleration and the g-forces sprawling me onto the floor. It's a real chore climbing into a moving car's seat while handcuffed, but, once accomplished, at least I was alone and could contemplate my options. The limo's windows were opaque and there were no inside door or window controls; I could tell from the lack of exterior noise that the windows were probably thick Lexan and I had no hope in hell of breaking them. I was separated from the driver by another sheet of the same indestructible substance. Since I still seemed to be stuck in a bad detective novel, I tried to fish around under the carpeting for a paperclip I could bend into an intricate key shape and somehow use to unfasten the handcuffs behind my back. No dice. I thought there was something I could do with my teeth, too, but I hadn't paid enough attention to miraculous escape methods in the movies. Plus I wasn't sure what I'd do if I could get the cuffs off – gnaw my way through the seat into the trunk and then flash Morse Code S-O-S signals by plugging and unplugging the taillight bulbs? I could tell from the empty-pockets sensation that my cell-phone had been taken away, so there'd be no calling Johnny Law to tell him that I was ready to drop a dime on Charlene and make a deal, provided they'd swoop down and save me from whatever nightmare fate Charlene and the Evil Twins had waiting for me at the other end of this limo ride. Since my only option was to try to get comfortable and await the inevitable, at which point I'd try to bullshit my way out of trouble, that's what I did.

After about an hour or so of freeway driving, the limo slowed, drove over some rough road, then halted. The door opened and some more of Charlene's uniformed thugs hauled me out into the chilly nighttime air. We were in the desert somewhere – no city lights the tipoff – apparently at an abandoned airport or military base. I figured we were probably somewhere near Edwards Air Force Base, although it was conceivable I'd been driven at extremely high speed across the Nevada or Arizona border. The thugs frog-marched me to a huge, rusty steel hangar, one of those early-Cold War corrugated-steel jobs thrown up in a hurry to house nuke-delivering shit like the F-102 and B-36. Inside was a brightly lit space, illuminated by many banks of complicated-looking lights – a film studio of some sort, I figured. In the middle of the vast expanse of concrete floor was a little, one-storey house. Something about it looked very familiar. Then I snapped to reality: it was an exact replica of the Richard Nixon Birthplace house, just like the one Frank Nixon had poured his parsimonious smalltime merchant's heart into building beneath the soul-bleaching Yorba Linda sun, according to one of my many long-winded internal rants on the subject. In fact, it was possible that Charlene had ordered her forces to steal the *real* Nixon birthplace – the nice old ladies operating the joint probably hadn't prepared for the brazen theft of the entire building by a crew of heavily-armed giants in tight-fitting polyester uniforms.

The goons were heading me straight for the Nixon House; I'd given up trying to talk sense to them – the only communication they seemed willing to undertake involved walkie-talkies and monosyllabic cop-grunts – and was just letting the wind blow me where it would. Waiting for my chance. Sooner or later, I'd see Charlene, and I'd try to get through to whatever vestigial trace of sanity she still had and derail her Blaze of Glory madness.

The Nixon Kitchen looked just the way it had in 1910, except for the gigantic electro-hydraulic apparatus suspended from the ceiling and taking up a large fraction of the room's space. It looked like some sort of industrial digging machine, but made from polished medical-grade stainless steel, with braided steel hoses and slick-looking anodised fittings. It was an unsettling sight, but not as unsettling as the realisation that I was to be strapped into the thing. The goons removed my cuffs and sliced all my clothes off with those scissors emergency-room personnel use to strip accident victims. I struggled, but I might as well have been an arthritic kitten as far as my strength counted against those hormone-enhanced goons; they looked like the East German shot-putting squad, circa 1956.

I knew Charlene was listening somewhere. 'Hey, Charlene, weren't we supposedly running this little venture *together*?' I called. 'Like, I thought we had an *understanding*.'

No answer. The goons got busy strapping me into the machinery, which looked ready to tear me apart at the touch of a button. I was getting pissed. 'And, by the way, *partner*, I hear you went running to The Man, tried to make a *deal* to save yourself from the slammer. *I* told The Man to go fuck himself when he tried to get me to rat you out – I'll spend five years on the rockpile before I rat my *partner* off! So who's standing on the moral high ground here?' This approach probably wasn't worth much, given that the true sociopathic/megalomaniacal dictator didn't give a squirt of fermented cat piss about moral high ground or anything else that smacked of altruism. *Weakness*. But I figured her true California-hipster nature was still there somewhere and it was worth a try. Anyway, if this truly was the beginning of the Blaze of Glory – and if I was the first log to be thrown on the fire – I wanted to give her something to think about in the lonely nights when she got old and started counting up her sins.

The goons left the room and I was naked, bound to the scary-ass hydraulic mechanism by countless leather straps criss-crossing my body every few inches and fixing me in place so firmly I could do little more than breathe; even my head was clamped into place. Suspended, facing downward and hovering a few feet over the Nixons' kitchen table. I hung there for a few minutes, wondering what was next, and the door from the Nixons' parlour opened. In walked Charlene. She was rigged up in a strange, futuristic-looking bodysuit studded with wires and sensors and connected by a thick cable to some humming machinery in the parlour – gear I'm pretty certain never graced the original Nixon house.

'Hey, Charlene, babe, how's it going? Just felt like dropping in on Frank, Hannah, and the boys for a big Yorba Linda-style dinner?' I asked in a joking-but-not-really tone. 'I'd come over there and give you a big hug, but as you can see I'm, uh, indisposed right now.'

She looked seriously spaced out. The End Times were here for her, I sensed. 'Eddie, I gave you my *heart*. And you *broke* it. I needed you by my side for the Final Days, but you rejected me.' She was near tears.

'Well, shit, Charlene, why not give it another chance? Maybe we could settle down in the suburbs, have some kids, maybe head to Vegas now and then when we get a wild hair and pull a few handles –'

'You joke about it, but you can't hurt me any more. You see how Sux-M-Owt.com is fading out? Our great venture dying of arteriosclerosis? Our empire was *poisoned* by you, just because you *hated* me and didn't want me to get what I wanted,' she pouted. I realised I was at the mercy of a temperamental trust-funder with a head full of delusions of grandeur mixed with all the angst of a 12-year-old girl rejected by her junior-high sweetheart.

'Uh, I think the empire fell apart because we couldn't answer questions like 'Where did all that money go?' or 'How do we plan to make a profit?' Not because I wanted to mess you up. Hell, I wanted the thing to keep rolling for*ever*!' I almost started a rant about her whacked-out slavery scene in the Geek Basement and how that was the *real* reason we started attracting so much unwanted scrutiny, but this wasn't the time or place to start dishing out Hard Truths to the woman who could do who-knows-what terrible things to me with the device into which I was strapped. 'By the way, what *is* this thing your muscle boys have stuck me in? And what's with your batshit outfit?'

'I had this machinery built for us to use with our slaves, once we'd set up our kingdom in the desert.' Oh, Christ, the Manson trip, only with about a hundred thousand times the budget ol' Charley had had at his disposal, and fifty times as many 'soldiers'. 'We could have made love to each other through the slaves, using this equipment, so you wouldn't have to actually *touch* me. Just like we did with Violet.'

I sighed. 'We could have had a plain old missionary-position fuck in a standard-issue four-poster bed any time you'd wanted to – my nuts were *burning* for you! For almost two years! In fact, we could still *do* that if you'd get me out of this thing –'

'But not *my* way!' she shouted. And she was right. I wouldn't play her goofy slave game, on either end. At heart, I was still true to my core, stoner-California-boy karmic values, flaky as they were, while she had never had any. 'So now we're going to play with it a little bit, before we all go out in the Blaze of Glory.'

'Sheee-it! Your fucking Blaze of Glory is the craziest goddamn thing you ever came up with! Get your head together and our stories straight and we'll walk with fucking probation. Then we can start another setup just like the original Torment, Incorporated, before the investors fucked it all up!'

'No, they're closing *in* on us. We have no choice. Die on our feet rather than live on our knees.'

I groaned. Our conversation effectively ended at that moment, because Mimi and Corinne entered.

Friendly greetings between them and Charlene. I was stuck with crazy Charlene and her strange contraption and apocalyptic delusions and the Evil Twins, who saw me as an entertaining toy.

'Who wants to go first?' asked Charlene, flipping some switches on the machinery's control panels and a few more on her suit. I felt and heard the hydraulic rig come to life, shaking me a bit as hydraulic fluid charged up its lines and cylinders. I could sense its enormous strength. Real fear shot through me, but I tried not to show it. To my horror, the fear crystallised in my parts and I felt an erection building.

Mimi and Corinne noticed the thickening, with approving glances. They carried on a quick whispered discussion that culminated in a coin toss. Mimi won. Now what?

'All right, Mimi, you can go first,' said Charlene. Mimi quickly stripped off her clothes, folding them neatly and stacking them on the Nixons' kitchen counter – no need to wrinkle those fine custom-tailored threads. The sight of her classy, nicely-proportioned body, every curve in its place, got me to full hard. I tried to think of Nancy Reagan naked, warthogs fucking in a pool of shit, and other counter-erectile imagery, but to no avail; the fact was that I was red-hot for all three of the nutcase females in the room and couldn't help but be stiff as an axe-handle in the circumstances. Mimi climbed onto the Nixons' kitchen table, a few feet beneath me. On her back, she reached up and traced the outlines of my muscles with her fingertips. My arms, chest, stomach, thighs. I felt like howling but kept my cool. Corinne leaned against the wall and fired up a smoke, watching. Charlene fiddled with some controls on her outfit and the machinery shifted my entire body downward, toward Mimi. Charlene's arm moved out in a caressing motion and the machinery forced my arm to do the same. Her fingers opened and mine did as well – there was no point in resisting the mighty strength of the hydraulic cylinders, so I just relaxed. My fingers did exactly what Charlene's did, and I explored the surfaces and crevices of Mimi's body as Charlene saw fit. It was a variation on one of those 'virtual reality cybersex' deals that you heard so much bullshit about in the mid-90s, only one that was set up to allow women to fuck each other with a man's body.

'Amazing!' panted Mimi, enjoying the attention. 'A marvellous invention, Ms Cabrillo!' I realised that the same engineer who'd built the original fuck-machine – the one that imparted a simple in-and-out motion to the body of the hapless Code Monkey tied to it – in the first version of the Geek Basement must have been the twisted genius behind this far more elaborate version of the same concept. It was probably one of the Code Monkeys, I figured, working for banana primate pellets and the time to eat them; the beautiful finish on all the exposed metal parts indicated the labours of someone under heavy compulsion to do a perfect job *or else*.

Mimi half-sat and began working on my cock with her pointy tongue-tip. Oh, she knew what to do, all right – restricting her licking to the areas of the shaft with just sufficient nerve endings to make me crazy for *more*. Meanwhile, Charlene was getting fancy, running my fingers through Mimi's hair and other tricky moves. She wasn't doing quite as good a job as I'd have done on my own, but it was good enough to stimulate Mimi to greater heights of passion. I wondered if Charlene's output had some kind of tactile feedback mechanism, so she'd be able to sense the amount of pressure exerted; if not, she might end up making me crack a bunch of Mimi's ribs or something. Not that I'd have shed any tears over that, of course.

Mimi's tongue action done, she reclined back on the kitchen table with legs spread. Charlene's engineer hadn't figured a way to clamp my tongue and control it, so she couldn't make me give Mimi some face (although I would have done so had she manoeuvred me into position; I'd want to prove that the voluntary, non-Charlene-controlled parts of me could do a better job of pleasing a woman than the parts controlled by her lunatic Fuck Machine Mark II). Mimi didn't really need it, anyway, she was ready to go as-is.

Charlene lowered me slowly toward Mimi, who grabbed my cock once it came within panoche range and began rubbing it up and down the lips, rasping me a bit with her fur until enough wetness coated the head and made the friction smoother. Charlene pushed her hips forward very slowly and mine pushed down in unison. Mimi got my schlong all lined up properly – good thing, too, because the great strength of the machinery would have snapped my member in half like a celery stalk if it wasn't aimed right on target – and Charlene pushed it in slowly. A quarter-inch in thirty seconds, then another quarter-inch.

Mimi dug it, pushing up with her hips. Charlene dug it, too, but controlling the equipment took so much attention that she couldn't really relax and feel real pleasure, another drawback of the whole setup that would probably cause difficulties in her proposed Manson Family-esque desert compound. Mimi lifted her face for a kiss and probed for my tongue with hers; I kissed back. My tongue was all I controlled, and I was going to use it, even though Mimi deserved less active participation on my part. Charlene was pulling me back slightly with every upward thrust of Mimi's hips. Teasing her, not letting her get any extra penetration for all her efforts.

'Oh, *mon dieu,*' Mimi moaned, wanting more. There was no point grabbing me and pushing me deeper; not only did Fuck Machine Mark II provide no way for her to get her arms around me, but it would have been pointless for Mimi to match muscle with it. We would dance to Charlene's tune. Corinne watched Charlene do her sister with my body, fascinated. She would be next, I realised. In fact, there was no telling how long this would go on – if I lost the ability to get hard after pumping the Twins with a month's worth of semen, Charlene could keep the party going with my fingers and toes.

Charlene wanted to tease Mimi for a long, long time, but after a half-hour or so she was getting hot herself and wanted to get some good in-out action rolling. She got me in a few more inches and stopped retreating from Mimi's counterthrusts. Since I didn't have to pay any attention to what I was doing with the rest of my body I could concentrate on phallic sensations as I never had before during the act. I tried to calculate the depth of Mimi's strongest vaginal muscles, to imagine the slight ridges inside her, all that good stuff that's so hard to analyse when you're going at it with your whole body. Charlene humped air and my body followed suit, slipping it to Mimi with more and more force. Finally I was bottomed out on each downstroke and the Nixons' table trembled beneath the onslaught. Mimi came, than came again, crying out more than I'd expected from such a cool customer. I held back, sensing that Charlene wanted to see if she could work the equipment in such a way as to make me come on command.

After a few more minutes of all-out cervix-pounding rutting, I realised that my schlong would be worn down to a stump by the time Charlene got through having her jollies with Fuck Machine Mark II. I let go, allowing the climax to build quickly. When Charlene realised what was happening, she pulled me out of Mimi so she could watch my semen land on her belly; Mimi kept it coming, milking me with some hand action.

Next it was Corinne's turn. She stripped and took her sweaty twin's place on the table. I felt spent, but some judicious mouth work by Corinne and my gear was standing tall again (Corinne's style was rougher, less subtle than her sister's, but quite effective). Charlene, having mastered the controls while Mimi lay beneath me, went for a long, slow, barely moving fuck this time, with both Corinne and I ready to break down and plead for some *satisfaction*. This time, Charlene would hold still each time it seemed Corinne was about to bust one – training for control of future desert-compound slaves, I assume; keep them under the spell of the Maximum Leader, etc. After an hour or so, Charlene got a nice side-to-side/in-and-out sequence going that resulted in a harrowing mutual climax for us.

I got a half-hour breather and then it was back to Mimi. The Evil Twins were enjoying this experience like they'd never enjoyed anything before – this was even better than putting the Pizza Slaves through their paces on a hot, busy Friday night at Colonel Sausage. I was in pretty solid shape, sexually speaking, but I didn't think I'd be able to hold up under an all-nighter on Fuck Machine Mark II. But what choice did I have?

But Fuck Machine Mark II was just the introduction to Charlene's plans for me. After about six hours of remotely humping the Evil Twins, Charlene summoned the goons and had them unshackle me from FMM2. The Twins left. I was shaky, head lolling, exhausted. What next?

'Oh, Eddie, I wish it hadn't come to this,' she said apologetically. *Come to what?* I wondered – so far things had been weird and exhausting, but if this was the worst of it I was home free. Maybe playing with her new toy had purged thoughts of the Blaze of Glory from her head and I'd be free to go. 'It has to be this way – you *forced* me!' she said. She pushed a couple of buttons on her control board.

That didn't sound good, and it wasn't. I heard some thumping and heavy footsteps from the next room. The Nixons' parlour door opened slowly. When it opened fully, I gasped in horror. It was the Vacuum Nixon, but twice as big as the one I'd built, with a complex, mobile face expressing a range of emotions running from rage to psychotic fury. Its eyes rolled crazily. Nine feet tall. No vacuum hoses and no wires – a totally self-contained Nixon robot. I wished she'd never seen the original Vacuum Nixon – obviously she'd figured I had a weird fixation on Tricky Dick and decided to go right for that perceived weakness in my makeup. Not under Charlene's direct control, either, I snapped immediately that her crew of traumatised Code Monkeys had directed all their fragmenting mental states into the code that would operate the Nixon (the Autonomous Nixonian Operating System, as I found out it was called later) and it was ready for action, ready to take on the world and kick its ass.

And I represented the world, probably a combination of Helen Gahagan, Lyndon Johnson, and Woodward & Bernstein all rolled together. The Nixon took a lurching, Frankensteinian step toward me. I backed up against the kitchen cupboards. There was no escape.

'TRAITOR!' it boomed. 'HAVE YOU EVER BEEN A MEMBER OF THE COMMUNIST PARTY?' it demanded. I quivered in abject terror, huddled naked in the corner of the Nixon family kitchen. There would be no reasoning with this creature, the vengeance of the Code Monkeys poured into a brain-addled interpretation of the soul of the former President. Then it got worse; its massive hands, literally the size of Virginia hams, reached for its pants zipper and pulled it down.

'No!' I screamed. 'Dear God, Charlene, call him off me! I'll do whatever you say, I'll join you in the desert compound and ride herd on your slaves, but *please call him off*!' The Nixon extracted, or rather *unrolled*, a pulsing robotic phallus about the size of a stack of twenty tuna cans. It glowed red and smoke hissed from the gaping peehole. The Nixon took another step toward me. 'SOVIET SPY!' it shrieked, pointing an accusing finger at me while the other hand jiggled that massive member my way. It didn't take a real vivid imagination to imagine the game plan.

Charlene sobbed. 'I *can't* stop it, Eddie. It *has* to be this way – it's in the programming that it can't be stopped once I start it.' She sniffled, then looked defiant. 'It would have been different if you'd really loved me.'

I scrabbled through the Nixons' cupboard, looking hopelessly for some kind of weapon that would miraculously prevail over a thousand-pound killer sodomising robot programmed by three dozen programmers driven around the bend by months of sexually-tinged abuse. I threw cans of oatmeal and peas, cooking utensils, and the rest of the contents of the cupboards at it, much like the panicking characters in 50s sci-fi flicks always did when the space alien closed in on them. All the crap bounced off the Nixon like so many gnats. Desperate, I kicked a leg off the kitchen table and took a huge Reggie Jackson cut right at its head. The wood splintered like a matchstick on the Nixon's skull. It lurched ever closer, making my soon-to-be-victimised asshole clench tighter than a clam's. 'BUM! YOU'RE A COMMIE BUM!'

Then, just like in the movies where the alien is chased off by the Army right before it kills the hero, the Nixon house's front door burst open from the force of several big G-Man boots. A bunch of burly guys in FBI windbreakers stood there, M-16s drawing down on us. 'Freeze!' they screamed as the Nixon turned toward them, hesitating. These strangers must be Commies, too, it was thinking. But it was programmed to ream the Main Commie; that was the Prime Directive. I threw myself to the floor figuring everyone in the room was about to be blasted into something resembling a cheese grater by the weapons of a squad of Feds confronting a nine-foot-tall Richard Nixon in a little 1910 house in an airplane hangar.

But it never came to that. The entrance of the armed, screaming Feebies presented the Nixon's processor with an unforeseen situation and it locked up, confused. The Code Monkeys had cut some corners with the programming, fortunately. 'COMMMmmmmiieeee . . .' it droned out, like an LP slowing to a halt. Toppled forward, like an axed tree, and slammed to the floor with a bone-rattling crash and cloud of dust. We were under arrest, as it turned out – the cops had been tailing us for days. City of Irvine, City of San Jose, County of Orange, County of Los Angeles, State of California, Securities and Exchange Commission, Secret Service, FBI, you name it, they had a piece of our ass. I was so relieved to be spared from the embrace of the Mighty Nixon that I *welcomed* the arrest.

Charlene and I went peaceably. Mimi and Corinne were already waiting in the back of an unmarked Crown Victoria sedan, and the goons were in an L.A. County Sheriff's paddywagon (it turned out we were about 100 yards from the Los Angeles-San Bernardino County border) and Charlene and I were stuffed into another Crown Victoria slick. We were under arrest for hundreds of counts of fraud, embezzlement, and a smorgasbord of other white-collar wrongdoings. Our rights were read to us. I didn't care; the Sux-M-Owt.com nightmare would be ending soon.

We were hauled back to Santa Ana. Charlene and I said nothing to each other; we hardly made eye contact. But the gears were turning, each of us determined to come out on top of the ensuing mess. Shit, I hadn't stolen any money; I'd made it clear all along that I didn't give a flying fuck about the money. The cops dragged into the County Jail. A gauntlet of photographers and TV cameramen, hundreds of the fuckers, were waiting outside the building as they hauled us out of the Crown Vic. The first of many such ordeals; it hadn't occurred to me before that we were going to be a huge, screaming-headline nationwide *story*. As the cops shoved aside the press weasels, I pasted a huge phony grin on my face and locked one eye shut tight, so every photograph would show me with a shit-eatin' 48-tooth smile and my face screwed into a massive, kiss-my-ass wink. Then we did the famous *perp walk*.

Charlene did the more traditional hide-your-face-from-the-cameras routine, which made her look like she had more to hide. Which was true, to my way of seeing it, but since she was sexy and mysterious and probably evil and I was just some goofy guy who jumped on the dot-com gravy train (as the world saw it), it was not in her interest to appear even *more* mysterious. I didn't understand at the time that nobody gave a fuck about the Geek Basement or any of Charlene's dictatorial craziness (at the time; when the blizzard of civil suits rolled in later on we heard endless stories, mostly bullshit, about Charlene's empire). All they cared about was the money. Close to a billion bucks! All gone!

So they booked us, took mug shots, made us put on bright orange prison outfits, the whole bust routine – the cops were pretty careful not to be too rough, figuring correctly that we probably had some good lawyers – and then they shoved me into a windowless, fluorescent-lit room with a little blond-wood table and one of those big wall clocks that changes the time every minute with a TICK of the minute hand. The ventilators hummed. Then the door opened again and Charlene was shoved into the room with me. The door slammed and I heard cop-shoes walking away. Alone at last. She sat down in one of the chairs, across the table from me, and leaned forward on her elbows, exhausted.

I knew the room was bugged. Obviously they were hoping we'd talk secret insider stuff about Swiss bank accounts, gold bullion stashed under floorboards, etc. Since the money was long gone, squandered on the Sux-M-Owt.com dream, there wasn't much we could talk about that would incriminate us. But I figured we might as well keep our mouths shut – don't give them *anything*. I made a bunch of 'they're listening, don't talk about anything serious' gestures to Charlene, who seemed to get the gist.

She was dressed in shapeless prison scrubs, like what medical personnel wear, only bright arrest-me orange and stencilled with ORANGE COUNTY INMATE across the shoulders. Her hair was sticking out crazily and her makeup was smeared all to hell. She smelled like stale angry sweat. She didn't look evil or haughty or fearsome – just a tired, pissed-off young woman in a bad outfit. But she looked good. I wondered how long they'd give us together.

She was thinking much the same thing. She leaned toward me to whisper something. I gave her my ear, cautiously – maybe she was setting me up to take the fall while she walked.

'This is the last time we'll be together for quite a while,' she whispered. 'In fact, when we get out they may make it a parole condition that we can't have any contact. That's usually what they do in conspiracy-type cases like this.'

'So what's your point?' I whispered back, looking around for hidden lip-reading cameras. 'Anyway, they got nothing on us. We never stole any money. It was all legit.'

'Oh, they'll find *something*. Since we couldn't go out in a Blaze of Glory, they're going to try to get us with the death-of-a-thousand-cuts deal. But I'm not mad at you about the Blaze of Glory thing any more – I understand you had your own ideals . . .'

I almost went off on her about the stupid Blaze of Glory Manson/Jim Jones thing, but what would have been the point? We were busted. It was *over*. Now we just had to work out the endgame to avoid serious prison time.

'Well, there's no point in getting our stories straight, because there's *no story*,' I whispered. 'What could we say? There's no money! I'm not gonna lie about *any*thing, except maybe my dope sources.'

'I know,' she said. Her breath in my ear was getting me hot. 'So the only thing left to do is to give me a kiss, like you've wanted to all this time. Like you should have done when you were the Dope Dealin' Pizza Dude. It's our last chance – we'll probably end up betraying each other so we might as well do it now while there's still something sweet about it.'

I was startled. 'A kiss? Think they'll kick in the door and pry us apart with billy clubs?' I was thinking I might be able to get a bit more than just a kiss before they dragged me into my holding cell. I knew my future cellmate would want to know all about what the mysterious Charlene Cabrillo was like, and why disappoint him?

She was getting excited by the idea of the cops watching on their secret video monitors. 'Yes, just give me something to think about while I'm staring at you on the witness stand.'

'All right, where do you want your kiss?'

'Do I have a choice?'

'Sure, I'll plant a nice smooch anywhere you want,' I said. 'I'll linger appropriately, tongue action, the whole enchilada. Our last chance, as you said.'

'Oh, if it's going to be just *one* I could never decide on the spot,' she replied, warming to the game. 'Can it be an area requiring removal of clothing?'

'Anywhere on your body,' I whispered back, flicking her earlobe a bit with my tongue tip as I said it. She dug that. 'Only keep in mind that Johnny Law will probably be watching, maybe even videotaping it for some kind of all-cop porno channel.'

'I'll need one on my mouth, but there are other spots I'd wish I'd chosen, later on during those lonely nights in solitary,' she said. 'How about *three* kisses – then I'll have something to remember when they're sweating me down, trying to get me to testify against you.'

Like she wouldn't, anyway. But I wanted it. 'All right, three. Where's Kiss Number One gonna be?'

She pulled her inmate shirt down a bit, exposing an interesting bit of cleavage, and tapped a spot just below the collarbone, on the upper slope of her left breast. 'Right here. That's a spot I always wanted you to touch.'

I leaned over and kissed the spot, gently. Explored the texture of her skin, the taste of her, with my tongue tip. Nothing slobbery or uncouth – no hickeys or toothmarks. She liked it. She reached for my hand and pressed it to her breast as I worked. No bra – probably took them away from female inmates to prevent them from hanging themselves by their lingerie – and her nipple swelled pleasantly on my palm. I didn't want to get us too hot, since I felt fairly certain that we'd be neck deep in coppers as soon as we started getting too heavy in our actions.

I broke off, pulling back. 'OK, how about Kiss Number Two?' I asked. She put her hands behind my neck and pulled me to her. I'd kissed her on the mouth once before, back in her office when we were fooling around with Bitsy, but this was different. Nothing to fear from her here; we were simply man and woman swapping some spit in the police station before the cops started pulling our fingernails out. We got into it for quite some time; if the cops didn't have video they'd be getting suspicious of our long silence.

What I didn't notice was that she'd worked her orange scrub pants off while I sucked on her tongue. Kicked them off under the table. She broke off her kiss and climbed on the table, half-naked. Spread her legs in most shameless fashion and announced, 'Kiss Number Three, Eddie?'

And that was the scene when the door popped open and a bunch of pissed-off cops and district-attorney personnel pulled me off her, just as I started to apply tongue to pussy.

'God damn it, what the hell's wrong with you perverts?' one of the DAs yelled as they wrestled the pants back onto Charlene and slammed me against the wall. *Perverts?* I thought.

So that was the last time I saw Charlene one-on-one. As she predicted, we're barred by court order from seeing each other once we're out of the can. I won't bore you, dear reader, with the story of the trials, Charlene ratting me off and me counter-ratting her off, both of us being truthful about the money but trying to blame the other for coming up with the *idea* of Sux-M-Owt.com. You know what happened at the trials as well as I do, unless you were completely isolated from popular culture for the last year. But as I reenter the world, having Paid My Debt To Society, I will hope that my story has opened a few eyes, maybe even a few hearts. Although I will be pursued by a rapacious pack of lawyers squealing for civil damages measuring in the hundreds of millions, I will continue to create my art and attempt to make a living from it.

Glossary

Brah: Bro, brother.
Brew 102: A weak, watery Los Angeles beer.
Burden, Chris: Southern Californian performance artist, in many ways the inventor of the genre.
Chingado: Mexican Spanish exclamation of anger or awe; roughly translates to 'Fuck!' or 'This is fucked!'
Crown Victoria: The Ford sedan used by all American police agencies.
Dube, doob: Marijuana cigarette.
Dumpster: Industrial-sized rubbish bin.
Hesh: Short for *Hessian*; a greasy, long-haired, amphetamine-abusing aficionado of headbanging guitar rock.
Jerntz: Marijuana cigarettes.
La Migra: The Immigration and Naturalization Service; the scourge of illegal aliens throughout the American Southwest.
Loadie: Stoner, dope fiend.
Man in the gray suit: A shark.
Nibley: Marijuana.
Olde English 800: A ghetto malt liquor; the 'OE' praised in countless gangsta-rap anthems.
Pacifico Claro: A cheap Mexican lager, popular in border towns.
Phishhead: Fan of the band Phish.
Primo: Hawaiian beer, an icon of 70s California mellowness.
Salvation Army Santa: Homeless alcoholic who rings a bell and solicits donations for the S.A. in front of public places during the Christmas season.
Sand Hill Road: The epicentre of Silicon Valley dot-corn-boom venture capital in the late 1990s.
Schlitz Blue Bull: A cheap, particularly foul high-alcohol beer, associated with accidental firearms deaths throughout rural America.
Tallcan: 16-ounce beer can (the 12-ouncer is the standard American size).